Our Blue Orange

A R Merrydew

To Karen and all of our children

"Time is an illusion"

—ALBERT EINSTEIN

To Anne

I hope you enjoy the story

26/06/16.

Acknowledgements

In preparing this book for publication I have had the good fortune to deal with following people who have been paramount in helping me get my work in print.

Firstly I would like to offer my thanks to Peter O'Connor of Bespoke Book Covers for his great book cover and on-going support with publishing.

My thanks also to Richard Sheehan for his copy editing skills and turning round this work precisely on time and offering such an in depth report.

For his formatting skills and boundless enthusiasm, my thanks to Matt at Candescent Press who added the final touches and made the pages come to life.

And finally, to my wife Karen whose insight and continued support over the years actually made this novel come to life.

CHAPTER 1

Lately, Nigel Prentagast was having problems sleeping. On a good night he may have been fortunate enough to savour three or four hours at best, and although his mother had tried to fuss over him with remedies for his insomnia, he had repeatedly shunned her help. Nigel alone knew the reason why he was incapable of sleeping at night, and he wasn't about to discuss it with his mother or anyone else for that matter.

The burden that he carried was making him ill, and that particular Monday morning, as he sat staring at his ageing monitor with sunken bloodshot eyes, he knew that numerically it was simply a question of time before someone else learned of his discovery. Sliding his trembling hand across the keyboard, he nervously tapped a key and waited. The vast bank of servers in the data hall behind him hissed and chattered as he peered nervously at the printer on his desk. The single page of text clattered into existence and slipped into his hand. Finally, the enormous machine that Nigel had served throughout his working life had regurgitated the evidence he had been dreading. There was something very wrong with the mainframe, and now he had the proof. The dejected programmer stared at the document, swallowing hard at what he read.

'Is there something wrong, Prentagast?'

Nigel turned and gazed up at his supervisor, a deep furrow ploughed across his wrinkled brow. 'Sir, I think you need to read this,' he said, nervously handing over the mainframe's dissertation of its own wellbeing.

The supervisor examined the text with black bead-like eyes. 'Who else has seen this?'

'No one, sir,' Nigel said, his voice faltering.

'Turn off your screen and wait here,' he hissed.

Sat behind his workstation, Nigel stared at the cables and pipes jostling for position on the walls and ceiling in this dingy, sweaty room. They swept in from above and below like the arteries of a great beast he had served diligently for so many years. It was as predictable as the mainframe's ability to control the weather systems far above their vast colony. There was little space, if any, for some cheery picture to remind him of a more invigorating place. It was in reality a forgotten backwater, a place where men who rarely saw the light of day or sensed the sweet smell of fresh clean air came to serve their kind. All that mattered was the mainframe and the colony far above their heads. There was but one objective and that was to work and serve the vast machine without question.

Nigel looked again along the neat line of work stations stretching into the distance. There were still those empty chairs. In the past week there had been the others, four of them –no, five. He reflected on the muffled conversations his fellow programmers had had with the supervisor, conversations similar to his own. He had tried not to watch their ashen faces as they switched off their monitors and left. They had not returned. Nigel glanced up at his supervisor and the two suited men standing beside him; now it was his turn.

As Nigel Prentagast entered the basement lift, his heart pounded in his chest. His supervisor tapped in floor one hundred on the panel and the four men ascended, silently staring at the elevator doors. Beads of sweat amassed on Nigel's forehead, dripping into his eyebrows and filtering down upon his eyelids. He wiped the back of his trembling hand across his face and smeared the residue over his cheeks. The inevitability of what lay ahead overwhelmed him.

In the half-light of a room on basement level thirteen, deep beneath the Ministry, the chromium-plated fingers of a metallic hand flexed themselves with human dexterity. With engineering precision, the motorised thumb and forefinger disconnected a solitary lead from a nearby data port and let it fall to the floor.

CHAPTER 2

Far above the discarded data lead on basement level thirteen, the normal Monday morning turmoil ensued in the foyer of the Ministry. Swept along in a sea of bodies, Godfrey Davis headed for the lifts as his mobile phone vibrated in the breast pocket of his jacket. Managing to break free from the stampede, he stepped to one side towards the tranquil haven between the entrance doors and inspected his phone. The text message was from his wife, Gloria: *'You have forgotten your sandwiches again. Have lunch at the canteen instead.'* Godfrey considered the prospect of another lunchtime meal with overcooked potatoes, watery greens and that brown sludge they called gravy. The staff canteen meals were considered the last resort and were avoided at all costs; in fact, hunger would be a more favourable option. That was unless he could manage to slip away to the little restaurant across the plaza where they served that delicious aubergine pasta with olive oil and basil, and maybe a glass of fine red wine from the south of the colony. Godfrey closed his eyes and took a deep breath, imagining the aroma of his alternative lunch.

'Good morning, Mr Davis. May I say how wonderful it is to see you here today. Sir, your tweed jacket is an excellent choice of tailoring for such a fine morning, especially as we have an eighty-nine percent impossibility of precipitation today, and your red bow tie is such a contrast of colour, without a doubt. On behalf of myself, my fellow doormen, and the management, I would like to welcome you to this fine establishment and wish you yet another splendid day at work here at the Ministry.'

The android gazed on with empty eyes, his plastic features controlled by wires and motors that pulled a distorted smile across his face not that dissimilar to a man suffering from flatulence. Godfrey looked the machine up and down as the thought of lunch evaporated. It was the same script he had heard last Friday and the Tuesday before that, when he had made the mistake of loitering too long near one of the Ministry's robotic doormen. It was in fact the same repartee he had heard all of his working life, and the realisation made him feel slightly angry. Godfrey reminisced about standing proudly beside his father when these innovative machines had first been unveiled. He had been barely eight years old. The fleet of androids had been his father's brainchild, and at the time they had been heralded a triumph of engineering and an asset to the colony and her people, but now? With the march of time, fifty years had passed and little had changed. The androids were still in service, tipping their caps as personnel entered the Ministry and operating lifts with their polite congenial tone, just as they had been programmed to do five decades earlier. Godfrey had taken his father's role as the Ministry's inventor and had tried hard to follow in his footsteps, and yet sometimes he felt he had a mountain to climb. If he were to ever achieve such an accolade as his father had, he would have to come up with something very special indeed. There had been a host of things Godfrey had attributed to his personal portfolio of inventions, most notably the moving pavements that had proved so popular with commuters across the metropolis. There was also a self-writing pen set that would take down any dictation in your own hand once it had been programmed to do so. But Godfrey still sensed a gap between his own achievements and those of his father when he looked back across his career at the Ministry. He would have to do something monumental and do it soon if he were to surpass him. Retirement loomed just a few years away; if his latest offering to the colony of Llar and her people failed to produce the benefits he believed it could, then he and his career would slip silently into obscurity. His thoughts were interrupted.

'Sir, is everything all right? Are you unwell?'

'Sorry, I was miles away,' answered Godfrey, who stood looking slightly perplexed, scratching his chin.

'Sir, I must inform you that you have not left this spot.'

Godfrey smiled sympathetically. 'Trust me, I have.'

The puzzled doorman stared back at Godfrey. His plastic eyelids with their chipped paint flickered as best they could to form an expression of bewilderment. His cheeks were cracked from a trillion smiles and greetings, baring testament to his lengthy service age.

'May I get you something, Mr Davis? Shall I dial up the mainframe and summon you a medical team, or would you like a chair to rest on for a while?' The android pivoted at the hips. 'Maybe I can get Rupert to bring you a nice glass of iced water?'

'No, thank you, I'm fine. By the way, who is Rupert?'

'Rupert is my colleague, sir.'

Another android approached them, looking blankly into space. 'Your glass of iced water sir, as requested.'

'Actually, I didn't ask for one,' Godfrey politely informed him.

His associate immediately went on the offensive. 'Thank you, Rupert, but no one actually asked for a glass of iced water. It was merely an offer, a suggestion, a proposal, a proposition, nothing more,' he said curtly. 'Mr Davis is not in need of this water, so please take it back.'

Confusion set into Rupert's circuits. 'But I heard you request a glass of iced water.'

'I did not, Rupert,' the android said firmly.

'You did too, Norman. I heard you.'

Godfrey looked on, spellbound. 'You both have names?'

'Of course we do,' Norman said in a matter of fact sort of way. 'Why wouldn't we?'

'Perhaps because you are both machines,' mumbled Godfrey.

'Well I am Norman and this is Rupert.'

Both of the androids offered out a plastic hand, and Godfrey found himself involuntarily accepting their gesture. 'How long have you had names and who gave them to you?' Godfrey asked, slowly stumbling in disbelief over his own question.

The pair looked at one another blankly. 'I don't know really, forever I guess', said Norman, and Rupert nodded in confirmation. There was an awkward silence.

'So, are you in need of this water, sir, or shall I send it away?' Norman asked.

'Actually, no, not as it happens, but if it's a problem…'

Norman turned and gave his mechanical cousin a sneer. 'See, I told you so. He does not want it. You can take it back. Now go and do something useful.'

Rupert's hips and legs became a flurry of motors and moving wires intent on erecting his metal skeleton to its full extent. 'Don't talk to me like that. I am only doing my job.'

'Doing your job? Please, do not make me laugh,' Norman retorted. 'You've spent longer in the Service Department than you have manning these doors lately. And when you are here you make mistakes all the time, just like with this glass of water,' he said pointing. 'If you ask me, I think you need a level twelve systems check out.'

Rupert frantically searched his memory banks, and the result of the search made his head twitch uncontrollably. 'But a level twelve systems check out is a permanent shutdown. I would cease to function anymore.'

Norman threw his head back and made a noise like loose change falling down the back of a radiator. 'Oh what a loss that would be,' he guffawed, trying to perfect his human laugh and failing miserably in the process.

Godfrey stood like an impotent referee listening to their bickering; he was totally dumbfounded. His briefcase slipped lethargically from his hand and plopped onto the floor beside him. These machines had never been programmed to argue, or bicker, or chastise one another or anyone else for that matter. Their behaviour was far beyond the remit of their original programming.

'What in the name of Llar is going on here? Have you all gone completely potty?' Godfrey blurted, his face turning a shade of crimson.

Rupert huffed like a naughty child being reprimanded, and he scuffed his shoe to and fro across the floor. 'He started it.'

Norman stood bolt upright. 'Liar, you started it. You brought that glass of water.'

Godfrey positioned himself between the two mechanical doormen. He was aware that people entering the Ministry were beginning to take an interest in the proceedings.

'Look, I have no idea what's got into the pair of you, but I have got to get to my office. Now, I want you to calm down and be friends, shake hands or something.'

Godfrey's desperate words seemed to mollify the pair, and after reflection, Norman held out his hand. Rupert promptly held out the glass of water.

'I have told you once already, stupid, we didn't want the water.'

Rupert's circuits were unable to absorb anymore of Norman's caustic comments and his head began to twitch from side to side as his right leg began to vibrate, shaking faster and faster until he managed a quite remarkable tap-dance rhythm. His shoe, no longer able to stand the pace, leapt from his foot and shot through the air, ricocheting off the foyer wall before striking another android on the head. The android, which had been standing harmlessly next to a lift, immediately collapsed in a heap on the marble floor. The whole foyer of the Ministry froze and fell into a hush as everyone stared at Godfrey and the two doormen.

'Look, just hurry up and sort yourselves out, will you,' exclaimed Godfrey, and he left the fracas as fast as his legs would carry him, tumbling headlong into an open lift close by. 'Floor eighty-three,' he snapped.

The lift android shrugged and closed the doors; his head pivoted from side to side and his eyelids blinked in quick succession.

'What?' Godfrey asked.

He pressed a button and the lift began to ascend. 'Nothing,' he said, staring at his passenger's mouth.

'So what is it that you find so fascinating about me then?'

'Nothing,' said the android, trying to look as demure as possible.

'Is it my nose?'

'No.'

'Is it my tongue?' Godfrey said as he produced his yellow-stained appendage and wagged it from side to side.

The lift android contorted his face as far as he could in a look of complete disgust. 'No.'

The lift arrived at floor eighty-three and the doors slid back into their recesses. Godfrey stepped out and turned back. 'Definitely not the tongue then?' he asked.

The android shook his head as the doors closed between them.

In the foyer, a crowd had gathered to watch Rupert's impromptu dance routine. It was becoming something of a sideshow.

'Right that is it,' Norman cried out, 'I am calling maintenance. You clearly have a major malfunction.'

Rupert's leg thrashed to and fro completely out of control and smoke began to pour out of the top of his trousers. A huge shower of sparks suddenly shot down his trouser leg and his sock immediately burst into flames. The entire assembly made the sound that crowds make at a firework display.

Norman's processors made a quick calculation. They concluded that there was only one course of action that would remedy the situation. Snatching the glass of ice-cold water from Rupert's hand, he doused his colleague's burning sock. As a puff of smoke floated high into the foyer, Rupert's leg quickly returned to normal and the crowd let out a sigh of relief. Clapping their hands vigorously, they dispersed and continued on their way.

'Thanks for your help, Norman. I needed that.'

'It is all part of the service. Now let me dial up the mainframe and get you off to the Service Department. We'll have you as good as new by lunchtime.'

While Norman rolled his eyes and blinked out a message to the mainframe, Rupert gazed out across the huge entrance foyer, past the milling crowd towards the lift that Godfrey had entered. He glanced down at his foot, which was still steaming from his embarrassing malfunction. 'I hope the Service Department can repair me this time, Norman. Look at the mess I'm in.'

'You'll be fine. They can fix anything downstairs with a spot of paint and a new uniform,' Norman told him confidently.

Rupert remained unconvinced as he looked soulfully at the floor.

'Anyway,' Norman said, attempting to lift his friend's mood, 'did you see Mr Davis's teeth?'

'I know, weren't they to die for?' agreed Rupert enthusiastically. 'It must be a new fashion gimmick.'

Norman nodded in agreement, and the two androids stood for a moment deep in thought, gazing wistfully into cyberspace as the vapour from Rupert's sock drifted silently across the foyer.

CHAPTER 3

One hundred floors above Godfrey Davis and the fracas occurring in the foyer of the Ministry, a widescreen monitor in the presidential suite played the video footage of an aerial catastrophe. The camera switched from the images of smoke, flames and wreckage to the familiar presidential lectern festooned with chromium microphones. Flashes of light from four dozen cameras lit up the media room, splashing the President and the wall behind him. He gazed solemnly around, clutching a handful of papers.

'Ladies and gentlemen, my fellow countrymen,' he started, 'I would like to take this opportunity to offer my deepest sympathies to the families of the victims in today's tragedy. As you all know, further meetings were scheduled this afternoon between the Reformist Party and this administration, and in light of this tragic event, sadly these discussions will no longer be possible.' The President drew a deep breath as he glanced down at his notes while the room continued to illuminate with sporadic bursts of light. 'I am deeply shocked,' he continued, 'by the news that our fellow politicians have been taken from us in such an unfortunate way, and I have directed the full resources of this administration to investigate what has happened and report back to me personally. I will now ask you to direct any questions you may have at this time to our press spokesman. Thank you and good evening.'

The President gave a solemn nod at the assembly, and then, turning, he slipped through the doors behind him and into the

Ministry. The video footage faltered and the screen went blank.

'So what do you think?' asked the President, looking away from the monitor on his office wall. 'Was that convincing enough?'

The President's aide stood in the shadow of the huge velvet curtains that hung beside the windows of the presidential suite. He gazed out through the fine linen nets across the crowded skies above the metropolis. He was deep in thought. 'You were perfect, sir, as always. In fact, for an event that hasn't even happened yet, you were superb.'

The President gave a little huff of contentment. Jack Marsden always said the right thing, even though it was probably a lie.

'Though I do have one small reservation, sir,' Jack continued.

'What reservation?' the President asked defensively.

Jack approached his leader's desk and continued. 'Do you think it wise to have used the mainframe for this little production? After all, we do have something of an anomaly at this present time.'

The President stood and angrily slammed his fist on his desk. 'I've waited so long to see the back of these people I can almost taste it, Jack. I just wanted to see what it felt like standing there facing our citizens and telling them of this tragic news.'

'Let's just hope nothing goes wrong to spoil our plan,' Jack said. 'I'm sure I don't have to remind you what the consequences would be if the mainframe disgorges this little snippet of information into the public domain.'

The President wafted his hand across the space in front of him. 'Too bad. I've done it now and I enjoyed every second of it.' He reflected on Jack's statement and then grunted impatiently. 'How much longer do you think it will take to fix that damn mainframe, eh? I thought we were supposed to have our best people on it.'

Jack shrugged his shoulders impassively. 'Perhaps longer

than we would like, especially if we continue to remove the programmers who know too much.' In an attempt to reassure the President, Jack smiled confidently. 'Everything will be fine, sir, I'm sure. This tragedy will occur in three days' time as we agreed. There's not a problem.'

'Good,' said the President returning to his leather chair. 'I just wish we could get all of them on board my shuttle at the same time. It would certainly help to eradicate any opposition for years to come.'

'We will,' Jack confirmed.

The President turned and cast a shrewd eye across his aide. 'Do you really imagine for one moment you could do that?'

'Yes, sir, I do.'

The President shook his head slowly, his eyes glowing with anticipation. Jack never stopped amazing him with his ingenuity. 'Tell me, how are you going to manage to entice them all on board? They're not mice, you know, and they won't fall for a piece of cheese.'

Jack felt confident. 'I had planned to tell the Reformist Party that you are ready to meet their demands and, of course, invite them to a presidential banquet afterwards'

The President raised his eyebrows, his eyes glinting at the simplicity of his aide's trap. 'How do you sleep at night?' he enquired, breaking into a laugh.

'Very soundly, thank you, sir,' Jack replied. 'Now, if we have nothing left to discuss, I have some final arrangements to make. There is still a lot to do.'

The President picked up the remote control for his monitor. 'Actually, Jack, there is. You see, while I was dabbling with that miserably idiosyncratic mainframe to produce my tragic announcement, I dug up some old video footage of you, would you believe?'

Jack smelt danger. 'And what footage might that be, sir?'

'Oh, it's just some old newsreels I found, so I mixed them in with pictures of some burning wreckage and added in some new dialogue. Here, let me show you, it's really rather good.' The President motioned his head at the screen on the wall. The picture of Jack Marsden in his crisp black suit faltered transiently and then stabilised as the commentary began.

> 'Early this afternoon, the presidential shuttle crashed, killing all of those onboard. I am unable at this time to reveal the names of those involved in this tragedy until their families have first been notified. The Ministry would like to confirm that the President was not – I repeat, was not – one of the casualties in this disaster. The presidential shuttle was enroute from the Tower Hotel where it had collected members of the Reformist Party for further negotiations with the President's administration. Unconfirmed reports indicate that the shuttle suddenly lost altitude after an explosion and crashed near the city centre. The President would now like to make a statement.'

The monitor went blank.

'The mainframe, for all its faults, made a pretty convincing job of your voice, don't you think?' asked the President as he gave his aide a cold stare.

Jack's eyes were locked on to the blank screen. Deep inside, the anger swelled up within him, though when he spoke he didn't let his emotions give him away. 'That fits in nicely, sir, with your announcement,' he said calmly.

The President nodded and gave Jack a parting glance. 'We're about to incinerate our opponents and I need to have your complete attention on this one. Do you understand me?'

Jack managed to execute an election-winning smile. 'Of course, now if there are no further matters you wish to discuss, I have to make arrangements.'

'Fine, carry on, but take some advice with you; trust no one,' said the President through an iron glare.

He considered the absurdity of the President's comment and wondered if his leader had considered his own advice when he had used the mainframe for his forthcoming announcement. 'Sir, no one will connect this tragic event to you or this administration, I promise you,' Jack told him.

'Connect this event to "*us*", Jack, and this administration,' the President coldly corrected him.

'Absolutely,' Jack said, desperately trying to suppress his anger.

The President paused. 'One last question before you go.'

'Yes, sir.'

'That latest programmer that they sent up earlier, what have you done with him?'

'He no longer represents a threat,' Jack told him, and nodding politely, he left the office.

As the President's office door closed silently behind him Jack took a deep breath. He was livid. The President had deliberately orchestrated that footage for one reason and one reason alone, to ensure that evidence of his involvement was embedded in the mainframe. If the President fell, then he would fall with him, and with the mainframe becoming more unstable by the hour, that fall could happen at any time. He quietly strode along the corridor to his office, acknowledging the sea of personnel withdrawing from his path. He walked with purpose, an air of confidence written across his face for all to see. Very shortly, all of the players on the Jack Marsden chessboard of life would be exactly where he wanted them, and those that were not would no longer present a problem to the smooth running of the colony.

His eyes narrowed at the thoughts coursing through his mind. The President had played his hand and his cards were now on the table. As for blackmailing Jack Marsden, that was a foolish move for anyone who wanted a long and prosperous life.

CHAPTER 4

As Jack Marsden left his meeting with the President on the one hundredth floor, Godfrey Davis arrived at his office still slightly flustered from his experience in the foyer downstairs. The door to his office was wide open, and a battered cleaning trolley was parked to one side in the corridor. Ethel the cleaner was behind with her schedule again, which was nothing unusual. She was a short stocky woman with muscular arms the product of whisking her mop across countless floors. Her pleasant disposition and warming smile greeted Godfrey every morning when he arrived at his office. Ethel would talk endlessly as she cleaned, recounting conversations with her two sons who had grown up and moved west. She told Godfrey stories of her bedridden neighbour whom she cared for in the afternoons and shopped for regularly twice a week. Over the years the pair had developed a friendship through working at the Ministry, and though it was entirely platonic, Godfrey felt somehow that he knew some of the most intimate details of her life. Often, as he prepared himself for his day, he wondered if Ethel deliberately took her time cleaning his office just to talk to him, not that he minded. Listening to her early morning discourse had become part of the fabric of his day at the Ministry, a reference point that indicated all was normal in his world.

'Good morning, Ethel.'

'Morning, Mr Davis, I'm nearly done,' she informed him.

Godfrey hesitated, looking perturbed.

'Where's your briefcase?'

'I must have left it in the foyer when I was talking to those two androids,' he mumbled. 'I'll ring downstairs and get them to bring it up later.'

Ethel squeezed out her mop and brushed the back of her hand across her forehead, disturbing the fringe of her tinted auburn hair. 'Tomorrow's the big day then. I suppose all the top brass and the President will be there?'

Godfrey gave her a vacant stare, and for a brief moment he thought he saw her squint and stare at his mouth. 'How in the name of Llar do you know about the demonstration, Ethel? It's supposed be a secret.'

Ethel carried on moving her mop to and fro across the marble floor as a distraction. 'Everybody knows about it, Mr Davis. Mainly the people that shouldn't, I must admit, but nonetheless they do. The Ministry has always been the same as far back as I can remember; it's like a leaky bucket, this place, and it will never change.'

Godfrey skilfully stepped over Ethel's mop, slid gracefully on the wet floor and closed the office door. 'Have you any idea of the trouble I would be in if security find out that a cleaner knows we are having this demonstration?'

'What do you mean, a cleaner?' Ethel said, turning her head in a questioning pose.

'What I meant was…' Godfrey stammered.

Ethel rallied her mop, which was almost as tall as her, and pointed the handle at Godfrey's chest. Her green eyes shone like fiery polished emeralds. 'Are you inferring that as a cleaner I am in some way inferior, Mr Davis?'

Godfrey felt his cheeks change colour as he grinned nervously.

'I'm sorry, but I fail to see what there is to smile about,' she told him, waving her mop defiantly.

Godfrey placed his hand on Ethel's shoulder. 'Look, I'm

sorry, I didn't mean to offend you. It hasn't been a good start to the day so far. Gloria texted to say I have forgotten my sandwiches again, and then I witnessed those two pugnacious androids in the foyer, which made me forget my briefcase.'

'Whatever happens today, don't have your lunch in the canteen,' Ethel advised him. 'They have that pie again, the one you can't put a fork in. And as for androids, I caught two of them skating up and down the corridor on my trolley this morning like a pair of kids. I had to chase them off with my mop.'

'Something's not right with them, that's quite clear,' Godfrey agreed. 'But what's making them behave so erratically?'

'I'm sorry, Mr Davis, I have no idea. I'm only a cleaner, remember? I'm not an engineer like you.'

There was clearly only one course of action he could think of to resolve the situation. 'I think we need a cup of tea, Ethel, don't you?'

'Now you're talking my language, Mr Davis. I'll get the kettle on,' Ethel said beaming. Before she had retrieved the cups from the top of Godfrey's filing cabinet, there were three knocks on the office door. 'Come in, sweetheart,' Ethel called out, 'and mind the floor, it's still wet.'

The young woman standing in the doorway was Semilla Smith. 'Morning, Mr Davis, morning Ethel.'

'I knew it would be you,' Ethel said warmly.

Semilla was an office runner on the eighty-third floor, and for the past two years she had also been Ethel's lodger. When Semilla had moved to the metropolis and started her studies at the university, she'd had the good fortune to meet Ethel and the pair had become close friends. The arrangement worked perfectly for both of them. Ethel again had someone to mother in the absence of her sons, and Semilla found a sense of family that she missed so much being in the metropolis. At weekends in her spare time, Semilla would visit her grandmother in the outer suburbs. It had been just such a visit the night before that had produced a present from her grandmother that Semilla now wore.

'Is that the outfit you told me your gran was making?' Ethel asked as Semilla pirouetted in the open doorway.

'Yes, isn't it amazing?' she said. She glanced at Godfrey and her eyes widened.

'What is it?' Godfrey asked her rather bluntly.

Semilla's eyes darted across to Ethel for support. 'Nothing, Mr Davis, really,' she said, sounding far from convincing. Several awkward looks were exchanged and Semilla tried to change the subject quickly. 'So there's only one more day to go before the demonstration then? By the way, how is your wife?'

For his age Godfrey was still remarkably nimble. The speed that he managed to drag Semilla into the office and slam the door left both of the women with looks of astonishment. The door to Godfrey's office shut with such an impact that a small insignificant painting of a duck flew from the corridor wall and bounced off the head of a passing android that promptly collapsed in a heap on the floor.

Godfrey went to the sanctuary of his desk and sank into his office chair, feeling thoroughly desperate. He propped up his forehead with one hand and contemplated the enormity of this conspiracy, which he had convinced himself is what it had to be. No one could have a day like this and see their career survive at the end of it. His life was taking a terminal nosedive over tomorrow's demonstration in front of the President, and if one other person dared mention it, he would surely lose the plot completely.

Semilla and Ethel stared at poor Godfrey, looking lost behind his office desk, while the kettle finally boiled.

'Have this nice cup of tea,' Ethel said, putting a large

steaming mug in front of him. She offered him the biscuit tin as two more knocks sounded on the office door. The door swung open and the doorway was filled by a large portly man with a huge bushy moustache and ruddy red cheeks.

'Good morning, Godfrey, how are we today? I see you have some charming company this morning,' he said, smiling at Ethel and Semilla. 'By the way, did any of you know there's an android lying on the floor out here?'

Godfrey glanced up from his piping hot beverage. 'Good morning, Charlie. I have had better day's, thank you,' he said, his head hung low as he stared into the steam rising from his mug.

Charlie Albright, sensing the body language, raised his eyebrows. 'Did I say something wrong?' The commander was Godfrey's oldest and dearest friend and the pair had worked together at the Ministry for more years than either of them cared to remember.

'No, not at all in fact you're the only one who hasn't wished me well with the President's demonstration tomorrow.'

Charlie's huge bushy eyebrows and wayward moustache remained tilted skyward. 'But apart from you and I, only a handful of people know about tomorrow,' he said, slowly entering the office.

'Not so, Charlie,' Godfrey said, taking a sip of his tea as he glanced across at Ethel and Semilla.

'Well, if you really want to keep a secret don't write about it on the pad next to your phone. I can read you know,' Ethel said defensively.

Godfrey remembered his call from Commander Albright, and the irony of the situation rapidly sank in. Ethel was correct. He had written about the pending demonstration on his notepad.

'I accept I may have been somewhat remiss in writing down details about tomorrow, but I'm now considering putting a notice on my office door to advertise the event. If we get enough interest perhaps we could organise tickets and have a raffle too. Even better, perhaps if we ask the androids really nicely they could spread the news around the entire Ministry for us.'

Semilla coughed nervously. 'Mr Davis, the androids already are. That's where I heard it from.'

Godfrey's grip on his teacup eased and hot tea began to cascade into his lap. His muffled cry was accompanied by a small gust of wind that swept through the office from the open window, disturbing some papers on his desk, sending them tumbling like autumn leaves to the floor.

'Is everything all right, Godfrey?' said a voice from the doorway.

Everyone in the room froze, and the moment was punctuated perfectly by the sound of a solitary falling pencil as it came to rest on the marble floor.

CHAPTER 5

....

Jack Marsden had just entered the presidential shuttle compound by the time the pencil had come to rest on Godfrey's office floor at the Ministry. The mere sight of Jack's level one pass opened doors almost before he arrived at them. Everyone in the colony knew him, though perhaps not on a personal level. With his face strewn across every magazine and newspaper distributed amongst the masses, it was hard not to. Whenever the President was filmed at a civic function, Jack Marsden would be somewhere in the background. Invariably he would be stood with his hands clasped behind his back, impeccably dressed in one of his sharp suits, crisp cotton shirts and smiling for the media cameras.

Jack was, in real terms, as famous as the President, and, in reality, almost as powerful. He tried hard to play down the rumours that he was in fact being groomed by the President to replace him when the time came. Jack was single, forty-two years old with dark unassuming features and the demeanour of a complete political professional. He was, however, beneath the facade of polite handshakes and attentive looks he gave civic dignitaries, a thoroughly ruthless entity. He unquestioningly achieved the goals his President desired and sometimes even a few of his own, flawlessly, efficiently, and without compassion. He knew that with power came privilege and had come to revel in both. Whenever the need arose, Jack would faithfully undertake any task required of him to maintain the life to which he had become accustomed. And this morning he stood in the secure compound where the President's shuttle was kept safely in its hanger, to complete a clandestine task that surpassed even the most suspect of duties he had ever undertaken in the past. He was here to plant a device that would, in one single act, completely annihilate the president's political opposition.

The guards at both the outer and inner security gates had not the courage to ask Jack if they could inspect the contents of his briefcase. No one questioned Jack Marsden's comings and goings, not if they wanted a quiet trouble-free life. And everyone that came into contact with him soon learned they preferred to have just that. When Jack arrived in the hanger, he gazed up at the huge elliptical green craft. It stood motionless, propped up by its three telescopic legs, light spilling from the windows along the length of the fuselage. To one side, the stairs leading to the cabin were unguarded and the door was open to air the interior.

Jack had been on this shuttle many times before, mainly on official visits across the colony, and he knew the layout intimately. As he climbed the stairs he stopped halfway and took a precautionary look around the empty hanger. It paid to be cautious under the circumstances. He was, after all, about to be the sole architect of the deaths of thirty-odd people. Looking up and down the aisle, he made his way directly to the cockpit. Jack took one last look behind him and stepped inside. Placing his briefcase on the portside seat, he removed his suit jacket and slipped it over the backrest. He opened the briefcase to reveal a rectangular black steel box that filled the case. From the lid of the case Jack removed a memory stick and plugged the device into the port of the on-board computer in the centre of the instrument panel. The computer responded. 'Good morning, I have detected some new software. Would you like me to download this?' asked the computer.

'Yes, I want the software downloaded,' Jack instructed the machine.

Moments later, the on-board computer confirmed Jack's request.

'Good, now encrypt the software before the mainframe registers this on your daily backup.'

'The download has now been encrypted.'

Taking the black steel box out of his briefcase, Jack cautiously examined one end. Hesitating, he cast his eye over a small black switch. Once this device was armed there would be no going back. The President's political opponents, the crew, and almost certainly a score of innocent bystanders on the ground, would be annihilated when the shuttle plummeted from the skies above the colony. For the unintended victims, Jack considered it was simply a case of collateral damage, nothing more. He flicked the switch and the pulsing glow of an inconspicuous red light confirmed the device was now armed. Kneeling on the floor, he placed the device beneath the portside pilot's seat, slipping the box out of sight. Jack stood and stretched himself as a tiny bead of sweat rolled down between his shoulder blades. 'Now, computer, with your new software, can you detect the remote device?' he asked.

'Yes, I can.'

'Good, then close down for now,' Jack told the machine as he turned for his jacket.

'Sir, may I be of assistance?'

Jack spun round to see an engineer android that was now standing behind him.

'Sir, I was not aware of any work being undertaken here in the cockpit today, not according to my work schedule.' The android glanced down at the open briefcase. Jack's reactions were swift and fatal. Grabbing the android's head between his powerful hands, he twisted it sideways in a short snapping motion, severing the main link to its motherboard. The sparks cascading from the android's mouth only lasted a few seconds before the machine went limp and collapsed to the floor. The smell of burnt wiring and molten solder filled the air as Jack slammed the lid of his case shut. He felt no fear, merely anger that he had been so careless and not checked the rest of the shuttle before he began his act of sabotage. He stared down at the limp lifeless form in front of him as the smoke drifted around the cockpit. Now there was another loose end to tie up.

Several minutes later, and looking utterly composed, Jack entered the compound security office. The two guards were watching a football match with their backs to the door and had no idea he was standing behind them.

'If it's not too much to ask,' Jack started, and the two men leapt to their feet. 'We have an android down in the President's shuttle. He collapsed while we were inspecting the craft for its next flight. Go and remove the android now and get rid of the smell of burning.'

'Sir,' said one of the guards, standing to attention, 'we'll get someone on it right away.'

'Not someone, you, and do it now,' Jack barked in a peremptory tone.

The two men grabbed their caps and ran from the office into the hanger and towards the shuttle. Jack waited until they had reached the cabin door and entered, before wandering casually over to the bank of recorders for the security cameras. He selected the disc marked presidential shuttle and removed it. Jack passed the outer security gate, nodding to the guard in his kiosk, and he was back in the street with his mission accomplished. He broke into a steady stride until he reached the corner of the block. The smell of fresh coffee filled the air as he glanced over the street vendor's wagon. He grabbed a large black coffee and a croissant and planted himself on a nearby bench. To any passers-by, he was just another man in a suit.

CHAPTER 6

As Jack Marsden walked calmly away from his insidious mission on the presidential shuttle, Godfrey and his colleagues stared at the figure standing in the entrance to his office.

'I see we have quite a gathering here this morning, Godfrey. Forgive me, if I had known I would have come later,' the President said, displaying one of his most charismatic smiles. He sauntered into Godfrey's office, offering his hand to Ethel and Semilla as the two women curtsied, both blushing at their leader.

The President wasn't a particularly tall man. In many cases, the vast majority of the people he met actually left him at a disadvantage, and he found himself looking up at them. These encounters had a subliminal effect. Some said, in private of course, that it honed a feeling of inadequacy within him and accounted for his short-tempered and somewhat aggressive nature. He wasn't the sort of person one would meddle with, even at the age of seventy. Adept at using the words he spoke, he was able to tease and transform a crowded function room into a gathering of loyal and grateful followers. And when he had their commitment and their vote, of course, he would barely acknowledge them afterwards. Over the years, he had earned the dubious reputation as being the longest-serving President the colony had ever seen. However, there were many people who knew of his shady and underhanded tactics in the world of politics and they were not taken in by him. They lived in anticipation, waiting for the day when this man succumbed to nature's law and passed into the next world.

'And conveniently we also have Commander Albright here this morning,' the President said, nodding at his salute.

Godfrey shot to his feet the instant the President walked into his office, his heart pounding deep within his chest. He dabbed vigorously at his damp tea-stained trousers. This was the pinnacle of imperfect timing, Godfrey thought, and for a terrible moment he considered that the President may have overheard the conversation in his office.

The President strutted towards Godfrey, standing awkwardly beside his desk. 'By the way, why is there an android on the floor in the hallway?' He glanced in the direction of the damp patch on Godfrey's trousers. 'Is everything all right?'

Godfrey's throat became an arid wasteland, and the only moisture at hand was his tea-drenched trousers. 'I spilt my tea, sir.'

The President surveyed the rest of the office as Godfrey sifted through a dozen excuses why the pending demonstration had been leaked. Most of them seemed plausible to him, though he feared none of them would appease their leader. He considered the androids; they were to blame, of course, and even Semilla could confirm that. Godfrey's mind and heart raced in tandem as he desperately tried to concoct a sentence plausible enough for the President's ears.

'Sir, I can explain, please, it really…'

Clasping his hands behind his back, the President focused on the array of diplomas and photographs mounted on the office wall, ignoring Godfrey completely. He stood looking at one particular photograph, which was pride of place above the others. It was Godfrey's graduation day, his father and mother standing proudly either side of him as he held his diploma humbly in front of the camera.

'He was a great man,' the President said, nodding at the photograph.

'You knew him?' Godfrey asked, thrown completely by his statement.

'Sadly, only for a short while. I joined the Ministry just before we lost him, so to speak.'

'I had no idea,' Godfrey replied.

'You have truly followed in your father's footsteps, Godfrey. If he were here with us today he would be very proud of you. Unfortunately, though, I haven't come here today on a social call,' the President said, taking a deep breath. 'We have a much more serious issue to resolve, one of immense importance to the colony and its security.'

'Sir, if I could explain. You see, the leak is not directly my fault, the androids ...'

The President threw his head back and laughed out loud, his rounded face depicting a look of amusement at Godfrey's statement. 'No, those ridiculous mechanical servants of our great colony are not my concern, not today. Besides, the Ministry has always been very leaky when it comes to secrets, though thankfully not all of them.'

'I told Godfrey that this morning, sir. The Ministry has always been the same all the years I've worked here,' Ethel piped up from the corner.

'Yes, quite,' the President said, acknowledging Ethel's statement as he glanced disdainfully across the room at the old cleaner clasping her mop. 'Anyway, what I have come to discuss here today is a matter of the utmost secrecy, so perhaps you ladies would like to leave now and kindly close the door behind you?'

Ethel was clearly embarrassed. Nodding politely to the President, she took Semilla by the arm and they left the office together.

The instant the door closed, the President continued. 'Gentlemen, let me get straight to the point,' he said, addressing

Godfrey and Commander Albright. 'I am here this morning because we are currently experiencing a major security breach in our illustrious mainframe. At this time, the problem has been contained within the basement, and nothing so far has spilled out into the public domain. Fortunately, apart from Jack Marsden and I, only our programmers are aware of this problem.'

The President ambled across the office looking deeply perplexed. He turned, facing the two men. 'I am unable to divulge the fine details, as the data that the mainframe is now spewing out is top secret. It goes back to an era a long time ago and involves information so sensitive that it could rock the colony to its very foundations.' The President glanced up at Godfrey, staring briefly at his jaw before continuing. 'You see, the secret data I'm referring to relates to both of your fathers and certain work they undertook during their time here at the Ministry.'

'What work?' asked Charlie Albright.

The President gave Charlie a condescending look. 'As I have said, Commander, I am unable to divulge the finer details as the project was top secret. They may have passed away a long time ago, but the fact remains that it has come back to haunt us, if you will forgive the pun?'

'So why is the mainframe disgorging this information now? Has it got some sort of virus?' asked Godfrey.

'I doubt it,' Charlie said, 'the mainframe has so many levels of protection, it just couldn't happen.'

'I'm sorry to contradict you, Commander, but right now the mainframe has something monumentally wrong with it,' the President informed him.

'Have the programmers undertaken a full sequence of diagnostic tests?' asked Godfrey.

'Of course they have,' the President scoffed.

'And they found what precisely?'

'Nothing,' he said, becoming agitated.

'Are you sure?' Godfrey persisted.

The President's body language suddenly changed. 'Look, I'm not a technical person and I don't work on the mainframe. I really have no idea what the people who do work on it actually do. If they say they can't find anything then I assume they know what they are talking about, wouldn't you? There was one programmer who volunteered a theory. He tried to suggest that the mainframe was almost taking on a mind of its own.' The President smirked at them. 'I mean, how absurd is that?'

'Sometimes, sir, the most absurd things in science are the foundation for plausible theories, no matter how preposterous they may sound at the onset,' Godfrey said.

The President dismissed the statement with a sneer and wandered back across to the photo of Godfrey's graduation. The President looked intently at the smiling assembly. 'I want you both to think back to when your fathers worked here at the Ministry. Do you remember anything that they may have said about their work here, anything at all? Something they may have invented perhaps? Did they ever take any of their work home, for example?'

The commander stepped forward and stood beside Godfrey. 'For my part, sir, I can remember nothing my father ever spoke of regarding his work here. He would come home and my mother would say, "How was work today?" And he would say, "Fine, thank you," and my mother would say, "Just fine, nothing else?" And he would say, "No, just fine, thank you."'

'My father was much the same. He never spoke of his work either, apart from when he was developing the androids when I was a young boy,' Godfrey said.

'That comment only serves to remind me how old and outdated those androids really are,' the President said tersely.

Godfrey's faced clouded over. 'There was one occasion.'

The President quickly spun round. 'What occasion exactly?'

'It was nothing really, not a comment or a statement as such, it was more of a mood thing as I remember. There was something troubling him just before he died.'

'Sir, how can our fathers' work possibly have any effect on the security of the colony when they both passed away a long time ago?' asked Charlie.

The President ignored him and focused on Godfrey instead. His eyes darkened. 'Explain.'

Godfrey moved uneasily on the spot, wishing he had been more precise with his statement. He coughed nervously. 'My mother and I both noticed how reticent he had become. There was clearly something on his mind. My mother tried her best to talk to him, but whatever it was that troubled him, he had no intention of sharing it with her.'

'Go on,' encouraged the President.

'That was it, sir. He never told my mother or me anything, right up until we lost him.'

'Sir, with all due respects,' Charlie started, 'I am sure our fathers would never have done anything that would have brought harm to the colony or its people.'

'Really, Commander, is that so?' said the President. 'I wouldn't be here today wasting my valuable time, would I, if we didn't have a problem with the mainframe and your two patriotic fathers and their damned secrets?'

'And they were patriots, weren't they? True Llarinians to the very end,' said the android standing in office doorway clutching Godfrey's briefcase in his hand. 'They were totally trustworthy men, steadfast to a fault, and they never, ever once gave up the location of the XXL, even to the very end, did they?'

The three men turned and stared at the android, and the android stared back.

CHAPTER 7

Far out across the huge metropolis in a quiet tree-lined suburban lane, a matt black security transport hummed to a halt and planted itself delicately on the ground. The two men on board looked at the neat single-storey dwelling nestling in a manicured garden. It was the home of Nigel Prentagast.

'Your call,' said the driver as he produced a silver coin and flipped it in the air. He snapped it up as it tumbled down and slapped it on the back of his other hand.

'Heads', claimed the passenger.

The driver lifted his hand and glanced at the coin, then smiled to his colleague. 'You tell her, it's tails,' he said, slipping the coin into his suit pocket.

A few moments after hearing her doorbell ring, Nigel Prentagast's mother stood in the doorway of her home clutching a tea towel.

'Mrs Prentagast?'

'Yes.'

'We are from security at the Ministry,' the man said, producing a badge from a black leather wallet. 'We have been sent to ask you if you have any idea where your son is today.'

Mrs Prentagast looked bewildered. 'Why, he is at work, of course.'

'I'm afraid he didn't arrive for work this morning, Ma'am. There has been no record of him entering the Ministry.'

'Has there been an accident?' she stammered.

'No, Ma'am, there have been no reports of any accident. We have already checked the hospitals.'

'He must have gone to work; surely there's been some mistake. Where else would he have gone?' she said as the tears began to fill her eyes.

'Did he say anything to you or give you some indication there was something wrong before he left this morning?'

'No, nothing, nothing at all.'

The two men watched her twist the tea towel nervously through her trembling fingers.

'Did your son ever mention his work at the Ministry, Mrs Prentagast?'

'No, he never spoke of it. He said it was forbidden,' she replied, her lips quivering with every word.

'If your son makes contact, Mrs Prentagast, please let us know immediately,' said the security man, handing her a card. The pair nodded politely and made their way back down the path.

At the end of the lane, where the colony met the desert, the driver swung their vehicle round and hesitated, hovering side on to the barren wastelands stretching into the distance.

'You know, every time we tell that story, I wonder,' said the driver.

'Wonder what?'

'Whether they really believe it, or whether they know we are lying.'

The passenger ignored the statement as he imagined the emptiness of the Llarinian desert, slipping silently into a catalogue of horrors he could only begin to imagine.

'By the way, it was heads,' said the driver, breaking the silence.

'I know, you cheat every time.'

'I'm comfortable with that,' the driver said, laughing.

The transport turned and headed back towards the colony, casting up a cloud of dust behind it as it passed beneath the canopy of eucalyptus trees that stood either side of the lane.

Mrs Prentagast closed her front door and returned to her kitchen. She stared out of the window at the rose bushes adorning the borders of the rear garden, overcome with the news she had just been given. Clutching the rim of the sink with both hands, she remembered their morning routine. Each day was exactly the same; the only demarcation between them was a date on the calendar that hung on the pantry wall. Her son was a very precise man; he undertook the same habitual acts each day of taking a shower, dressing, making his bed and then seating himself at the breakfast table. Nigel would sit inaudibly consuming his cereals while she chattered on. He would ruminate his way methodically through his breakfast, drifting deeper in thought until her words passed silently over him as if he were in a vacuum. Lately, he had begun to take on the appearance of a man who was physically ill, and she'd known there was something eating away at him. The sound of the doorbell announcing the paperboy's delivery that morning was all that it took to set the hair on his neck bristling and a burst of adrenalin coursing through his veins. He had jolted back to reality, stared at his empty coffee cup and then glanced up at his mother who stood beside the cooker preparing the vegetables for their evening meal. Mrs Prentagast had carried on talking to her son until the front door had sounded his departure. She had turned and looked along the empty hall leading from the kitchen. Mornings like this had become a regular event, and she was only too aware that her son carried a burden he would not share with her.

Once, when Nigel had been a younger man and keen to impress his peers, he had relished the beginning of his week as a fresh opportunity. That had been a long time ago, and now his daily routine merely served to mark the beginning of another ordeal. The thought of facing that room beneath the Ministry and serving his colony were of no inspiration, not now, not after all these years. He had convinced himself that there was nothing left for him to look forward to. Any form of promotion that would have elevated him to a better position and a more salubrious place to work had long since passed him by.

This small sinewy man with thinning grey hair had only ever had one passion in life, and that had been for numbers. Nigel had always had a sharp eye for figures even as a child. He had excelled at school from an early age and his teachers were quick to realise his ability. Nigel had by all benchmarks been fortunate enough to benefit from something akin to an idyllic childhood. They had been happy days, happier than those he had experienced of late, and he would often reflect upon them when there was a lull in his workload. Then suddenly his father had died and life changed irrevocably. The dream of leaving home and starting a life of his own stalled until he could guarantee that his widowed mother would be able to cope alone. But she never had, and Nigel continued to live at home where he had grown up in the outer suburbs of the great colony of Llar. With the passage of time, he had come to consider his mother to be more of a burden than a responsibility, though he remained unable and unwilling to change the status quo, bound instead by a sense of duty. The thought of finding himself a wife and raising a family were far behind him now. He had mulled over the prospect in those early years from time to time and eventually discarded it as he no longer deemed it an issue worth considering. He knew the effect on his mother would have been devastating. As the years passed by, Nigel had become withdrawn, shunning the few friendships he had made as he slipped further into the abyss that had become his life.

Mrs Prentagast's eyes flooded with emotion. There was something else outside of the secure little cocoon she had built for the both of them that she had no control over. It was something embedded in her son's mind that had tormented him lately. She had heard him late at night calling out in his sleep as he lived out a private nightmare, muttering words, incoherent words, all except for one: 'Mainframe.'

With a sense of utter desperation she sat herself down and began to weep as the casserole she had prepared for the two of them simmered on the stove.

CHAPTER 8

Two guards, responding to the President's phone call, burst into Godfrey's office, stood to attention, and saluted. 'Reporting for duty, sir,' they both shouted enthusiastically, as if it were the first action they had seen in a long while.

'At last, it's so kind of you to turn up,' snapped the President. 'I want you to arrest that android and put him in solitary confinement, now,' he said, nodding in the general vicinity of the android that was standing beside Godfrey's desk.

The two guards stared blankly at their leader. 'I don't know that we can do that, sir,' replied one of the guards.

'Why not?' muttered the President, staring down at his shoes and trying desperately to keep his temper.

'Sir, technically, the android is a machine.'

'But I am not a machine,' the android stated. 'I am an individual.'

'Ah, yes, of course, that's right,' the President said as he scowled at the android. 'I'm sorry, didn't you say you had a name? What was it?'

'My name is Arthur,' the android replied proudly.

Both of the guards looked utterly bewildered.

'That's right,' said the President, pursing his lips. 'Now, I seem to remember telling you, Arthur, not to utter another word. Do you remember that, just before I phoned security?'

'Yes, sir, I do,' Arthur confirmed cheerfully.

The President strode across Godfrey's office and glared at the guards. Harry and Burt quickly stood to attention.

'Let me get this straight. I have asked you to arrest this android and you are telling me you can't because it's a machine, correct?'

Harry and Burt stared at the ceiling. 'Yes, sir.'

'What buffoon made up this ridiculous rule then?' enquired the President sarcastically.

'It was our inventor, Reg Davis, when he constructed us,' Arthur said gleefully.

Commander Albright confirmed Arthur's statement. 'He's correct, sir; it's Llarinian law, it's written into our constitution. Godfrey's father had the foresight to realise that they may look humanoid, but they are still machines. For goodness' sake, it would be as ridiculous as arresting a vacuum cleaner, wouldn't it?'

The President sighed deeply, shook his head, and stared at Godfrey. 'I might have known your father would be mixed up in this somewhere.'

'I'm not a vacuum cleaner,' blurted the android, stamping his foot on the floor. 'I am an individual and my name is Arthur.'

'When did they get names?' the President asked Godfrey.

'I have no idea, sir,' Godfrey told him nervously.

The President began to wander to and fro, gazing out of the office window to the busy skies of the metropolis and beyond. 'So, to summarise, we have this idiotic android that is clearly a security risk to our great colony. We have two security guards who won't arrest him because he's a machine and protected by our glorious constitution, and then we have me, the President of the colony, who is getting very, very angry,' he shouted.

'I am not an idiot,' exclaimed Arthur.

The President swiftly raised a finger. 'I know, you're an individual, aren't you?'

'Yes,' replied Arthur proudly.

'Good, then as an individual you represent a risk to our

national security and that is why I am going to do this.' In a moment of pure frustration, the President plunged his hand into Burt's holster and grabbed at his pistol. 'Give me your weapon.'

'I'm sorry, sir, I can't do that; it's against regulations.'

The President gave Burt a menacing look. 'Really, and so is throwing a guard out of an office window eighty-three floors up.'

Burt reluctantly released his pistol from its holster and handed it to his leader. The President grabbed the weapon and pointed it at Arthur, and everyone with the exception of the android himself took cover. Without any further hesitation, he aimed the large chromium pistol and pulled the trigger.

Godfrey's office resonated to the sound of a dull metallic click as the trigger mechanism operated once, twice, three times and then repeatedly in quick succession. Everyone in the room, and Ethel and Semilla, who were watching from the open office door, stared at their leader in disbelief. The President, realising he was making a spectacle of himself, turned and pulled a bemused face at his audience. 'Oh dear, I think it's empty,' he said.

There were some remarkable facts that surrounded the history and construction of Burt's standard issue Phlegm-O-Matic guard's pistol, a weapon of unique concept and as yet unrivalled in the history of the colony.

Firstly, the designer of this idiosyncratic pistol was a backroom technician called Dave, a man of no notoriety whatsoever, who shortly after the weapon's incorporation into the arsenal of the great colony of Llar, died tragically while opening a family-sized tin of pilchards. Dave, however, before his demise, had a monumental head cold at the time he was designing the weapon. He thought it would be symbolic, and something of a stab at their authoritarian society, to name his creation after the greenish-yellow propellant contained within the cartridges. The name stuck, somewhat like the deposits in

Dave's handkerchief, and before long the weapon had a title forever revered amongst the security forces across the colony.

This pistol in fact became legendary, a triumph of technological advancement, though it couldn't boast of many kills. In fact, during the weapon's entire service history throughout the colony, it couldn't boast of any at all, not a single one. Gifted with the ability to hold a conversation, the Phlegm-O-Matic became a firearm with outstanding capabilities. Thanks to the software designed by Godfrey's father, the weapon had had its original lethal intent somewhat diluted. This menacing-looking firearm had, in real terms, more of a penchant for weather reports than for annihilating people and would happily impart its knowledge of pending precipitation, or other inclement or favourable conditions, to the end user. For those who were intent on harming their fellow man, there was another downside to achieving their end goal. This remarkable piece of engineering and design also had a say in the annihilation of a chosen target, if in fact the situation ever arose. This feature naturally offloaded some of the end user's guilt if it were proven later that the target was actually innocent of any misdeed. Nevertheless, the *guilt override mode* could prove to be a tedious option when trying to talk the weapon into performing the task for which it had been originally designed. There had been many exponents of this original concept, and some called it pure genius that the weapon was, thanks to its software, actually more in control of a confrontational scenario than, in fact, the user themselves.

The technology behind this pistol was an adaptation of artificial intelligence based on Advanced Robotic Silicone Evolution. Sometimes, when the weapon was proving difficult, Dave often referred to the pistol by its acronym, especially when it failed to obey commands. Occasionally, on a particularly good day, Dave referred to the pistol as *'nice A.R.S.E'* although these compliments during development were unfortunately few and far between. He did, though, from time to time, telephone Reg Davis to inform him of his partial success in getting the pistol to follow requests and actually fire a shot at a cardboard target. These telephone conversations were in reality a rare occurrence as Reg knew only too well how his software would infuriate rather than facilitate the user at achieving their request to operate.

Designed on a basic short-circuit principle, the cartridges in the magazine housed two separate compartments each with an equal number of positively charged Nanobots and an equal number of negatively charged Nanobots. Each of these feisty little characters, oblivious to their actual role in the grand order of things, had strapped to their backs an unhealthy quantity of plastic explosives. The concept was that when these brave but foolhardy little creatures finally impacted on their target, they would sing three rousing choruses of the Llarinian national anthem, join hands, and detonate immediately afterwards.

'We were Nomad's in the Desert,'
'We were lost and now we're found,'
'So here's to Mick and the Dheybar,'
'It's time for another round.'

The result of joining hands in a circle caused a short circuit that detonated their backpacks and created an aperture the size of a dinner plate in the unfortunate target. This sequence of events, needless to say, took place in nanoseconds and was oblivious to the human eye.

The President slapped the gun and shook it vigorously several times as everyone in the office ducked again, and this time, Arthur, realising the severity of the situation, decided to join in as a precautionary measure.

'What's the matter with this confounded weapon?'

'Sir, the safety catch is on,' Burt pointed out as he cowered in fear, desperately trying to stay away from the business end of the pistol.

The President glanced at Burt and raised an eyebrow, and then, inspecting the pistol, he flicked the safety catch off.

The Phlegm-O-Matic immediately chirped into life. 'Good morning, user, this is the Phlegm-O-Matic Weaponry Corporation here at your service. I am glad to report that it is another fine day here in the wonderful colony of Llar, with clear blue skies, a light refreshing breeze, and an eighty-nine percent impossibility of precipitation. The barometric pressure today is 1015 hectopascals, making the climatic conditions just perfect for annihilating the target of your choice. How may I assist you?'

The President stared at the pistol in abject disbelief. 'I don't want a weather report, I just want you to shoot that wretched android,' the President said as he waved the gun around in the general direction of the desk where Arthur cowered. The android's face contorted in an expression of impending doom.

'I am sorry, sir, I cannot do that,' replied the Phlegm-O-Matic after some hesitation.

'Why not? You're a gun, aren't you?' queried the President in a derisive tone.

'Yes, sir, that is technically correct. However, you will have to follow the Phlegm-O-Matic Weaponry Corporation's procedure for end users,' the pistol informed him.

'What procedure?'

'Sir, first of all would you please ring our helpline for assistance,' the pistol continued.

'Helpline?' muttered the President, staring at the pistol in his hand. 'I'm not trying to buy my wife a sofa.'

'Sir, I understand that, but all I am trying to do is point out is there are other alternatives to shooting an unarmed, defenceless android. If our lines are busy then please hold and listen to our recording of Burt Bimblefek's *'Let's talk this over'*, which, I might just add, is a cheerful little number intended specifically to reduce the stress in confrontational situations.' The LED screen on the top of the pistol's barrel illuminated and rang an 0800 number several times as the President gazed at the gun in utter disbelief.

'I want to shoot this bloody android, not make a phone call, you arse!' he screamed.

'Ah, yes, I see you are familiar with Advanced Robotic Silicone Evolution,' chirped the pistol with a cheery voice. 'Then, sir, you will understand exactly why I am unable to action your request.'

The President surveyed his audience and shrugged his shoulders before turning back to the chromium pistol in his hand. 'Sorry,' said the President sarcastically, 'I think I've missed something of paramount importance here. Perhaps you would be kind enough to explain yourself?'

The Phlegm-O-Matic cleared its throat with a small cough. 'Technically speaking, Arthur and I are related.'

From the doorway of Godfrey's office, Ethel and Semilla both gave maternal sighs as the motors and wires in Arthur's plastic face produced an enormous smile. The President's head dropped, his chin touched his chest, and very slowly he began to laugh, quietly at first, then louder and louder until his eyes began to fill with tears. The situation had become utterly surreal. There he stood, the leader of the largest most advanced civilisation imaginable, and he was being dictated to by a pistol that was related to an android and thought it was doing everyone a favour by offering them a weather report.

The President rallied himself; he raised his head and twisted it several times to stretch his neck before looking down at the Phlegm-O-Matic resting in his sweaty palm. 'Related?' he asked.

'Sir?' the weapon replied.

'You and the android, you're related?'

'Yes, sir, we are. My software was also designed by Reg Davis,' confirmed the Phlegm-O-Matic.

'Marvellous, Godfrey's father again,' huffed the President, shaking his head as he stared venomously at the inventor's son on the other side of the office. He paused, clearly deep in thought, then, carefully considering his next question, he homed in on the uncooperative weapon. 'Can I assume you are sophisticated enough to have some sort of user menu?'

'Oh, yes, sir, I do,' said the Phlegm-O-Matic proudly. 'My user menu consists of kill, maim and destroy.'

The President nodded at Godfrey and the others watching intently, indicating progress was being made. 'That's good, so let's go with the kill option, shall we? Kill has such a permanent ring to it, don't you think?'

The Phlegm-O-Matic was silent as it considered the President's request. 'So you would like the kill option, then, if I understand you correctly?' it said finally.

The President calmly inspected the fingernails on his other hand. 'I believe that was the option I requested.'

The Phlegm-O-Matic seemed preoccupied.

'What is it now?' screamed the President, holding the pistol at arm's length.

'I am sorry, but while we have been speaking regarding your option choice, I have contacted the mainframe regarding the chosen target, and I must inform you that it has suggested an alternative option,' replied the pistol with a nervous tone.

'And that is?' hissed the President.

'The mainframe has suggested a bunch of flowers, a big hug and an apology,' the pistol informed him enthusiastically.

The President was filled with rage and his blood pressure soared.

'Sir,' continued the pistol, 'I am sorry if this disappoints you. However, I do have a say in any decisions regarding live firings. My programmer wrote this into my software, in particular the guilt override protocol.'

'Then if your programmer were here right now I would shoot him too!' screamed the President.'

'No, sir, you would not,' said the Phlegm-O-Matic firmly. 'My programmer wrote in a clause—'

'I'm not interested!' the President shouted as he gave the assembly in front of him a frenzied glare. 'No wonder this weapon has never been used in anger. It's a damn pacifist.'

Burt bravely attempted to defuse the situation with a suggestion. 'Sir, now that has been settled, could I please have my gun back?'

The President ignored the guard, and holding the pistol close to his lips, he spoke in a sibilant tone. 'Now listen to me very carefully, I am going to aim you at that android over there and I am going to pull the trigger. We'll have no guilt override mode, no mention of a bunch of flowers, a big hug or an apology, and no more weather reports, all right? And if you refuse or miss or give me any more excuses I will have you immediately placed under a very, very large mechanical crusher.'

The Phlegm-O-Matic gulped loudly.

'So,' said the President with an air of confidence, 'have we selected the kill option?'

'Not quite, sir,' the gun whispered back.

'And we are ready at last to fire, a task for which you were, I believe, constructed?' continued the President, ignoring the weapon completely.

'Actually, no, sir, I am having something of an anxiety attack. It's just the thought of that monstrous crusher,' the pistol responded, sounding extremely nervous, and the Phlegm-O-Matic immediately went off with a very loud bang.

The section of ceiling that had been in the flight path of the Phlegm-O-Matic's shell collapsed to the floor, showering the entire assembly in fine white dust and plaster. The sound of falling debris bouncing across the furniture and floor filled the room, and several smaller pieces finally came to rest in Charlie's large bushy moustache.

'What are you doing?' shouted the President staring down at the pistol, which was now shaking in his hand. 'I hadn't pointed you at anything yet!'

'I am so sorry, sir, there was a minor overload in my fear circuits. I do apologise,' the pistol replied quivering.

The President squinted through the haze of dust hanging in Godfrey's office as he levelled the pistol towards Arthur's head. 'Now, stop messing me about and shoot this android.'

The Phlegm-O-Matic cleared its throat and attempted to sound dominant. 'Sir, I cannot, my protocol will not allow that.'

'You will,' demanded the President, holding the chromium pistol firmly.

'I will not.'

'Shoot that android now! This is your last chance,' shouted the President, his face crimson with rage.

'Sir, I can't do this. Please be reasonable,' stammered the pistol.

The President tried to override the trigger without success, then, screaming out loud, he took the petrified weapon by the muzzle and threw it at Arthur with all his might. Fortunately, the President was as proficient at throwing objects as the Phlegm-O-Matic was at shooting them, and the gun sailed past Arthur's head with room to spare and demolished one of the office windows instead. The Phlegm-O-Matic quickly reached terminal velocity, plummeting downward guided briefly by the light breeze, which it had itself predicted earlier. It tumbled towards the entrance where Godfrey had previously entered the Ministry eighty-three floors below.

Outside the main doors of the Ministry, and standing proudly to attention, Rupert had returned from his visit to the Service Department. His leg had benefited from being rewired and the mainframe had shared some new downloads with him, leaving him feeling brisk and assertive. Rupert was complete with new trousers and, of course, a new pair of socks and shoes. He was now a proud android with a purpose, gleefully welcoming personnel as they entered the Ministry.

The impact of the pistol dislodged Rupert's cap, simultaneously ejecting his mechanical dentures and sending them reeling across the plaza, where they landed spinning out of control next to the discarded weapon.

'I can't believe this!' screamed Rupert with his teeth chattering around in a circle.

'I am sorry. It is not my fault,' protested the Phlegm-O-Matic, soulfully lying on its side. 'I was thrown out of a window by a psychopath eighty-three floors up.'

Rupert was unimpressed. 'I'll give you eighty-three floors up. Come here,' he said, seething and grabbing at his teeth, which were now firmly embedded in the weapon's muzzle. As he rolled his eyes and dialled up the mainframe, his circuits coursed with anger. Thanks to his earlier downloads, this was a new experience for the old android. The Phlegm-O-Matic, meanwhile, was frantically whistling Burt Bimblefek's melody *'Let's talk this over'*, as its only form of defence.

CHAPTER 9

It had never occurred to Godfrey before how utterly lonely and abandoned the suburban multilane pavements were at that time of day. As he made his way home with the rest of the city still at work, Godfrey had the demeanour of a lonely clown that had just crash-landed from a fairground cannon. His jacket was still covered in white plaster from his office ceiling and his greying hair was dusty. Godfrey struggled to come to grips with the events of his day, his head hung low as he stared at the pavement. He mulled over the accusations the President had made about both his and Commander Albright's father, and the thought left him feeling hollow inside, deep to the pit of his empty stomach. He simply couldn't comprehend how they could have been involved in something so subversive. There was also the question of the device that they were alleged to have created, which Arthur had referred to as the XXL, that now threatened their great colony. He could only hope his leader was wrong and that there had been a terrible mistake, but they had all seen another side to his character. Godfrey and his colleagues had watched helplessly as the President had smugly ordered the guards to remove Arthur with his mouth securely taped over. The android had been dispatched to a secure facility where he would be, according the President, 'dealt with later'. Godfrey could only imagine the poor android's fate, which was almost certainly to be beneath the jaws of that mechanical crusher the President had earlier promised the Phlegm-O-Matic pistol.

Semilla had been instructed to organise a maintenance team

to repair the ceiling and window in Godfrey's office. She, like her co-workers, had been sworn to secrecy and was forbidden by the President to discuss anything they had seen or heard. They were all under no misapprehension as to the consequences should they even utter one word of the events they had witnessed or the conversations they had heard. Throughout the aftermath, Godfrey had sat on his sofa, his throat sore from the dust, as teams of tradesmen came and went from his office. The ceiling had taken shape and soon looked as good as new, and the fumes of fresh paint that hung in the air had further irritated Godfrey's throat. The window had been replaced quietly and efficiently, and before long it was as if nothing had ever happened there at all. Semilla had been supportive and had fussed over Godfrey, making him cups of tea. 'Everything will be all right, Mr Davis,' she'd said. Although he could barely hear her voice over the commotion of hammering and cleaners vacuuming his office, Godfrey had understood Semilla's instructions as she later ushered him out of the building, informing him that he had been told to go home early. She had smiled at him sweetly as they stood outside the entrance to the Ministry. 'Get yourself home, Mr Davis, and get some rest. You'll feel better then.'

The moving pavements that led away from the metro station out to the suburbs finally delivered him to the sanctuary of Dusty Bottom Lane. Moving silently towards his home, Godfrey felt as if he were in a bubble. His whole day seemed like a sequence of clips from a terrible film as he watched his life take one unbelievable turn after another. It was as he arrived at the gate of his home that the true impact of the day finally hit him and his legs began to give way. He staggered slowly to the rear of the house, where his wife stood folding washing by the clothesline. Gloria caught a glimpse of her husband's face and she realised something monumental had happened.

'Are you all right?' she asked.

Godfrey shook his weary head. 'It's just my throat,' he said. 'It's very sore.'

Abandoning her laundry, she and her husband entered their kitchen, where Godfrey sat himself down at the kitchen table. Gloria immediately spooned two large doses of cherry-flavoured cough medicine down him, accompanied with a stern warning. 'This medicine is very potent, so no more today, okay?' Godfrey nodded obediently.

Eventually, after the cough medicine and a large bowl of hot chicken soup, Godfrey managed to croak out the events from his disastrous day. 'The man is a psychopath, Gloria,' he said as his wife listened intently, 'and this business of my father being responsible for some device that could destroy the colony is totally preposterous.' Never in his entire life of serving Llar and her people had his faith and trust in the colony been so profoundly questioned.

The phone rang in the hallway. Gloria's mother, in her usual nosey fashion, had been loitering at the base of the stairs to see why her son-in-law had returned home from work so early. 'If you're trying to sell double-glazed windows, you're too late, we've already got them,' the old lady told the caller.

Fortunately, Gloria intercepted her mother before she could continue. 'Yes, my husband is here,' she said, 'who shall I say is calling?' She wandered into the lounge looking perplexed. 'It's for you, but the caller refuses to give their name.'

Godfrey ambled sluggishly into the hall and picked up the phone.

'Are you listening carefully, Godfrey?'

'Yes, but who is this?'

'It's more a question of who you are,' replied the voice.

In the background, Godfrey was certain he could hear the familiar sounds of the Grand Plaza in the heart of the metropolis. 'Look, I've had a rather distressing day,' he started.

'I know,' agreed the voice, 'and there will be many more to follow, but you will endure. The prophecy is quite specific.'

'What prophecy?' Godfrey muttered.

'You will understand soon enough. Now, rest tonight, and tomorrow I will meet you at the roamer's statue on your way to work, and all will become clear.'

Before Godfrey could ask another question, the phone went dead. He replaced the handset and considered the caller's promise to contact him again tomorrow. Whatever Tuesday had in store for him could wait. He wandered back into the lounge and sat himself down in his favourite chair, kicked his shoes off, adjusted the cushions and drifted off to sleep.

Early that evening, Gloria gently shook her husband's shoulder and informed him dinner was ready. He and Gloria ate in silence; there was little to discuss. Godfrey's day had eclipsed any cordial chat that they would have normally had over dinner, and Mother too, sensing the atmosphere, said nothing as she ate. She chose instead to hover over her meal, glancing at Godfrey now and then, tittering as she prodded her fork into the vegetables on her plate. Godfrey knew only too well he was the butt of Mother's ridicule. However, for once he felt too enfeebled to challenge her or retaliate in any way.

Shortly after dinner, Godfrey excused himself from the kitchen, telling Gloria he was going out to check the vegetable garden. As he left the kitchen, he discreetly removed the cough medicine bottle from the worktop and closed the door quietly behind him. Godfrey sat down on an upturned bucket next to his carrots and took a very large swig of Gloria's cough medicine. He had always liked the taste of cherries, but he couldn't remember them ever tasting as good as this. The night air was warm and laced with the scent of roses. He took a deep breath and stared at his vegetable patch beneath the light of Llar's pathetic little moon. The thought of that poor android being disposed of concerned him, as Godfrey loathed the prospect of disposing of perfectly good machinery. The problem was that the machine now had a name, which somehow made it worse. But at that precise moment the warm night air, mixed with the cherry vapours of the intoxicating medicine, began to addle his senses.

Godfrey watched, bewildered at first, as a lettuce began to grow in the soft soil beside his feet. It grew larger and larger until finally it stood at nearly the height of a small man. Godfrey widened his eyes in disbelief at this manifestation, and he gave the lettuce a gentle prod with one finger to test its authenticity. What a day, he thought, smiling to himself. He had mediated a fracas in the foyer of the Ministry with a pair of pugnacious androids, his father had allegedly been the inventor of a weapon of mass destruction, and his psychopathic President had demolished his office. And finally, an unknown caller was about to reveal a prophecy to him tomorrow, which would involve days just as peculiar as this one. His smile broadened at the prospect as he stared at the monstrous vegetable stood in front of him. Slowly, the lettuce uncurled a large outer leaf, and with the grace of a toreador courting a bull with a cape, it revealed its face and elf-like grin.

'The snow's just perfect tonight, Godfrey. Do you want to come skiing?'

Godfrey opened his mouth as he attempted a reply. Instead, he collapsed, falling gracefully face first onto the ground as the remains of his bottle of cough medicine spilt over his carrots.

That night, Godfrey Davis enjoyed himself immensely, skiing with his new friend Rodney, an iceberg lettuce, on the slopes of a giant vanilla ice cream. It had been without a doubt the most bizarre day of his life. But there were still stranger days to come.

CHAPTER 10

At the precise moment Semilla had ushered Godfrey out of the Ministry, Rupert had wandered into the Service Department deep beneath the building. He made himself comfortable in a maintenance chair as a service android came over and plugged him into the mainframe.

'Where are your teeth?'

Rupert rummaged in his jacket pocket and produced his mechanical dentures. 'Please don't start on at me, I've had a bad day,' he replied as his teeth chattered around in his hand.

The service android slipped Rupert's dentures back into place and the old doorman flexed his jaw. 'That's more like it. Now, let's get down to business. What I want is a new paint job on my—'

'You will have to wait your turn, chummy, there are others in front of you,' the technician android informed him, exerting his authority. 'We have a queue, you know, and besides, the paint technician is taking his break right now.'

'Taking a break?' queried Rupert. 'Since when do *we* get breaks?'

'It's a new directive from the mainframe.'

'Marvellous,' Rupert muttered as he glanced sideward at the line of other maintenance chairs. To his left sat another soulful example of his mechanical brethren completely unconscious. In the chair to his right, another android sat clutching a small insignificant picture of a duck tight to its chest.

The android with the picture smiled. 'Hi, I am Barney.'

'I'm Rupert, pleased to meet you,' he replied, eyeing him up and down. 'What happened to you?'

'I'm waiting for counselling. I was brutally accosted by a flying picture of a duck in the corridor on floor eighty-three this morning. It just flew off the wall and hit me for no reason.' He held up the remnants of a broken picture as proof of his demise. 'And Piers, sitting next to you, he was struck by a flying shoe in the entrance foyer earlier this morning. He has been unconscious ever since.'

Rupert quickly sat back, hoping that Piers didn't have his old shoe in his pocket for evidence. 'Seems to be the day for flying objects, pictures, shoes, guns.'

'Guns?' shrilled Barney in excitement.

'Yes, a Phlegm-O-Matic pistol hit me on the head and knocked my teeth clean out. That came from floor eighty-three apparently. Nothing to do with your little mishap, was it?'

'No, nothing to do with me, but I wish I had been there to see that. I bet that was really scary?'

'Yeah, well, it is all part of the job,' Rupert said casually.

'Don't worry, gentlemen,' offered the service android turning his back to grab a probe from the bench, 'we will have you both as good as new in a jiffy.'

In the chair beside Rupert, Piers began to stir. His hand came up to feel his forehead. 'What happened to my head? My circuits are killing me.' he groaned. 'That's it, now I remember, there were these two androids fighting, and then this shoe flew through the air…and…'

Rupert slipped his left hand smartly behind Piers' chair and disconnected his lead to the mainframe. Piers immediately slumped back and his hands fell limply beside him.

'That one is a complete head case,' the service android said as he turned and inserted a probe into Barney's ear. 'He has been in here all morning and now he's totally delirious. Obliviously a major circuit malfunction.'

Rupert raised his eyebrows and slid silently back in his chair. 'I suppose so.'

The door of the Service Department swung open and another android stood surveying the gathering and taking stock. 'Not more work, I hope?'

'This is our paint technician,' the service android said, nodding to Rupert.

'That's great.'

'So what are you here for?' asked the paint technician as he approached Rupert's chair.

'I was hit on the head by a flying gun and my teeth were damaged. I will need to have fresh paint,' explained Rupert. He leant forward to enable a hushed question. 'By the way, would it be possible to get one of them painted blue?'

'Which one, upper left six?'

'How did you know that was the one I wanted?' Rupert asked with a stupefied expression.

'Easy, I painted another android's tooth earlier and he was most specific. He said it was a fashion statement. You must know him, he works in the entrance foyer too.'

'Devious bastard,' snapped Rupert.

The paint technician frowned. 'No, actually, I think his name was Norman.'

Shortly after the Ministry had closed for the evening, Rupert finally emerged from the Service Department with the teeth of his cyber dreams. His little excursion, though, had not been without incident. There had been a terrible commotion while he was having his teeth repainted, when Piers had finally regained consciousness. The technician android had been forced to call for backup after Piers had lunged at Rupert and was trying to strangle him. Piers had accused Rupert of all manner of things, which of course he vehemently denied. Rupert had suggested instead that the blow to Piers' head had in fact rendered his circuits temporarily insane.

Rupert stood gazing at his reflection in the glass panel of a department door further along the corridor. The Testing Department was now closed until the morning and the corridor lighting created an almost perfect mirror. He raised his upper lip for a view of his new acquisition. 'I will show Norman he is not the only one,' he muttered to himself.

Several steps further down the corridor, Rupert's dentures began to rattle. They shuddered around in his mouth, making his eyes wobble up and down. The lighting along the passageway flickered, and as he turned to glance behind him, a flash from the Testing Department illuminated the corridor.

'Must be a problem with the lights again,' he said under his breath.

Still, it wasn't that important right now. What was important was to get back to his section and charge himself ready for the morning. He couldn't wait to see Norman's face tomorrow when he arrived for work in the main foyer. He imagined his colleague's expression and smiled to himself. 'Systems check out level twelve?' he muttered. 'Over my blue tooth.'

CHAPTER 11

Jack Marsden yawned and looked up from his desk. It was late and he was tired. He hated feeling fatigued; it made him feel vulnerable, and late nights in this office brought back a host of memories he would rather have forgotten a long time ago. Many years earlier, it had been the hub of his father's political life, and even now, after its reformation, Jack could still feel the presence of the man he had taken over from.

Bernard Marsden's office had been an austere room, and it matched perfectly the character of a man who had spent his entire life serving the colony with a passion. The wood-panelled walls had been littered with a lifetime of photographs and memorabilia spanning his career. Famous faces had hung like trophies marking one man's rise to power, and for Bernard Marsden this room had been a shrine and a testament to the commitment he had shown to the administration.

Jack let his heavy eyelids close, remembering just how ill at ease he had felt here in the past.

'I have some news for you,' Bernard Marsden had said, skipping any formalities. His eyes had been fixed on a report in front of him as he sat at his desk.

Jack held his breath, awaiting his father's verdict. He had an idea why this meeting had been arranged and the best diplomacy had been to stand to attention, remain silent and continue to sweat.

'It seems from this that you have exceeded my expectations,' his father had continued.

Bernard Marsden had been a master of protocol that regulated his demeanour and his way of life. That too had included his relationship with his son. He had been a shrewd man who despised weakness and failure, and subsequently the two men had never been close. Although his son had never failed him as such, Bernard sensed an inherent weakness in his character and never missed an opportunity to parade it in front of him. For Bernard Marsden, Jack was simply a product that had been groomed to one day fulfil a particular task and that day looked even closer than ever before. His dark eyes had flashed over the pages of the report in front of him.

'So,' Bernard had asked, glancing up from the papers on his desk, 'do you know why I have summoned you here today?'

Jack had gazed above his father's head like a sentry on parade. 'Yes, sir, I think so,' he'd replied.

'Think so or know so?' Bernard Marsden had snapped. 'You still have that tendency, that indecisive streak, just like your mother had. Be more assertive.'

Jack had raised his chin. 'I know why I am here.'

Bernard Marsden had given a sneer, and pointing at the chair next to his son, he had commanded him to be seated.

'It would seem that very soon you will maintain our family's proud heritage and serve the colony. The name Marsden will be upheld in the halls of power in this great nation of ours for another generation. That is, of course, if you have the stomach for it?'

Bernard Marsden had leant across his leather-inlayed desk and thrust the report into his son's hand. He'd slid a cigar from a hardwood box on his desk and lit it up, surrounding himself in a cloud of acrid smoke. Jack had flashed over the report; it seemed the whispers he had heard were true. His father had continued puffing.

'You need to take a wife. It would be good for your image.

The people you will work with would make an issue out of your bachelor status, especially as you're about to become a member of the President's cabinet. It will have an adverse effect on your career.'

'I hadn't considered it,' Jack had replied, taking a deep breath at the thought of family life.

Bernard Marsden had stood and paced slowly to and fro behind his desk. 'Consider it something you need to do if you want to get on,' he'd hissed. 'What happened to that pretty little thing you were with after college?'

Jack had leant back in the chair; he'd tried to distance himself from his domineering father and the pungent smoke. 'We see one another occasionally, but there's nothing between us anymore.'

Bernard Marsden had blown a long, slow cloud into the air. 'She is a photo opportunity you can't afford to miss. She's the right stock. I've made some enquiries into her family and their background. Organise a dinner reunion to rekindle your relationship.'

'We never really had a relationship to speak of,' Jack had lied.

Bernard Marsden's face had swollen with anger. He was not use to getting anything else but his own way. 'You misunderstand me, boy. I'm not making a suggestion. Have you any idea of the favours I have had to call in to get you this appointment?'

Jack had felt his shoulders slump; his worst fears had been laid before him. His father's network of political contacts had engineered his new opportunity and he was now nothing more than another of his father's political pawns.

'I heard rumours of this appointment and I had thought if they were true they were based on my own achievements and not something you had engineered.'

Bernard Marsden had stormed forward and slammed his fist

down upon his desk. His lifeless eyes shone like black beads with all the empathy of a shark. 'There is nothing in the world of politics that is as it seems, don't you understand that? You would wander in the political wilderness forever if it weren't for my name and my contacts to help you. Sometimes I wonder if you are really the right calibre for the task ahead of you. There are too many of your mother's genes in you, young man, and mark my words they will be your downfall unless you're very careful. You need to suppress them, and suppress them soon.' He had angrily walked back towards his desk and flicked a chunk of ash into the ashtray. 'Let's get something perfectly clear, shall we? You need to understand a few lessons about politics from someone who knows.'

Jack had taken a deep breath at the thought of another of his father's doctrines. He'd heard most of them before.

'Let me ask you,' Bernard Marsden had continued, 'just how many of your friends do you still see from your college days?'

The question had perturbed Jack slightly. At his best count there were less than the fingers on one hand. He had hesitated to answer.

'Not many of them, Jack, I bet, and the reason for that? The reason is that they are off pursuing their own lives and careers. They're not interested in you anymore, or what you're doing. That is, of course, until you make the papers and they think you can do something for them. One day you will realise that people come and go, they pass you by like strangers walking across the plaza. Never mourn their passing, embrace it. Take from them if they have something to offer and discard them if they haven't. Never trust any of them. Trust is a weakness they will use against you.' He had re-lit his cigar, puffing heavily until the end glowed red. 'You need to become an island in a sea of men if you are going to survive. There will be decisions that will come back to haunt you at night, and your private remorse will be a measure of your greatness. For your enemies, your reputation will make them think twice about taking you on.'

'Sir, with respect,' Jack had said, 'I have no enemies, as far as I'm aware.'

Bernard Marsden had choked out a cloud of smoke and laughed heartily. He'd propped one hand on his desk to steady himself, then turned and smiled for the first time since Jack had entered his office. 'That's good, but starting the day after tomorrow, your life will be full of them when you enter the world of politics at this level. I'm warning you; what I'm telling you is based on experience you won't find in your college books. Trust me, there's no margin for error here if you wish to succeed. Listen to some wisdom from someone who knows what he's talking about.'

Jack had run his tongue across his bottom lip, wondering what to say next. He had sensed his time with his father was over. 'I promise you I will do my best to serve you and the colony, you have my word on it.'

His father had huffed. 'Actions speak louder than words, and I should know, I've been a politician all my life. I'm counting on you, so don't let me down.'

Jack had raised himself from the chair and glanced across to where his father had stood staring into his own private world.

'Sir, may I leave now?'

Bernard Marsden had waved his cigar indifferently at the door, avoiding eye contact with his son.

Jack had turned the handle on his father's office door and paused momentarily. 'One last thing, I was wondering if perhaps tomorrow you would accompany me to Mother's grave with some flowers. It's the anniversary of her passing.'

Bernard Marsden had turned his head slowly and gazed at his son; his eyes were cold and lifeless. 'I have meetings all day.'

Jack opened his eyes and wondered why he continued to torture himself over the past. Since that conversation, he had slowly become as ruthless as his father, moulded by the world of politics and the people that existed within it. The prediction had come true, and somewhere, with the passing of time, Jack had become his father in all but name. The world he had inherited was every bit as dangerous as Bernard Marsden had told him it would be, and somehow he had survived it.

The knocks on the office door brought him back from his thoughts as the mainframe supervisor walked in and stood beside his desk. He handed Jack a single sheet of paper. He glanced over it, grabbed a pen and signed it.

'This one makes six in total,' replied the supervisor. 'We need to move them as soon as possible.'

Jack sighed at the prospect. 'There will be no one left to work on the mainframe at this rate. We will dispose of them all as soon as we can. I will let you know when.'

The supervisor nodded. 'Yes, sir.' And he turned and left.

Later, Jack stood at the open door of his office. He was finally about to go home for the night. Tomorrow was the anniversary of his mother's passing. There was no one left in his life now that he could ask to accompany him to her grave, and even if there were, he simply couldn't go. He had meetings all day.

CHAPTER 12

As Jack Marsden closed the door to his office, Burt and Harry were preparing to end their shift. It had been a long day, and with the added excitement of the morning's events in Godfrey Davis's office, quite a tiring one too.

'I'll see you in the morning,' Harry said, clasping the handles of his bag and heading for the door of the locker room.

'Don't you want a quick tipple at Dave's Bar on the way home?'

'After this morning's fun and games, no thanks, I'm going straight home,' Harry replied, and he left.

Burt gazed dejectedly across the empty locker room as the door closed silently behind his companion. The prospect of going home to an empty flat was already bringing him down. If he left now he would be indoors in an hour or so and struggling to find something in the fridge to eat. He missed his wife cooking, though by all accounts she hadn't missed him since she had left. Burt and Mary had been married for a decade and had a daughter who they both loved dearly. Burt was a good provider, and even with his meagre wages, the family never went without. Over the years they had grown apart, and although they had tried to stay together for their daughter, eventually it became too much for Mary. One day he came home to a note and her empty wardrobe. Burt took a deep breath and put his private thoughts behind him. He grabbed his holdall, switched off the lights and left.

Basement level thirteen was an eerie place at night when

everyone had gone home, and Burt had no intentions of loitering down there by himself any longer. The thought of a couple of whiskies to help him sleep when he got home seemed a more favourable idea. As he turned the corner near the androids' Service Department, he witnessed several sudden short bursts of light flickering across the corridor further down. There was only one other door the light could have come from: the Testing Department. He stood and thought for a moment. No one would thank him for spending his time off duty doing what he did when he was on duty, so he shrugged to himself and carried on walking. The sound of muffled laughter caught his ear and stopped him in his tracks. It too was coming from the Testing Department. Burt's curiosity took over. He lowered his bag to the floor and walked towards the door. As he got closer, the smell of something burning drifted across his nasal passages. The flashes of light were clearer now, flooding out through the frosted glass door. Burt could hear the sound of arcing each time the light splashed out into the corridor. There was someone welding in the Testing Department. He knew Godfrey had been sent home unwell that morning, and earlier he had seen Commander Albright locking up before he left for the evening. Blending his short rotund frame into the corridor wall, he crept forward and tried the handle. It was locked. He fumbled for his bunch of keys, and as quietly as he could he managed to unlock the door and let it swing open. The room was in total darkness, lit only by the shaft of light from the corridor. The air reeked of welding fumes, and in the half-light he could see the haze of smoke suspended in the room.

He swallowed hard. 'Who's in here?'

In the dark shadows away from the light of the doorway, something stirred.

'Who's in here?' he repeated, his heart racing as he fumbled for the light switch. He scanned around the empty workshop but there was no one. Slowly, one step at a time, he moved forward, peering here and there behind the benches and desks that filled the room. There was no sign of anyone hiding from him. He inspected the welding unit beside him. The welder hummed; it was still connected. There was something going on, he knew it, but there was no one to be seen. Burt slowly made his way to the door. Flicking off the switch, the workshop plunged into inky darkness. He stood staring into the pitch-black room. 'I know you're in here,' he said, and dejectedly he closed the door and locked it.

Across the emptiness of the Grand Plaza a small light flashed invitingly. Night-time in this part of the metropolis was a lonely affair. The neon sign broadcast its message that 'Dave's Bar' was still open, if only for one customer.

'Go on, Dave, just one more,' Burt insisted.

'This is your last one and then you go home,' Dave told him.

The barman came over and poured his customer another drink.

Burt downed the drink and put the empty glass on the counter. 'You wouldn't believe the day I've had,' he slurred.

'Is that right?' Dave said, slowly wiping a glass.

'No, I mean, really, you wouldn't believe me. No one would.'

The barman stacked the glass on the shelf behind him. He was beginning to wonder what had got into his customer. He had never seen Burt like this before. Placing the cloth neatly over a beer tap, he gave in to his curiosity. 'Try me,' he said. 'There's only you and me here, everyone else has gone home.'

Burt turned and glanced around the empty bar. 'You won't tell anyone, right?'

The barman leant across the bar top. 'Trust me, I would never tell another living soul. After all, we are friends, aren't we?'

Burt thought about it and beamed through the haze of liquor that surrounded him. 'That's right.'

The motors and wires in Dave's face pulled a typical android smile. 'If you can just hold on for a minute so I can plug myself into the mainframe, then we can talk while I download.'

CHAPTER 13

It was a nightmare of monstrous proportions, Godfrey thought as he stared at the bathroom mirror. He looked like he had died and come back to life again. His chin was unshaven, his eyes were bloodshot, and his head throbbed as if all of the blood in his body wanted to gatecrash his cranium simultaneously for one gigantic party. He vaguely remembered the night before, sitting by his vegetables finishing off that cough medicine. This morning, though, reality had a different order, and Gloria was far from impressed. She had woken him in the vegetable patch shortly before dawn with a washing-up bowl full of freezing cold water.

'If you don't like it,' she had said, 'I'm sure the vegetables will.'

Godfrey gave his mud-covered shirt a fleeting look as he stood in front of the bathroom mirror. His shirt was ruined and he was soaked to the skin.

'Are we back from the mortuary then?' asked a voice at the bathroom door.

Godfrey tried to ignore his ageing mother-in-law as he threw the soiled shirt into the bath. He wished the floor would open up and swallow her, but that was too simple an end. 'Please, Mother, not now, not this morning. I can't cope with you today,' he sighed, dabbing foam onto his stubble-ridden chin. 'I've got to go to work today.'

'If I were you I would go to the doctors instead. You look awful.'

'I feel awful.'

Mother gave a sinister chuckle. 'Oh well, have a good day anyway, happy shaving.' And she wandered off back to her room.

There was something wrong; his mother-in-law was being civil. Godfrey turned back to the horror story in the mirror. He popped out his bright red tongue; the cough medicine had left its mark for sure. And then he noticed it: a splash of bright blue lurking just beneath his upper lip.

Gloria heard the screams from where she stood at the kitchen table. She glanced up at the ceiling, frowned, and then continued buttering the toast. She wasn't in the mood for any of her husband's melodrama this morning. When she heard Godfrey thumping down the staircase, she made her way into the lounge. The door leading to the hall burst open and Godfrey stood with his face covered in foam.

'Look at this!' he said pointing at his face.

Gloria placed her reading glasses delicately on the end of her nose and gazed up at her husband's finger. It was pointing at one of his front incisors. 'Oh, that's novel, your false tooth has turned bright blue.'

'I know, but how?'

Mother sauntered into the discussion from the hall. 'What do you expect? You've been cleaning your teeth for the last three days with my haemorrhoid cream.'

Godfrey screamed again. 'I'm going to kill her!' he bellowed at Gloria.

'Now listen, you really need to be more careful. It's not Mother's fault you picked up the wrong tube to clean your teeth with, is it?'

'Or the wrong tin of foam,' Mother said dryly.

'What do you mean?' Godfrey begged, dabbing at his chin.

Mother could hardly contain herself; she was having the time of her life at her son-in-law's expense. 'That's not shaving foam, its Five Minute Tan,' she snorted.

The sound of screaming resonated along Dusty Bottom Lane, disturbing several dozen birds from their lofty perches in the towering eucalyptus trees that lined the pavements. Three doors away, Mrs Prentagast stood beside one of the trees and frowned. She looked up and down the lane and, discounting the noise entirely, she continued to nail her poster to the tree.

Gloria slopped the eggs onto her husband's toast as he sat down at the breakfast table. Mother was seated opposite him, grinning brightly. When Gloria had finished serving breakfast, she too took her seat. 'You will have to try and refrain from smiling,' she said. 'That's all you can do.'

Godfrey was shifting his eggs around with his fork, utterly disinterested in eating the produce of his wife's labour. 'And my chin, how do you suggest I hide that?'

'Just put the fake tan over the rest of your face,' his wife suggested.

'I can't, there's none left.'

'Then you'll have to let your beard grow, Godfrey, won't you?'

'But I've got the demonstration today and the President will be there.'

'Perhaps you should have considered that last night before you drank the rest of that cough medicine,' Gloria erupted.

Godfrey could tell by his wife's body language that she wasn't in the mood for taking prisoners this morning. She was right, of course, it was his fault entirely. He reflected on Gloria's words and tried to make amends.

'Thank you for my eggs.'

Gloria ignored him.

'They're really nice.'

Gloria continued to pay no attention to him.

'They're perfect.'

Mother surveyed the pair with beady eyes. 'Stop creeping, Godfrey.'

'Mother, that's enough,' Gloria roared.

'He always creeps. I told you when you first brought him home that he was a creeper. He creeps, and that's all there is to it.'

'Fine,' exclaimed Godfrey, standing up and thrusting his fork down, 'I'll be off then.'

'It's not that bad,' Gloria said, looking at her eggs.

'She's right,' agreed Mother. 'It's not that bad. It's terrible.'

Godfrey grabbed his jacket and stared angrily at his mother-in-law. 'It's bad enough you left your haemorrhoid cream in the bathroom, but fake tan? I look like a complete nerd.'

Mother laughed. 'You can do that without a blue tooth or the tanned chin.'

Godfrey stormed into the hall, and the sudden rush of movement sent his head into a horrific thumping fit. 'I'm off then,' he shouted, hoping for a response. None came.

Gloria and her mother heard the front door slam and then the front gate. They glanced across the breakfast table at one another. The two women burst in to fits of uncontrollable laughter.

CHAPTER 14

The metro was heaving as usual that morning as Godfrey braved his way to work. His balance deserted him several times as the carriage swayed from side to side, and his fellow commuters, distracted from their newspapers, gave the man with the tanned chin and the red bow tie a wide berth. When the moving pavements from the station finally disgorged him and the rest of their cargo, he spilled out of the unconquerable stampede and stood overlooking the Grand Plaza. Staggering to the roamer's statue, he propped himself up against the granite base, looking up at the monument towering above him. Children from schools across the colony came to hear the history of their civilisation from the hologram of their founder who had been the first to walk upon the fertile oasis. Godfrey felt awful, and for once in his life he conceded that his mother-in-law had been right. Instead of standing there waiting to rendezvous with his anonymous caller from last night, he should have been heading to the doctor's surgery. He felt far from normal; his head thumped in time with his heartbeat and his legs still appeared to have a mind of their own. The Grand Plaza was now a seething throng, and at some point he had to negotiate it to get to the Ministry. Godfrey closed his eyes; it was a daunting prospect in his current condition.

'Are you still drunk?' said a voice.

'No I am not,' Godfrey said, his eyes still firmly closed. 'I just have a monumental hangover.'

'What happened to your chin?'

'So kind of you to mention it,' Godfrey sighed as he opened one eye and cast a squint over the hologram standing clutching a wooden staff. To his right quivered the small pear-shaped hologram of the legendary desert creature, the Dheybar. There had to be another anomaly in the mainframe, he reasoned, one that enabled Mick the Roamer's hologram to ask questions. Godfrey cautiously surveyed the two figures either side of him. 'How do you know I was drunk last night?'

'We watched you stagger over to our statue.'

Godfrey rubbed his face and tried to concentrate. 'Look, thank you for your observations, but I need to get to my office, so if you will excuse me.'

'But we need to talk, Godfrey, about my phone call yesterday evening. You do remember me calling, don't you?'

Godfrey went to shake his head in disbelief and then thought better of it. 'That was you?'

'Yes it was.'

'But you're the tour hologram. You can't make phone calls.'

'Perhaps a couple of days ago that was the case but it now seems that I can. Don't ask me how it happened, I haven't got a clue. Nevertheless, it was me and I did phone you.'

Godfrey took another deep breath and his head began to spin wildly. There was something desperately wrong here and this had to be something to do with the mainframe.

'Now listen to me carefully. I know about your future,' Mick said, leaning on his staff. 'You are destined to do great things for the colony and her people. You are the one in the prophecy.'

This was all too much for Godfrey to comprehend in his present mental state. He closed his eyes and sincerely hoped that when he opened them again both of the holograms would be gone.

'You will travel north to the home of your ancestors,' Mick continued.

'What?'

'The truth will unfold before you when you reach the oasis. Trust no one and tell no one of our conversation. You are the chosen one and your destiny awaits you.'

Before Godfrey could attempt another question, Mick's quivering form and that of his odd little companion faded and silently disappeared. Godfrey leant back against the statue's granite base and observed the Grand Plaza and the Ministry beyond. Yesterday had been the worst day of his life and now already this morning it appeared even that could be eclipsed. He had an ominous feeling things were about to get worse and there was nothing he could do to change it. Accepting his fate, he re-entered the early morning skirmish.

The foyer of the Ministry was busier than usual, and for some reason there were large queues in front of all the lifts. There were no lift androids at their posts and far across the other side of the foyer, beside one of the entrance doors, Godfrey caught sight of Norman and Rupert standing face to face. They appeared to be having another tiff. The body language was definitely out of context to their usual behaviour and Rupert was waving his finger vigorously under Norman's nose. It was clear all was not harmonious.

'You really are the pits, Norman. You deliberately slipped away while I had to stand here debilitated yesterday morning, waiting for the Service Department to collect me.'

Norman folded his arms in defiance. 'It is not my fault you tried to incinerate yourself, is it?'

'Regardless of my minor mishap, you jumped at the chance to get yourself a blue tooth, didn't you?' Rupert said as he grated his plastic dentures with annoyance.

Norman raised his head and gazed out through the glass doors impassively. 'You had the opportunity too, so don't blame me that you didn't think to ask. Besides, someone has to be first with a new fashion idea, don't they?'

'It wasn't you, though, was it? It was Mr Davis,' Rupert scoffed.

Norman waved his mechanical hand dismissively in the air and turned away from his colleague. Across the foyer he noticed Godfrey standing patiently waiting for the lift. His expression suddenly mellowed. 'So, Rupert, if we were both to acquire the next fashion idea at the same time, we would be quits then, would we?' he said, nodding in Godfrey's direction.

'You are kidding me,' exclaimed Rupert, gaping in amazement at Godfrey's tanned chin. 'Of course we would, we're friends, aren't we?'

Norman smirked at his mechanical colleague. 'Ring the Service Department and tell them that we have technical problems and we are on our way down.'

'I have already called them, let's go.'

The two trendsetters immediately abandoned their posts and headed to the nearest service stairs and the basement.

When Godfrey finally made it to his office, Ethel was standing in the doorway looking up and down the corridor. 'Morning, Mr Davis, thank goodness you're okay. I've been so worried about you all night.' She peered up at Godfrey's bloodshot eyes and tanned chin. 'What happened to you?'

'Is there any coffee?' he asked, collapsing onto his office sofa.

Several minutes later, Godfrey was cupping his hands round a large mug of strong black coffee.

'You should be at home in bed, you look awful,' Ethel told him. 'Besides, you can't really wander around the Ministry looking like, well, like that.'

Godfrey sighed. 'I really don't have a choice, Ethel. I'm conducting the demonstration today.'

Ethel looked left and right as if there were spies hiding under the sofa. 'I spoke to a colleague of mine on the way in this morning. He told me the story of what happened to him last night when he was leaving the Ministry.'

'What story?'

'He found someone up to no good in the Testing Department.'

Godfrey closed his eyes and counted to ten. 'Does this "something" have anything to do with today's demonstration for the President, by any chance?'

Ethel chewed her lip and frowned.

'Who else knows about this?'

Ethel gave him a demure smile.

'The President was right about one thing, I suppose,' Godfrey said. 'There's nothing sacred at the Ministry. I suppose everybody must know by now?'

'Eh, not quite, Mr Davis. I haven't seen Doris yet this morning on floor thirty-seven.'

The mood took him and he managed to laugh. Godfrey was beginning to see the absurdity of the whole situation. As the coffee vapours drifted up past his tanned chin, the office door burst open and Semilla hovered in the doorway. 'Morning, Mr Davis. Sorry I didn't knock, only we have a little problem and it will be here very shortly to search your office.'

'What?'

'Security are on their way up.'

'Oh good grief,' Godfrey blurted. 'What are they after?'

'The XXL,' they both said in unison.

Godfrey and Semilla left Ethel to clean up his spilt coffee as they hurried along the corridor to the lift. The pair stood watching the lift indicator above their heads counting down the numbers, and as it got closer to their floor the lift slowed.

'Security,' they agreed.

Slipping swiftly round the corner, they peered back to see the lift emptying its consignment of security guards, who promptly marched off in the direction of Godfrey's office.

'That was close, Mr Davis.'

'Thank you for your help, Semilla. I really couldn't handle those oafs at this precise moment.'

'Why don't you get down to the Testing Department and I'll give you a call there when the coast is clear.'

Godfrey thanked her and slipped into the empty lift. As the doors closed silently, he wondered how poor Ethel would manage with security plundering his office. He felt a sense of guilt that he was not there to support her, though in reality his presence would make little difference. But knowing Ethel as he had for so many years, he knew she would give them a hard time. Minutes later, he arrived on basement level thirteen and found that the corridor was unusually busy. There were dozens of androids walking purposefully in the same direction. He followed them, and turning the corner he stopped dead. Stretched out along the entire corridor stood a line of Llar's mechanical servants patiently waiting to enter the Service Department.

'Good morning, Mr Davis, how are you today?' said one of the androids.

'I'm fine, thank you,' mumbled Godfrey in an automated fashion.

The android turned to his colleague behind him as Godfrey drifted past. 'Did you see that? Did you see his chin?'

Godfrey immediately broke into a trot. He turned his head towards the corridor wall, trying hard to reduce the area of his face that was visible to the androids. His paced quickened. Turning the next corner, Godfrey saw the entrance of the Service Department. He slowed and caught sight of a newly installed electronic numbering system from a delicatessen's counter as it illuminated the figures 457. He heard a buzzer sound. The numbers flashed. The next android looked at his ticket and then at Godfrey as he passed by. Smiling broadly, the android marched into the department. Godfrey took stock; he became aware of a hundred faces staring at him. The identical mechanical servants of his colony beamed as one.

'Good morning, Mr Davis,' said a multitude of voices. Godfrey's head began to thump again and his balance faltered. The pit of his stomach knotted as he burst into the Testing Department and slammed the door. The android holding ticket number 457 stepped proudly into the Service Department.

'And you want what exactly?' said the service android, raising an eyebrow.

'Same as the others, I guess.'

'Upper left six in bright blue?'

The android slipped into the service chair and nodded in confirmation. 'And if it's not too much trouble, can you paint a tan where my stubble line would be?'

The service android looked puzzled. 'Where does that man get his inspiration from?'

'I have absolutely no idea,' grinned the android, making himself comfy in the chair. 'But I know one thing, when I walk out of here I'll be the first.'

The service android pulled the trigger on his airbrush. 'You sure will be.' There was a hiss, and a fine mist of blue enamel paint hit the air.

A short while later, the android with ticket number 457 walked past the queue of his fellow mechanical cousins. He screwed up his ticket and threw it casually over his shoulder. His walk was slow and fluid, his legs seemed like elastic. He acknowledged the line of gaping faces as he passed by, nodding nonchalantly.

'What number have you got?' Rupert asked as the android passed by them.

'Ticket 879,' Norman replied.

'Typical,' announced Rupert, watching the latest client of the Service Department amble past. 'You come up with a new idea and, guess what, someone else has already thought of it.'

Norman nodded. 'Just goes to prove there's no such thing as an original thought.'

The two androids huffed, and with sagging shoulders they continued to wait their turn.

Godfrey, meanwhile, stood with his back against the department door, his eyes closed, his stomach churning. What in the name of Llar was going on and why were those wretched androids so intent on copying him? He had little time to consider any other options as a voice from across the room distracted him.

'Good morning, Godfrey.'

Godfrey's eyes opened in an instant and he glanced over at his inventions lined up on the back wall of the Testing Department.

'You look awful, Godfrey,' said lamppost Number Nine, hovering serenely towards the nearest workbench. The face on its plastic beacon twisted in a look of concern. 'Shall I call a doctor?'

Godfrey's heart began to race as his legs slowly gave way. He stepped back, leant against the wall and slid gracefully to the floor. 'You can hover?' he whimpered.

'That's correct, Godfrey,' he confirmed. 'We all can.'

'But I never made you like that,' Godfrey stammered.

'Oh, that is only one of several modifications we have made on ourselves.'

With the prospect of the imminent demonstration, the revelation sent a shiver through him deep to the pit of his stomach. Unable to cope, his nerves subsequently treated his shirt, his jacket and part of his trousers to a completely new colour scheme.

CHAPTER 15

As Godfrey headed towards basement level thirteen that Tuesday morning, Ethel stood with her mop in the doorway of his office. She stared icily at a beefy-looking sergeant with a shaven head. 'Over my dead body you will,' she seethed. 'You're not walking on my wet floor. Come back later when it's dry.'

The sergeant's cranium was as devoid of diplomacy as his head was lacking in hair. He stood snorting like an angry bull. 'Listen, I have my orders and there was no mention of any wet floors. Now move aside and let my men do their job.'

'I'm warning you,' said Ethel, holding up her mop defensively.

The sergeant towered over her, and with one quick lift under each arm, Ethel found herself dumped in the hallway. 'Okay, men,' he hollered, and marching into Godfrey's office, he promptly skidded on the wet marble floor and landed with a thump on his backside.

'I told you it was wet.' Ethel sniggered loudly. The old cleaner watched from the corridor as the anger rose inside her. The guards began searching Godfrey's office, tearing out draws from his desk and filing cabinets and discarding them on the floor, spilling their contents in every direction. Semilla returned and gave Ethel's arm a reassuring squeeze and she peered around the door frame.

'He can't come back and see this,' Ethel whispered. 'You need to go and find an android and get him to put out a message for Godfrey. Tell him not to come back until after lunch when I've had a chance to clean up.'

Semilla nodded and whisked off along the corridor. Turning the corner by the lifts, she conveniently collided with one of Llar's mechanical servants.

'Just the person I want,' she said, stopping the android in his tracks. 'I need you to find Godfrey Davis and give him a message. It's very important.'

The android seemed more preoccupied with getting into the lift. 'I am sorry. I have to go to the Service Department. I have a malfunction.'

'What malfunction?' quizzed Semilla, grabbing the android's arm.

'Eh, it's my neck, look.' The android swivelled his head from side to side with exaggerated effect.

Semilla seemed unconvinced. 'You're putting that on, there's nothing wrong with you.'

'How do you know that?'

Semilla raised an eyebrow. 'I'm a woman and I work on the powers of deduction,' she told the uncooperative android with a frown furrowed across her forehead. 'Now, find Mr Davis. He should be in the Testing Department.'

He complied, and rolling his eyes backwards, his eyelids fluttered several times. 'Yes, he is in the Testing Department; the mainframe has confirmed it.'

'Are you sure he is still there?'

'Of course I am sure. Four hundred and twenty-two of my fellow androids also saw him enter the establishment.'

'Blimey, the Service Department must be busy this morning?'

'It is, and that is precisely where I am off to now,' the android said, pressing the lift button.

'Now just hold on a minute, I want you to send a message to him on the Testing Department phone.'

The android stamped his feet and gasped impatiently as Semilla leant over and spoke in his ear. He rolled his eyes a second time and fluttered his eyelids in quick succession. 'There, are you happy now? May I go?"

'Are you sure you sent that message?' Semilla said with air of mistrust.

He nodded. 'Of course I am sure. Unlike you, I'm an android and I work on the power of induction,' he said with a sneer, and slipping into the open lift, he promptly disappeared.

On basement level thirteen, the door opened in the Testing Department and Charlie Albright sauntered cheerily in. 'I say, you must be keen to start today, Godfrey, you're here rather early.' His smile quickly faded when he noticed his colleague's vomit-covered torso and trousers. 'Good grief, are you ill? I hope you haven't been eating those wretched doughnuts from the canteen, have you?'

Godfrey raised himself to his feet as Charlie handed him a wad of paper towels from a nearby dispenser. 'I wish it was that simple,' Godfrey said, cleaning himself up, 'but I have a feeling it's worse than that.'

Charlie wondered what could be worse than the canteen doughnuts. 'By the way, what's going on with the androids this morning? Most of the little blighters seem to be queued up in the corridor.'

Before Godfrey could answer, the office phone rang. 'Good morning, Testing Department, Baz speaking. If you need a test then come to the best. How may we help you? Mr Davis? Certainly, I will get him for you.' The lamppost hovered serenely across the workshop floor. 'There's a call for you, Mr Davis, on line two.'

Charlie stared with his face frozen in disbelief. 'Good grief, they can hover, did you see that? That's marvellous. I would never have thought of that. When did you make that modification?'

Godfrey calmly wandered across to the desk and picked up the handset and placed it against his ear. He looked at Charlie. 'I didn't.'

'Voice recognition required,' instructed the metallic voice of the mainframe.

'Godfrey Davis speaking,' he said slowly.

The automated voice continued. 'Recognition confirmed. You have one new message.' Godfrey glanced at Baz's grinning beacon and shook his head. 'Mr Davis, this is Semilla. Please don't come back to your office until Ethel has tidied it up. Leave it until after lunchtime.' Godfrey replaced the handset. 'Marvellous, it looks like security are making a proper job of wrecking my office.'

Charlie was on a different track. 'So, if you didn't make this modification to the lampposts then who did?'

'What in the name of Llar are they looking for?' Godfrey said, ignoring Charlie as he paced the floor. 'They can't possibly believe my father would have concealed this XXL in my office, surely?'

'For goodness' sake, Godfrey, are you listening to anything I say? So if it wasn't you who made this modification to them, then who did?'

Number Nine gave a nervous cough. 'Well, actually we did.'

'That's impossible!' snapped Charlie. 'You chaps are devoid of any arms, hands and digits. You couldn't possibly do that.'

The lampposts silently hovered forward until they formed a line across the workshop floor. Sliding back the centre section of their columns, they each unfolded a perfect chromium-plated arm and hand. They flexed them in unison like the stringed section of an orchestra.

Godfrey scratched his aching head. 'How in the name of Llar did you manage that?'

'We bribed an android to assemble the first hand and arm on

Number Ten. After that, it was easy. Once he had the dexterity of you humans, he simply copied the prototype and installed one on each of us,' Number Nine informed him.

'What did you bribe the android with, exactly?' asked their inventor.

'The chemical composition of blue enamel paint actually. It seemed a reasonable trade-off at the time.'

The commander was thoroughly bewildered. He was struggling to comprehend the lampposts' new abilities. He looked them up and down before his eyes returned to Godfrey for some sort of explanation.

'It's simple, Charlie, they have been plugging themselves into the data ports when we go home at night. They must have been downloading from the mainframe for ages.'

'You really are clever little devils,' Charlie muttered.

'Pure genius, I would have said,' commented Number Six, the lamppost who called himself Baz.

Godfrey lobbed his soiled paper towels into the bin. 'I wouldn't mind betting that these fellows are the ones responsible for the anomalies we are suffering on the mainframe right now. It's more than possible that every time they have logged on, which I didn't want them doing until they were fully tested,' Godfrey said, raising his voice ever so slightly, 'they leave a trace of their artificial intelligence behind. Their little trips into cyberspace every night would seem a perfect reason why the mainframe has been acting so strangely.'

'Do you think that's why it's suddenly started disgorging information about the XXL?'

'I would say that is a very good possibility.'

The commander thought for a moment. The implications began to sink in. 'I suddenly feel very queasy.'

'I thought you might. The paper towels are over there. Welcome to the show.'

Godfrey sighed; the situation had become very serious. He looked across at the line of lampposts. 'Do you realise what will happen to you if our peers comprehend what you've done? The mainframe has been infected, possibly irreversibly, and now it, in turn, has infected every single machine that downloads on to it each night. The entire android fleet has gone completely potty, and thanks to you lot they're now running off to the Service Department to copy me,' he said, baring his teeth and pointing at his face.

There was a brief silence. Deep inside twelve artificial intelligence chips, the potential was mulled over silently. It seemed to be a question of significant substance to absorb all of them, but only briefly. Finally, Number Eight made a comment. 'Mr Davis, with respect, sir, you are our creator, are you not?'

'Yes, I am, unfortunately,' confirmed Godfrey.

'That fact is something we collectively thank you for and compliment you on. You have created a fine piece of engineering, if I can say so. However, as I understand it, you intended for my eleven clients and I to expand ourselves mentally as we learned from your society. Is that not correct?'

Godfrey looked bewildered. 'Yes, that's correct, but what do you mean by clients?'

'Please, Mr Davis, let me ask the questions here,' Number Eight said in a polite but firm voice. 'As I was saying, my clients have told you the truth of their nocturnal activities. They have kept nothing from you. True, they have been slightly nefarious in their actions, albeit with the best intent, and I might remind you they have undertaken this with your programming protocol. Under these circumstances, the defence council would ask for some degree of leniency when considering our sentencing.'

Baz chuckled. 'Number Eight has been studying law on the Llarinian Internet. He's our council.'

'Studying law?' Godfrey shouted as his face filled with colour. 'That's enough.'

'Sir, might I remind you that you are under oath,' continued Number Eight, who was clearly living out his courtroom drama.

'Under oath?' Godfrey blurted. 'What oath?'

Charlie Albright positioned his rotund frame between the raging inventor and his twelve creations. 'Just calm down, Godfrey, and let me handle this,' he said as he moved briskly behind the line of lampposts.

Godfrey quickly realised his colleague's intentions. 'That's a damn good idea. Disconnect their power leads. That will shut them up.'

Charlie stared back at his friend. 'But none of them are plugged in.'

'Kept nothing from us?' raged Godfrey.

Number Eight coughed loudly. 'There has been an oversight in our pre-case submissions,' he proclaimed. 'My clients claim the Fifth Amendment.'

The room echoed to the sound of tumultuous laughter and cheering as the lampposts erupted into a chorus of hoots and howls. Mechanical arms were extended and handshakes were freely exchanged, as the lampposts hovered to and fro across the workshop complimenting Number Eight on his splendid performance. Godfrey plonked himself down on a nearby stool as Charlie stood motionless, absorbing the spectacle. Finally, the commander succumbed to a session with his hip flask. His action, though, was somewhat inopportune. As he raised his flask towards the ceiling, the Testing Department door silently opened behind him. Standing in the doorway, with his entourage nestling behind him, was the President. The lampposts suddenly went very quiet, realising only too late the implications of the situation. The President casually wandered into the facility early and unannounced. His timing had been perfect. He had asked why there had been so much laughter, not that he objected, of course, but he felt the need to be let in on the joke. Charlie managed to put on an admirable performance and started to lie rather successfully, or so he had thought. Godfrey, meanwhile, sat trembling on his workshop stool.

The President, surrounded by his group, insisted on seeing an example of this new creation's capability, and that is when the proceeding took a massive downturn.

'Am I right in thinking your proposal is to have one of these machines on every street corner throughout the metropolis, Commander?' he asked.

'Absolutely, sir,' Charlie replied confidently.

'And they will interface with the mainframe?'

'That is correct, sir,' he informed him.

The President looked disdainfully across the workshop at the twelve creations standing silently in a line. Charlie, though, was full of nervous exuberance and attempted to show the benefits of Godfrey's creations by conducting a simple test. He advanced upon Number Nine to prove the new lampposts value to Llarinian society.

'Right, you need to imagine,' he said to the President and his eager companions, 'that you are walking down the road and you need directions to the post office.' The President nodded approvingly and coaxed the commander to continue. 'I need directions to the nearest post office. Can you help me, please?'

Number Nine responded favourably and gave Charlie, as he had requested, the exact directions from the very spot on which he stood. It included the lift to the ground floor, which exit door to traverse and the quickest route across the Grand Plaza. The entourage, who had crowded into the Testing Department, clapped vigorously. The President, however, seemed unconvinced at this perfect display of Godfrey's engineering prowess.

'So, what if I ask one of them to assist me as there has been a minor accident, for example?' said the President. 'An old lady has tripped and fallen and she needs an ambulance transport.'

'Not a problem,' Charlie said gleefully. 'Please come over here and converse with this fellow, he's closest.' He guided the President in front of Number Nine, but the President hesitated. He sneered at the commander and then deliberately walked along the line of lampposts until he reached Number Six.

'This one,' he said, grinning. 'I want to ask this one.'

Godfrey's heart sank still further as the President confronted Baz. He could almost sense the commander's fear as he stood speechless before his leader, his mouth agape.

The President proceeded with his request. 'You,' he said, 'get me an ambulance immediately, there's been an accident.'

Baz's light flickered as his features on his beacon contorted into a sneer. 'Didn't your mother teach you any manners when you were younger? Please and thank you wouldn't hurt, you know.'

The President glared at Godfrey and Charlie. 'Is this part of their normal protocol?'

Charlie flustered around his leader, trying to persuade him that this particular lamppost had a minor malfunction. Unfortunately, Baz was unable to remain silent.

'There's nothing wrong with me, Commander Albright,' he said just as the Testing Department phone rang again for the second time that morning. Baz just couldn't resist. 'Good morning, Testing Department, Baz speaking. Oh, hello darling, can you please hold the line?' The delinquent lamppost glanced at the President. 'If you don't mind, this is a private call.'

The President's head turned purple, just as it had the day before in Godfrey's office. His eyes bulged with anger. 'Who do you think you're talking to?'

'My nail technician, actually,' Baz informed him.

Unable to contain himself, the President lunged forward and kicked the base of the lamppost with his shoe. 'Comply with my request, you insolent fool!' he screamed.

'Listen, sweetie, if you dare kick me again you'll be the one who'll need that ambulance transport.'

Godfrey's body went limp as he slid slowly from his stool and landed on his knees, his head bowed forward in defeat. It seemed the perfect position for his forthcoming execution.

CHAPTER 16

The handful of bread landed in the murky green water of the lake and was immediately devoured by a group of ravenous ducks. The flurry of jabbing beaks finally abated and the water calmed as Godfrey leant back against the park bench. 'So that's that then, the bread's finished and so are we.'

Charlie crossed his feet and got comfy on the park bench. 'Look,' he started, 'this is more my fault than yours.'

'I designed them. I'm the one that's responsible.'

'Yes, and I was the one who was supposed to be testing them. That responsibility was entirely mine. I should have cottoned on before. It should have been obvious they were up to something.'

Charlie took a swig from the whisky bottle he had collected from the shop on their way to the park. He offered his bottle to his colleague, who shook his head. Godfrey instead raised his family-size bottle of cough medicine.

'Thanks, but no thanks. I'll stick to this stuff if you don't mind.'

The two men fell into their private thoughts, drifting through the events of their day as they gazed across the lake.

'I just can't get rid of the image in my mind of when Baz slapped the President,' Charlie said as he laughed. They both giggled at the vision of Baz, who had produced his mechanical appendage and proceeded to slap the President's hand.

'You are horrible, you are!' Baz had said in his haughty voice.

The lights around the park received a signal from the mainframe and illuminated for their nightly vigil.

'What was it that Baz said?' Godfrey asked, smearing away the tears from his cheeks.

'I intend to stand on better street corners and get insulted by better people than you,' Charlie said, reminding him. The two beleaguered men sank into an uncontrollable fit of laughter until the humour subsided and the reality of the situation set in. Their moods then became more subdued.

'What are you going to say to Gloria?' Charlie asked.

Godfrey shrugged. The truth was he had absolutely no idea how to approach the subject. He was already in Gloria's bad books over his little misdemeanour in the vegetable garden when she'd discovered him cuddling his crop of carrots. Now he had to try and explain this. His demise at the Ministry was going to send a ripple through their lives, and sitting there drinking away his sorrows with Charlie was hardly going to resolve the issue. It was, in fact, almost certainly going to make it worse. He took another long sip from his bottle and felt the warm glow of satisfaction slide down his throat. Gloria was a practical person and he knew her first concern would be in his ability to find another job and quickly. The bills wouldn't stop slipping through the letter box if he were between jobs, and although Gloria worked at the school, it was now only part-time. Her income alone would prove insufficient in supporting the three of them. Since Mother had arrived on the doorstep last year they had been burdened with supporting her too, not that Gloria minded one little bit. She now had someone female to talk to, especially at meal times, and he often felt ousted by his mother-in-law's presence at the table. She was an intelligent woman, an ex-university professor with a sense of humour that could cut paper, though normally it was aimed at cutting him instead. She revelled in watching him buckle under her veiled innuendos, which generally portrayed him as inept and useless. Her best attribute, Godfrey considered, was her private fortune secreted in the vault of a bank that she repeatedly reminded them about. *'One day, when I am gone, you will want for nothing,'* she would say, largely to see the effect on his face. Well, she really didn't have to loiter on his account, he thought. Godfrey glanced at his bottle of cough medicine; it was half-empty. Perhaps it was time to go home now.

He looked over at Charlie with the intention of suggesting they call it a night but his companion had become deeply pensive. His worried expression concerned Godfrey immensely. 'What are you so deep in thought about?' he asked.

'It's occurred to me that this whole thing is more far-reaching than it would first seem. The impact that the lampposts and their AI have had on the mainframe, so far, is unbelievable.'

Godfrey agreed. 'Please don't remind me. I feel bad enough about this as it is. Thanks to me and my wonderful lampposts, the entire contingent of Llar's mechanical servants has decided to adopt names for themselves. The mainframe is coughing out data implicating our fathers and some invention that could harm the colony, and we've been dismissed.' Godfrey leant forward, placing his elbows on his knees. 'Everything in the colony is connected to the mainframe. What else have I disrupted?'

'It's just…' Charlie started.

'It's just what exactly?'

'I wouldn't mind betting that the President and his minions in the basement haven't put two and two together yet. Right now they have no idea that it's the lampposts that are responsible for the anomalies on the mainframe.'

Godfrey turned and stared at him. 'You could be right, you know. The only reason my inventions are going to the crusher in the morning is because they humiliated the President at the demonstration.'

'Precisely,' Charlie agreed. 'So with the lampposts gone, they are no longer an annoyance to the President.'

'Or a threat to the mainframe,' Godfrey said.

'My money is on the fact they haven't realised what the lampposts have actually done yet,' Charlie said. 'Do you remember what our President said yesterday in your office? He stated that one of the programmers had a theory, and I quote, "the mainframe was almost taking on a mind of its own".'

'I remember,' Godfrey said. 'And the President scoffed at the very thought of it, didn't he?'

'He did,' Charlie agreed.

'At least we can't get blamed for that, can we? After all, ignorance is bliss, as they say.'

Charlie leant forward and pointed at a duck standing on the bank of the lake. 'Not quite, my dear boy. You see, that little fellow there, for example, knows absolutely nothing about secret information on the mainframe and devices called the XXL. He's completely safe and absolutely no threat to our leader at all.'

Godfrey blinked nervously. 'But when Baz threw that tantrum, he blurted out that he and his colleagues knew about the encrypted data that the President was concealing. We were present.'

'I know,' Charlie said with a solemn face. 'Ignorance may be bliss, but the problem is we're not ignorant and we're certainly not innocent. We're responsible for wrecking the mainframe, and sooner or later they will realise it was our fault. We know too much, Godfrey. We know that your inventions struck a blow right into the President's treasure trove of secrets and unveiled information from over four decades ago, which has certainly put him on edge. He is not the sort of man one wants to upset,' Charlie said with a frown. 'It almost makes you wish you were that duck, eh?'

Godfrey stared across the pitch-black waters of the lake. 'What is he going to do with us then?' he whispered.

Charlie Albright pondered the statement. 'That is a very good question, and one we will find out the answer to very shortly, I'm sure.'

Across the dimming light of the park, the first shadows of the evening were being cast down; the night would soon be upon them. It was a poignant ending after spending an entire lifetime working for the Ministry, to be ejected from their respective jobs, dismissed by their furious leader, and sent home in disgrace until further notice.

Godfrey looked down at the file box by his feet, the remnants he had collected from his office after his dismissal. Wedged in amongst the diplomas and his broken crane lamp sat the picture of his graduation. The picture was cracked, courtesy of the sergeant and his men who had searched his office. Carefully prising it from the box, he stared through the shards of broken glass, gazing down at his parents and their ecstatic faces. 'Not so proud of me today,' Godfrey muttered.

Charlie agreed. 'Same for me,' he said, pulling a similar photo from his own file box of memorabilia. 'Thank Llar they can't see us now.'

The two men chinked bottles in the early evening air of the park as the ducks began to settle down for the night, and Godfrey, thinking of his trip home to the suburbs, carefully placed his old picture back in his file box. He hesitated. His hand lunged down into the box and he grabbed the photo again. His faced curled into a look of disbelief. 'What in the name of Llar?' he muttered quietly. 'It can't be?'

Charlie now had his curiosity aroused. He gaped at Godfrey's stunned expression. His friend was almost traumatised. 'What's wrong?'

'This photo has been staring down at me from my office wall every day of my working life and I have never noticed it before.'

'Noticed what, for goodness' sake?' Charlie asked, becoming impatient.

'This photograph of my graduation. I think it holds a clue.' Godfrey babbled as he sat motionless, his vision locked on the broken remnants of his graduation photograph. Through the shards of broken glass, Godfrey noticed something white peering through. There were grey smudgy letters in pencil. Godfrey placed the picture beside him on the park bench. Then, carefully removing the rusty pins from the frame of the photograph, he separated it from the cardboard backing.

The commander looked thoroughly bewildered. 'What is it?'

Godfrey removed a small handwritten note hidden between the photo and the cardboard support. 'It's a note from my dad.'

'What does it say?' Charlie said excitedly.

Godfrey stared at the note; his face was ashen. 'It simply says, *"Go to the caves and find the tin."*'

'Give me your graduation photo, quickly,' demanded Godfrey.

Charlie handed over his photo. Godfrey looked at the two almost identical graduation photographs side by side, and the realisation of what he saw drained the colour from his face. 'The devious old devils,' he said quietly.

'What is it?'

Godfrey waved the photographs excitedly in front of Charlie. 'I think I know what the XXL looks like and where we will find it.'

On the eighty-third floor of the Ministry, in the office that had belonged to Godfrey Davis, Ethel sat on the sofa trying hard to compose herself.

'Please stop crying, Ethel. You'll set me off too,' Semilla said as she passed her another tissue and placed her arm reassuringly around the old cleaner's shoulder.

'I just can't believe that he's not coming back, Commander Albright neither,' Ethel sobbed.

'I know,' agreed Semilla. 'It certainly won't be the same around here anymore, that's for sure.'

Ethel dabbed her last tears away and gave Semilla a brave smile. 'Come on, lovey, it's late, let's get off home.'

There was a quiet knock at the office door and Burt the security guard peered into the room. He quickly entered, sheepishly looking back down the corridor outside before he closed the door.

Ethel stood up and clenched her tissue tightly. 'I can't believe you would come in here, Burt Brown. Why have you come back, to gloat? I hope you're proud of yourselves down in security. It's bad enough that poor man has lost his job, but wrecking his office before he left is despicable.'

Burt put a finger across his lips. 'Please keep your voice down. I shouldn't even be here.'

Ethel crossed her arms defensively. 'That's something we both agree on. So why are you here?' she hissed.

Burt tried to reassure her. 'I don't agree with this anymore than you do, but I wasn't involved in this, you know that.'

The old cleaner's head slumped and she stared down at the floor. She knew it was the truth and she also knew Burt was really a good man beneath that uniform.

'Mr Davis and the commander, do you know where they are now?' Burt asked.

'No, they left before it got dark,' Semilla informed him. 'What do you want them for?'

'This isn't over yet,' Burt said, his voice laced with concern.

'Why, what's going on?' Ethel enquired.

'If I get caught here I'll be for the high jump. They will probably dismiss me too if they find out I told you.'

Ethel gave him an exasperated look. 'Come on, Burt, out with it. We won't tell anyone, will we, Semilla?'

The young woman shook her head and leaned in closer, eager

to hear more. Burt looked anxiously at the door half expecting someone to walk in at any moment. 'The President has ordered the Testing Department to be sealed up. They are removing Mr Davis's inventions and taking them to the crusher in the morning.'

'For goodness' sake, Burt, please tell us something we don't already know!' Ethel blurted impatiently.

'Please keep your voices down. I was told something just now and that person promised me they wouldn't say anything for a few hours.' Burt moved in closer. 'You both know Mr Davis and the commander well enough to warn them,' he said in a virtual whisper.

Ethel gave Burt a puzzled look. 'Why do we need to warn them? Surely they know the inventions are going to be destroyed in the morning. Everyone in the building knows that.'

Burt nervously looked back at the office door again. 'My sergeant doesn't even know what I'm about to tell you.'

'Tell us what, for goodness' sake?' Ethel asked.

'The lampposts have gone missing.'

CHAPTER 17

As Ethel absorbed the news in Godfrey's old office, the President paced to and fro across the floor of the presidential suite. He was less than happy and he was not in the mood for taking no for an answer.

'I've never been so humiliated in all my life,' he raged, 'and if you had been there you might understand why I'm so angry.'

Jack was used to suffering the President's tantrums, though it didn't mean he liked them. 'We will sort this out, I promise you.'

The President stormed across his office and glowered at his aide. 'Just when do you think that will be?'

Jack drew a shallow breath. The President could be insufferable when he didn't get his own way, but for now he would remember his position and the limitations that it brought. The President strode over to his desk and poured himself a large drink, glaring back at his aide. 'I want you to make Davis and Albright disappear immediately. Do you understand?'

'Sir, with respect, we're treading on thin ice here. These men are too high profile to just disappear. They're not lowly programmers in the basement at the Ministry that no one will miss, apart from their families maybe.'

'Think of something. That's why you're here, isn't it, to think?'

'We need to remain calm. If anything leads back to this administration it could make you look very unpopular; people will start to demand answers.'

The President absorbed Jack's comment. He realised his temper would be his downfall if he made a rash decision. His aide was right as usual, and he knew it. Sipping his drink, he gave Jack another shrewd look as he sat down in his leather chair. 'All right, so where do we start? I take it you have a plan? After all, Jack Marsden always has a plan, doesn't he?' he said in a sarcastic tone.

Jack remained calm and silent. He was well versed at standing in front of raging politicians, though none of them had ever surpassed his father. 'Firstly, let us take stock of the situation, shall we? Godfrey Davis's office yielded nothing in our search for the XXL. We therefore need to widen our investigation.'

'Go on.'

'I will instruct security to search his home and that of Commander Albright too – something low profile.'

'And then?'

'I will personally undertake the disposal of the six programmers with immediate effect. As for those inventions that caused you such embarrassment today, they are locked away safely in the basement and are destined for destruction in the morning.'

The President was listening now; he was calmer and thinking more rationally. 'This just leaves us to eradicate the problem with the mainframe.'

'And, of course, the annihilation of our political opponents in the presidential shuttle.'

The President smiled from ear to ear; the thought of disposing of his adversaries made him almost euphoric. 'Looks like we have something of a busy week ahead,' the President said, raising his glass and toasting his aide.

Jack smirked, his patience and his experience had paid off again as he knew it would.

Shortly afterwards, Jack closed the door to the President's office and acknowledged the two security men standing patiently waiting for him to reappear. 'Go and prepare my transport. We are going to Area 21 now, tonight,' Jack instructed them as he lifted his phone from his pocket.

Shortly after a brief phone conversation, and descending the one hundred and one floors of the Ministry, Jack and his two security men left the underground parking complex in a matt black transport. He sat in the rear of the vehicle, surrounded by tinted glass, as they slipped silently through the metropolis, past the crowded streets bustling with the citizens of their great colony. The streets were so vibrant, so full of life, and the pageant made him feel despondent knowing the task ahead. The rain that came to pepper the windows only served to enhance his mood.

'It's not supposed to rain until 4 a.m. tomorrow,' the driver said as he flicked on the wipers.

'There's something wrong with the mainframe,' his colleague openly told him, forgetting who they had on board. Jack didn't say a word; there was little point in a reprimand. Everyone at the Ministry knew there was something wrong with the vast machine that controlled the colony. And day by day the problem was becoming more and more difficult to deny.

Several minutes later, the transport came to a rest, hovering patiently at a set of traffic lights serving a large intersection. Through the unscheduled evening rain trickling down the window, Jack caught sight of the cafe. It was still the way he remembered it, even after all this time. A young couple ran laughing across the street and into the shelter of the light flooding across the pavement. Lulled by the moment, he remembered a day from his past.

He had been sitting in the cafe gazing out of the window at the steady rain. There had been a constant stream of people slipping in from the afternoon's weather. They were mainly couples eager to spend a short while together around a warm beverage. He had drifted off. The sound of chinking crockery and mumbled conversations eased his troubled mind. Locked away privately, he had been considering the events of his day at the Ministry.

'So is this how the President's new aide spends his time?'

Jack had looked up at Rachael. She was standing smiling beside him, her raincoat glistening in the cafe's lights. He rose, helped her remove her coat, and kissed her.

'Sorry, I was daydreaming. It's been a long day.'

Rachael had nestled herself into a chair as a waiter attended their table, serving them with two fresh coffees.

'So, do you want to tell me about it?' Rachael had asked, stirring her coffee. 'You seem very distant.'

Jack had watched the steam rising from his cup. It seemed the perfect description of his current mood. He'd glanced up at his fiancée and given her a tired look. 'It's privileged information. I can't disclose it.'

Rachael had eyed him carefully. 'Okay, then sit and stew if it makes you happy.'

Jack had known there was no winning with her. She would have sat out his mood in silence until he decided to talk. Rachael was a master of patience. He had observed the other clientele in the cafe. The nearest people Jack considered were out of earshot.

'He is going to order the media to print and broadcast only what the Ministry has vetted and sanctioned.'

'What?' Rachael cried.

Several people at some of the nearer tables had turned and given them a fleeting look.

'Please keep your voice down,' Jack had whispered nervously.

Rachael had raised her pencil-thin eyebrows and stared across the table. 'So reporters like me are going to have their hands tied, is that it?'

Jack had run his tongue over his bottom lip. He'd hesitated as the waiter floated past. 'I shouldn't even be telling you. Nobody else knows about this. He asked for my opinion about adding this control, and when I told him, he shot me down in flames.'

'What did you tell him?'

'I told him that the colony surely had a right to a free press. I told him the truth. What else would I say?'

Rachael had stared across the table, her face barely containing the anger that smouldered inside her. 'He can't do that. It goes against every fundamental principle that built our colony.'

Jack had wished he had kept his mouth shut; their rendezvous had taken a massive downturn thanks to his loose tongue. 'Look,' he had said, 'why don't we go out for dinner tonight and maybe a nightclub afterwards?'

Rachael wasn't being bought off. 'Tell me something?'

'What?'

'Tell me what that the inscription says?'

'What inscription?'

'You know what inscription, the one on the roamer's statue in the Grand Plaza,' she had hissed at him across the table.

He had huffed and looked across at the waiter clearing the tables. 'It says *"We were the children of the desert and now we are free."*'

'And the rest of it,' demanded Rachael.

Jack's shoulders slumped. '*And we shall remain free for the rest of our days.*'

Rachael had stood up and grabbed at her raincoat. 'And that includes the press, Jack Marsden.'

Jack had half stood and motioned her to sit back down. He had nervously looked around the cafe, conscious they were drawing attention to themselves. She had sat again and he had leant across the table and held her hand.

'When he tells the Ministry to implement this control, what do you intend to do?' he'd asked, staring at her intently.

'This is censorship and it's a travesty,' she'd replied, 'and it will be down to journalists like me to speak out about it.'

Jack had felt his face lose its colour. 'You need to be careful. This isn't a game.'

She'd given him a look that was half surprise and half fear. 'He's just another politician, and politicians come and go. Let the people decide. After all, it's their colony.' Jack had frozen to the spot. The waiter had stood beside them with a pot of steaming coffee. Rachael had waved him away.

'I have a feeling this politician isn't going to go away that easily,' Jack had whispered across the table. 'He plays dirty, and he plays for keeps.'

'Do you know more than you are telling me?'

Jack had blushed and stared out of the window. His role as the President's aide was new, but the rumours at the Ministry were old. Outside, the rain had eased up, and the cafe had emptied except for them. Jack had stood and grabbed Rachael's raincoat and helped her on with it. As they left, he had slipped his hand into hers and they began to walk. After a short while, she'd stopped and turned to him. 'You didn't answer my question.'

Jack had frowned as he looked along the wet pavement behind them. 'You need to be careful, Rachael, very careful. That's all I can tell you.'

'Are you really that concerned over this issue?'

'I am,' Jack had said in low meaningful tone, 'with a passion.'

'Then I promise you I will be as careful as I can be, OK? But my articles may prove unpopular at the Ministry if the President makes this change to our lives.' They had continued walking in silence. Behind them, the waiter had turned the sign on the cafe door to 'closed'.

Jack watched the cafe slip past as the lights changed and the transport moved on. That encounter had been a long time ago, though it was still as vivid as if it were only yesterday. He laid back and closed his eyes, hoping the memory of that day would disappear into the darkness. If he could just sleep, even for a short while, it would ease his mind. This excursion was a long one, and Jack knew the route to their destination intimately. Jack also knew that when they reached their goal his nightmares would be waiting for him, just as they always were, on the other side of the colony.

CHAPTER 18

There was little point, he thought, in trying to hide the fact that he had been drinking again, albeit only cough medicine. The fresh evening air on the way home had oxygenated Godfrey's brain sufficiently, giving him a degree of complacency. He sauntered into the kitchen as Gloria glanced up from her stewing pot. 'So is this drinking cough medicine thing going to be a regular habit?' she said sarcastically.

'How can you tell it's cough medicine?'

Gloria frowned at her husband. 'Your lips are bright red.'

'Only if I do it often enough,' he said, tittering like a naughty school boy. 'Get it? Regular? Often enough?'

Gloria was not amused, and the humour, if any, evaded her completely. 'Where have you been? Your dinner is ready and you're completely sozzled again. What's going on, Godfrey?'

He thought quickly and rallied with a tactical defence. 'Yes, I am late, although technically I'm not completely sozzled. I know this to be true and I can prove it,' he said with an air of complete confidence.

'Oh really, can you?'

'Yes, I can, of that I am emphatic.'

'Then please do enlighten me.'

Godfrey beamed a huge smile that broadened his tanned chin to the limit. 'You see, Gloria, I haven't seen Rodney yet this evening.'

'Who in the name of Llar is Rodney?'

'I went skiing with him last night. He's a giant lettuce.'

Gloria saw red. 'That's enough. Now go and get a cold shower and then come down to dinner sober!' she shouted. 'I'll hear no more of this insanity.'

Her husband paused, wondering when it would be convenient to inform her that he had lost his job at the Ministry. He concluded that now was not the right moment, and wobbling off into the hall he managed to intercept the phone with perfect timing. 'Look, if you're ringing about double-glazed windows, we've already got them. Please check your records,' he slurred.

'What?' said a voice that was glaringly familiar. 'I'm not ringing about your windows. I have a message for you. You must listen. It's vital.'

'I beg your pardon? What message? Who is this?'

'I am trying to tell you something important, something very important. The message is "*grin a reply, most miss a soup*".'

Godfrey's pickled brain carefully considered this information. 'No, I think Gloria is making stew again, actually.'

'What?'

'Tonight's dinner, it's stew.'

'You don't understand,' said the voice, becoming agitated. 'This message is in code. Your phone is probably being monitored.'

Godfrey had a glazed expression. 'Look, I really have absolutely no idea what you are on about.'

There was a prompt from the kitchen. 'Godfrey! Shower! Now!'

'Look I have to go now, but thank you for your call. Goodbye.'

Shortly afterwards, Godfrey lay in a warm relaxing bath with his yellow plastic duck bobbing cheerfully amongst the foaming bubbles. He considered his day and giggled. So he was out of his job, big deal. They would have to give him another one. No one in Llar was allowed to sit about; everyone had to work. Maybe they would give him a job in the park looking after the ducks –

now that would be wonderful. He grinned to himself, lifting his big toe and tapping his plastic duck on the head. 'We don't care, do we ducky? Tomorrow's the start of a whole new day, isn't it?' We're going to redeem ourselves, aren't we?'

The duck, which now had a large cigar smouldering in the corner of its mouth, shook its head slowly. 'You'll never make tomorrow, fella, if Gloria catches you in this bath. You're supposed to be having a cold shower, remember?'

Godfrey eyes widened, but only briefly, as his head slid backwards and clumped the cast iron bath. He slid gracefully into the warmth that surrounded him. His nostrils were fortunately just above the waterline as he slipped into another drunken reverie.

Semilla stood beside the phone box staring at Ethel who was shaking her head in despair. 'Didn't he understand our code?' she asked.

'No, he didn't, not a single word of it. He was rambling on about stew for dinner or something.'

'What are we going to do now?'

Ethel raised an eyebrow at her colleague. 'We think of another code quickly and then ring him back. He must get the message sooner or later.'

Semilla nodded and produced a pad and pen from her bag.

Charlie Albright could have kicked himself for being so remiss. If he hadn't weakened and dropped into Dave's Bar after leaving Godfrey at the park, he may have been able to avert this. He only had himself to blame as his love for a fine malt whisky had been his downfall yet again. Crouching down still further behind the bush in his front garden, he listened to the sound of breaking furniture. The radios in the security transports parked outside his home babbled on about 714s and 715s in progress across the metropolis, none of which made much sense at all. It was all just security gibberish to him.

Suddenly, the sounds from within his house ceased. Then, the sergeant who had demolished Godfrey's office earlier that day came out, followed by his men. He hesitated on the porch, seeming livid that they had been unsuccessful in their search. 'It's pretty clear there's no XXL here,' he grunted.

From beside one of the transports parked in the road, another guard called out. 'We've got to get back to the Ministry, boss. Someone's broken into the Testing Department.'

The sergeant looked over at Harry and Burt. He didn't particularly like these guards, and though he couldn't put his finger on it, he didn't trust them either. 'You two take your transport and get over to that Godfrey Davis's house and continue searching. I want you to call me if you find what we're looking for, all right?'

Burt and Harry saluted as the burly sergeant pounded his way down the path. They watched their sergeant's transport whistle and hum off into the night, leaving them alone on the porch.

'Don't tell me what we've just seen in there is right, Harry? It can't be?'

They looked up and down the street a couple of times. They knew there was no need to destroy the commander's home, but everyone was too frightened to stand up to their sergeant. Besides, orders were orders. Harry sighed heavily. 'I'm just one man. How can I change anything? What can I do?'

Burt watched Harry walk off towards their transport. The flashes of blue and gold light silhouetted him against the darkness of the night. 'The President is just one man and he runs the whole of Llar,' he called out. 'Mind you, the way we've seen him carry on these last couple of days, I'm beginning to think he's no better than our sergeant.'

Harry hesitated and turned back to his colleague. 'I am a security guard. I am not the President. The man must have his reasons, and remember, we were sworn to secrecy about yesterday and what happened on floor eighty-three. I've kept my promise, and I've said nothing about it to anyone.'

Burt blushed. Harry was right. They had been forbidden by the President to say anything about the events in Godfrey Davis's office. He also remembered his late-night chat at Dave's Bar and how he had foolishly related his stories to the friendly android. Burt also considered about his earlier encounter with Ethel and Semilla. He silently hoped they had managed to warn Godfrey that his inventions had disappeared from the Testing Department. As he and Harry climbed into their transport, he felt relieved over one thing. Searching the Davis's house now would be a much more respectful affair with their sergeant heading off in the opposite direction towards the Ministry.

The two men drove across the vast metropolis towards the outer suburbs and the home of Godfrey and Gloria Davis, which, considering the events of the evening so far, was the perfect destination for Charlie Albright as well. Hidden behind the seats in the back of their transport, Charlie knew these nice chaps were going to take him straight there.

CHAPTER 19

The cast iron bath was cold against Godfrey's back; his shoulder blades and bottom were numb and lifeless. He peered with one eye at the bath plug and chain wound neatly round the big toe on his left foot. All of the water had gone and he was freezing. The plastic duck had perched itself neatly over his belly button and was grinning at him foolishly. Godfrey clambered out of the bath, grabbed his dressing gown, and shortly afterwards he stood in the hallway downstairs. He tried to compose himself in preparation for telling Gloria his news when suddenly the phone rang. His shoulders sagged as he lifted the receiver. 'Look, I'm sorry, but we are not interested,' he said curtly.

'Just listen,' said Ethel in a low, whispering tone. 'It's vital you understand this coded message.'

'Understand? Do you know you're the second person tonight who's rung up with a coded message?'

'*Sir Tight Lake*,' she said.

'What?' Godfrey asked, sounding slightly angry. 'You must have got the wrong number. Goodbye.'

Across on the other side of the metropolis, Ethel stood in a phone kiosk staring in to the handset. 'He still doesn't get it,' she said, glancing up at Semilla in disbelief. 'There's only one thing for it. We go to his house and tell him face to face.'

Godfrey wandered into the living room and found Gloria on the sofa reading a newspaper with her half-rimmed glasses poised on the end of her nose. She glanced at him with a look that clearly mirrored her foul mood. 'I see you've dressed for the occasion. Are we ready to eat at last?' she said flatly.

'Look, darling, there's something we need to talk about. It really is very important.'

Gloria folded the newspaper and placed it neatly on the coffee table. She wasn't being deterred. 'After we have eaten dinner! Now please go and call Mother.'

Godfrey obeyed and wandered into the hall as Mother appeared at the foot of the stairs. She looked her son-in-law up and down with her best grimace. 'So you're bladdered again, eh? I love it when you're like this. It's so much easier to pick on you.'

Strangely enough, Godfrey didn't feel annoyed or offended. He seemed to have an invisible resistance to Mother's abuse, a sort of force field. With the remnants of the chemist's cherry-flavoured remedy drifting through his brain, he imagined her swinging gently from the banisters on a stout rope, like a piñata, with him whacking her with a stick. The moment was sadly interrupted by a loud crash from the cellar. The dimly lit hallway was instantly pierced with shafts of searing light from the gap beneath the door.

Mother stared at Godfrey. 'So what have you blown up this time, Lofty?'

He approached the door and slowly clasped the handle. 'I can hear voices,' he whispered. As Godfrey eased the door open, they peered in cautiously. The cellar flickered with light, and muffled voices were clearly audible.

'Who is it?' whispered the old lady.

'How do I know? I can't see around corners.'

Mother scowled at him, and Godfrey suddenly had an idea. 'Look, why don't you go first and smile at them.'

'What?'

'Well they're more likely to be frightened of you!'

Mother sneered as the pair crept down the staircase into the basement, her gnarled fingers clutching the handrail. They went slowly downwards until they both stood upon the floor of the huge cellar. Suddenly the area was pitched into darkness. Godfrey felt his heart miss a beat as he ran his hand along the cellar wall, desperately attempting to find the light switch. Mother fumbled around in the blackness seeking out a support, and her hand instead located Godfrey's bathrobe.

'Show yourselves!' Godfrey blurted. 'I'm heavily armed, you know.'

A light in the corner suddenly burst into life, accompanied by a familiar voice. 'It's only us, Godfrey,' said Number Nine, excitedly hovering in front of the frightened pair.

Mother immediately erupted with a monumental scream and fell backwards onto the staircase, landing with a thump. Unfortunately, she failed to release her vice-like grip on her son-in-law's bathrobe and it flew off like the unveiling of a new acquisition in an art gallery. Godfrey gasped and clasped his hands over his groin as the cellar turned into utter mayhem. The lampposts laughed and shouted as the lights from their beacons flashed on and off in a barrage of illumination.

Mother screamed again, and still grasping Godfrey's bathrobe tightly in her hand, she ran up the staircase. Arriving in the hallway, she raised the robe at arm's-length, took a very large deep breath and screamed some more.

'How did you get here?' stammered Godfrey.

'It is a long story,' Number Nine informed him.

'I don't care how long the story is, I want to know and I want to know now,' he shouted over the top of Mother's screaming.

'We thought you might, especially as we've now decoded some of *The Great Book of Llar*,' Number Nine shouted back.

It was fortunate that Mother had chosen to take a breath and stopped screaming long enough or Godfrey would probably have never heard the doorbell. He pointed a finger at his errant inventions. 'Now just stay here and be quiet. I'll deal with you all later. You're in very big trouble.'

'There is another huge oasis on the other side of Llar,' Number Five told him, hovering forward and undeterred by Godfrey's reprimand. 'I couldn't get the coordinates, though. We had to disconnect from the mainframe and leave the Ministry in rather a hurry.'

Godfrey's addled cortex resonated to an orchestra of bells. Suddenly, his encounter that morning with the old hologram had some credence. 'It's in the north,' he uttered.

The lampposts turned to one another in amazement. 'How do you know that?' asked Number Nine.

The sound of screaming in the lobby upstairs abated briefly as Mother took another breath. The doorbell chimed again.

'It doesn't matter. I'll tell you later. I have to go.'

Godfrey leapt up the stairs, slamming the cellar door behind him. Mother was running up and down the hallway, her hands still gripped on her son-in-law's robe, screaming for all she was worth. She took another look at Godfrey's naked body and screamed even louder.

Gloria entered the hallway and tried to calm her mother as she cast an eye over her husband. 'Why have we got a security transport outside our home, and why are you naked?' she enquired.

Godfrey grabbed at his dressing gown, but Mother, who insisted on clenching it tightly, began a tug of war. Godfrey finally won. He slipped his garment on rapidly to cover his nudity. 'I was trying to tell you earlier, but you insisted that you didn't want to listen until after dinner, remember?'

The doorbell chimed three times, though it was barely audible from Mother's screaming. Suddenly, the old lady took several intakes of breath. 'The cellar is full of them, and they can

talk and fly. We're being invaded. We're all going to die!' she
hollered.

Gloria gave her husband a shrewd look as her mother began
screaming again. 'So how bad is this?'

'Bad.'

'Just how bad?'

Godfrey raised both eyebrows. 'Very, very bad.'

'Right,' Gloria said in confirmation, and she promptly
disappeared into the lounge. Seconds later, she reappeared and
took her mother by the arm. 'Come with me. You'll be safe in
here,' she said, guiding her hysterical mother into the lobby
toilet.

Shortly afterwards, Gloria stood next to her husband,
brushing down the arm of his robe. 'On the count of three,' she
said, 'you open the door and let me do the talking, OK?'

Godfrey was now very sober indeed, and with a sheepish look
he confronted his long-suffering wife and took a very deep
breath. 'I've been dismissed from the Ministry and the security
forces are here to ransack our home. They're searching for one
of my father's old inventions that's apparently a weapon of mass
destruction, and in our cellar there are a dozen stolen lampposts
that can talk and fly.'

Godfrey gave his wife a pathetic look and then he opened the
front door of their home.

CHAPTER 20

As Godfrey Davis's heart pounded and the front door of his home opened, the phone on the President's desk rang three times in a quiet unobtrusive tone. It was a call he was expecting from security; his visitor had arrived. And given the fact he had just discarded a tray that had contained his evening meal, it was indeed well timed. He had left explicit instructions with the security team that manned the lift in the underground parking that only one person would be allowed access tonight.

Entering from the ramp and the street above, this female guest rarely visited the Ministry, maybe two or three times a year, and then only at the request of the colony's leader. Miranda Short was far from vertically challenged, at a little less than six foot. With the aid of her block-heeled knee-length boots, she towered over most of the guards she encountered when visiting the Ministry. Her lifeless steel-blue eyes would leave you forgiven for thinking her only pleasure in life was inflicting pain and suffering on those she met. She was attractive and physically perfect; her contoured black motorcycle jacket and tight leather trousers accentuated her athletic figure. As she strode boldly beneath the coffered ceiling and across the parking bays towards the presidential lift, she remembered her last visit to the Ministry. It had been a messy affair for the security team, and the four men standing either side of the President's private lift this evening had all heard the story.

'Good evening, Ma'am. How are you tonight?' asked one

guard, moving forward, the trepidation in his voice clearly evident.

The President's visitor gave him a cold icy stare. Fear had already set in, and the hairs on the back of his neck were bristling. His heart palpitated as he awaited a reply. None came. Instead, Miranda stood and flexed her gloved fingers; the black leather glistened in the lights above the lift entrance.

'May I see your ID?' continued the guard, stumbling across his own words.

Miranda Short narrowed her eyes and shifted her stance. One blow is all it would take to dispatch him.

The older man to her left nodded at the lift. 'You're free to pass, Ma'am. There is no need for ID,' he said as he stepped to one side.

Miranda entered the lift, her eyes trained on her inquisitor. Her heart hadn't raised a beat during what could have been another ugly scene. She was a hardened professional, and while her reputation may have been known to the security forces in the colony, not even they knew where she came from. Miranda appeared when she was summoned, and in between she was nothing more than a ghost. As the lift began to ascend, she closed her eyes and pictured a place far from the metropolis.

On the southernmost tip of the oasis, far away from the lush green lands of the interior, sits a derelict township long since forgotten by the Llarinian people. As the colony grew year by year, so did this small hamlet. The influence of commerce changed the landscape while seemingly limitless deposits of granite were extracted for profit. Generation after generation lived and worked there toiling beneath the sun until one day the quarry finally became exhausted. The heyday of building across the metropolis had also come to an end, and the demand for granite had dried up completely. For the people of Stoneburg, it marked the end to a way of life they had known for centuries.

The machinery rusted and the abandoned buildings fell into disrepair. The desert laid claim to the streets, raining down thick layers of sand until finally most of it had been swallowed up completely. The families that had remained there slowly dwindled in numbers. Stoneburg was doomed and would never return to its former glory. Each year more and more of the inhabitants had ventured north, drawn to the metropolis and all that it offered. One couple, though, had chosen to remain and endure the harsh terrain and way of life in this sand-filled ghost town in the middle of nowhere.

They continued to live perched on a rise that overlooked what was left of the town, in a home that was part of a small farm that sustained the two of them. The house was a single-storey dwelling that had once been thrown together in something of a scramble. There was a large wooden door in the centre, with small windows either side offering a degree of light for the inhabitants. It was a squat structure that looked disproportionate and had weathered badly across the years despite being built from the very granite the men had quarried. Etched and pockmarked by the relentless desert wind, the roof constantly required attention. But, for Benjamin and Mary, it was the ideal location, and when the last family left Stoneburg, it, in fact, became perfect.

The couple rejoiced at the solitude now the town was finally theirs, although the euphoria did not last for long. Mary began to notice food missing from the pantry and small sandy footprints on the floorboards of their kitchen. Someone hungry was entering their home during the night. It didn't take long for them to catch the thief red-handed as they lay in wait, kneeling down behind their dilapidated sofa. The child screamed and hollered as Mary grabbed her while her husband lit a lantern to get a better look at their nocturnal visitor. The child was filthy, dirty, her blond hair matted and her thick cotton dress torn and stained. The girl was no more than six years old, abandoned by her family in their haste to leave like an unwanted pet. When the child stopped kicking and lashing out at her captor, she froze, staring at Mary with steel-blue eyes. The couple's childless marriage had left a void in their lives, and now it seemed there was a way to fill the emptiness that had prevailed for so many years. As the woman took her into her arms and comforted the new addition to their union, the girl sobbed heavily on her shoulder. With the passage of time it would prove to be the last occasion in her life that Miranda would ever cry.

Life for the three of them soon took on a new routine. Each day after breakfast, when Benjamin went about his farming duties, Mary took out her tattered books and she and Miranda would sit at the kitchen table and continue with her education. Mary worked hard with the child, her patience and devotion, before long, rewarded as Miranda became numerate, mastering the world of arithmetic. Her literacy skills grew and soon gave her the ability to read everything she could lay her hands on. When Miranda was not studying, her new father taught her how to tend to the farm animals and how to hunt in their remote wilderness. By the time she had reached eleven years of age, he had passed on his survival skills and his knowledge of the terrain. But the instinct Miranda continually displayed was not something she had learned, it was something unique to her and would one day give her the edge to exist in a world far more hostile than an abandoned township. The bond between Miranda and her adopted parents grew year by year and the love they shared for one another was as real as if she had been a daughter of their own. The years passed by and the routine of family life on the edge of the desert far from civilisation continued unchanged. Several times a year, Benjamin would venture north on horseback to visit the great metropolis. His trips took two weeks or so and Miranda always counted down the days to his return. He would arrive back with new books and gifts for both of them, pleased to be home again with his family on the edge of the desert.

One trip changed the balance of life irrevocably for the three of them when Benjamin returned home late one night. He had barely made the front door before he had collapsed, badly wounded. The story he told his distraught wife was that he had been attacked by several men who had attempted to rob him as he had left the metropolis. Mary sent Miranda out of the room while she tended her husband's wounds. For the first time since she had been that abandoned child, Miranda felt fear again as she had caught sight of the knife wounds on his back and arms. Her heart raced as the adrenalin flooded her veins. The panic was soon replaced by an intense anger and the desire to seek vengeance on those who had inflicted this suffering on her father. It took some months for him to heal properly. Most of the summer was spent convalescing, and during that time Miranda had attempted to find out more details of the night he had been attacked. Benjamin, though, was reluctant to elaborate, and before long it became apparent to her that there was more to this story than he was prepared to offer. As the season passed and the autumn winds once again returned from the direction of the desert, Benjamin saddled up his horse to ride to the colony. He kissed them both goodbye, allaying their fears for his safe return, but Miranda was unable to sense the sincerity in his words and in his eyes. Watching him ride off at dusk, her mind was made up. She had to know the truth, and to find it she had to follow him.

The express elevator delivered her to the one hundredth floor, and the lift doors slid silently into their recesses. The entrance hall of the presidential suite was a large and opulent room, adorned with plush sofas for guests waiting for an audience with the colony's leader. Vases of flowers embellished the secretary's large white marble desk and assorted tables that were adjacent to the sofas. Magazines and newspapers lay scattered beneath the floral displays, advertising a sense of disorder in this lavish room. The lighting was soft and diffused and the area devoid of personnel as she advanced upon the majestic oak doors leading to the President's office, her heels echoing her arrival across the marble floor.

'Miranda, do come in, it's such a pleasure to see you again, and it was so nice of you not to kill any of my guards tonight,' the President said as he advanced towards his guest. Taking her gloved hand, he play-acted at kissing the back of her wrist.

She shrugged impassively, saying nothing. For her, the President's greeting was as false as the man himself, and the pleasantries were clearly faked. Wandering back to the refuge of the sumptuous leather chair behind his desk, the President sat down. 'Can I offer you something to drink?'

Miranda walked up to the large mahogany desk and reached inside her leather jacket. She pulled out a disc and slammed it down in front of the President. 'This is the only reason I am here tonight, Mr President, so please, let's stay focused, shall we?'

The President shook his head slowly. 'Come now, are you still upset with me? You really can't blame me for wanting to get to know you a little better now, can you? Besides, the disc you have so kindly retrieved from my shuttle and delivered tonight is not the only reason you are here.'

Miranda's face clouded. Her eyes narrowed. Their last encounter had not been favourable and she was not about to forget it. 'Just pay me and I can go,' she snapped.

The President leaned over and opened the top draw of his desk and tossed a package in front of his guest. 'It's all there, but you may feel better counting it before you go.'

Miranda took up the package and stuffed it inside her jacket, ignoring the sarcasm as she turned to leave.

'Please, not so fast, we have other business to discuss. Now, come and be seated.'

'What business?'

The President lifted his brandy glass and took a delicate sip, motioning at Miranda to take a seat. 'In a few days' time you will hear of a terrible catastrophe. It will involve the deaths of a group of people who are becoming very tiresome with their continual demands.'

Miranda watched the President swirl the snifter of brandy around the glass as he cupped it in both hands.

'So where do I fit in?'

He moved forward in his seat, put the glass down and faced her across his desk. 'The disc you retrieved from the cockpit of my shuttle tonight is the evidence I will produce to convict Jack Marsden of the appalling act I have just mentioned. The camera I had installed in the cockpit some months ago will show just how low he will stoop to further his agenda in trying to take control of the colony. When I have Jack firmly behind bars, I will call on you to complete the final phase of my plan and eradicate him too.'

Miranda remained impassive. 'Really, and when will that be?'

'Patience. As I have said, in a few days' time. I promise you.'

Miranda stood and stared at the President. Clearly she loathed the colony's leader. 'Make it soon,' she hissed. 'I may not want to come back to this hole.'

'Oh, you will come back. You always do,' snarled the President. 'We need one another, Miranda, and that, whether you like it or not, is a fact of life.' His face produced his usual unctuous smile when he had the upper hand. 'I will be in touch,' he said, gesturing his hand towards the office door.

As Miranda Short hurtled down to the basement car park in the President's private lift, she carefully considered the information he had given her. From the breast pocket of her leather jacket she pulled out a copy of the disc she had delivered and flipped it over between her gloved fingers. The disc glinted in the lights above her head, flashing and reflecting across the lift compartment. It reminded her of a similar disc that had once changed her life forever.

Following her father had not proven as difficult as Miranda first expected. Although she was barely fifteen years old, her life on the edge of the desert had toughened her, and with her hunting skills, she had mastered the art of stealth. She hadn't been raised as a soft city dweller unable to cope without a button to press to summon all that she needed. Within an hour of his departure that night, she took a little food and a bottle of water, before quietly slipping out of the house without her mother's knowledge. She soon caught up with Benjamin, following the melodic thud from the hooves of his horse as it walked ahead of her in the darkness. She shadowed him for mile after mile, ducking into hedgerows and ditches as he stopped regularly, cautious of everything around him.

After two days of sleeping rough and keeping a safe distance to avoid detection, Miranda watched him leave his horse at a farm with a man whom he had evidently met before. The two men hugged like long-lost brothers and went into the farmhouse. From her position in an adjacent field, she could see the glass towers of the metropolis in the distance between the ripening maize that surrounded her. It was unlike anything she had ever seen before. The sky was littered with shuttles criss-crossing in the distance, small moving specks of silver on a pale blue backdrop above the city. Her father had described this place to her when she was a child and now it stood ahead of her, but there was no sense of excitement at the prospect of actually entering it. She remembered the wounds he had returned with that night, and the memory was enough to maintain her mistrust of the metropolis and the people that dwelt within it.

When Benjamin finally appeared at the door of the farmhouse again, he was clutching a stout canvas holdall. He strode off along the track that led to a low-slung structure less than half a mile away surrounded by more corn fields. Miranda watched him as dusk came and the task of remaining undetected became less demanding, and then she went closer to the solitary building. It was her first encounter with a metro station in the outer reaches of the colony. They were bland, characterless places and this one had an angled roof balancing on thin metal posts. There was no place to conceal herself from her father, so she knelt in the nearest field watching and waiting for her moment. She was tired and hungry; her food was now gone, so she carefully picked several corncob's, tucking them in her bag for a raw and meagre meal when she next had the chance.

The driverless train eventually arrived, silently gliding to a halt, but there were no passengers to disembark. As he boarded the empty train, Miranda seized her opportunity, running to the last set of doors and ducking down upon a seat eight rows behind him. She regulated her breath as she cautiously peered around the back of the seat in front of her. This was the closest she had been to him since they'd left the farm, and for the first time, she considered his reaction if he caught her there. The thought soon evaporated as the train pulled out of the station, quickly gathering speed. Instead, the motion of the carriage teased her into closing her eyes, and as the surrounding sounds became distant echoes, the warm blanket of sleep swept over her.

She woke with a start as the tunnel sucked the air from the carriage, making the doors and windows shudder. Lights were flashing past the windows as they tore along the track deep beneath the ground. From the opposite seat an elderly couple cast disdainful looks at the scruffy young girl who had woken so abruptly. There had been other stops and Miranda had missed them all, but her father was still seated on the train. Four stops later, he took his luggage and headed for the escalators. He emerged in the busy commercial area of the Eastern Quadrant, a neighbourhood notorious for organised crime and a haven for the dubious members of Llarinian society. It was barely policed by the security forces and tolerated by the President only because of some useful connections he had there. This was no place for a teenage girl on her first visit to the metropolis, but Miranda was no ordinary girl. As she slipped behind a row of colonnades that suspended a monstrous tower of glass and steel above her head, she absorbed the pageant parading before her. Transports hovered along wide multilane streets as three-dimensional images moved across the sides of buildings advertising their message to thousands of disinterested passers-by. Street vendors held out their trinkets, and flyers were thrust into her face in a barrage of commotion she had never before experienced. The aroma of food from a myriad of cafes and restaurants spilled out onto the pavements, adding to the torrent her senses struggled to absorb. For her, the colony was a nightmare, a tapestry of sounds, lights, smells and people jostling for attention. Miranda now understood why her father found such contentment on their farm; the metropolis was simply a living hell, where peace and tranquillity meant nothing and were merely words in a dictionary.

She caught sight of him entering a shop some thirty metres away, a rundown seedy establishment on the edge of a dingy passage leading away from the pandemonium. The windows hadn't seen a bucket and sponge in a long time, and as Miranda peered cautiously around the window frame, she could see that the shop was completely empty. She crept down the adjacent passage that led to the rear of the property, exploring the possibility of catching a glimpse of her father. The rest of the building was in even worse repair than the front. Fractured pipes hung precariously from walls no longer capable of discharging the rainwater from the roof, and the corroded rungs of the fire escape looked barely able to support the weight of a teenage girl, but they did. Miranda warily traversed the flat roof at the rear of the shop and spotted an open sash window at the top of a flight of stairs. She slipped over the frame, her feet silently landing on the floor, stopping suddenly in her tracks at the sound of raised voices from below. It was her father; he was arguing with two men in expensive suits. They crowded around him, and the larger of the two men prodded his index finger at his chest. Her father passed the man a shiny disc but the squabble continued unabated. Miranda couldn't hear what the argument was about, but something dark took her over when she saw him being pushed to the floor and kicked repeatedly. There was a flash of steel as the smaller man pulled a knife and moved forward. Miranda reacted, leaping over the banister, colliding with the pendant light and sending it swinging wildly to and fro in a crazy display of dark and light. Crashing down on the man, she sent him and his weapon reeling across the landing floor. Finding her balance, she grabbed at the shiny blade, wielding it in front of her, lowering her frame like an animal standing its ground and ready to defend its space. The blade glinted as the light from the hallway swung in one direction after another. The man who had kicked Benjamin turned and lurched forward at her, his right index finger pointing at her menacingly. He shouted words at her but she heard nothing other than the blood pounding against her eardrums in a deafening crescendo. In a swift curling motion, Miranda swung the blade, slicing off his digit below the first joint, and she watched it tumble, spilling blood in a shower of droplets that decorated the floor and wall. He hesitated, taking stock of his loss before his face filled with rage. Surging his bulky frame forward upon Miranda, he struck her across the face, sending her to the floor with a stinging welt. She lay face down, her head swimming, the taste of blood in her mouth and upon her lips as her attacker rolled her over and knelt menacingly above her, ready to strike again. Her reaction was automatic and pre-programmed. Before her assailant had time to strike again, the knife tore through his larynx in one clean slash, showering her in a warm fountain of blood. Grabbing at his throat, he tipped precariously, trying to support his mass with one hand on the banister before crashing down the steps of the half landing. By the time his lifeless hulk came to rest upon the dilapidated floorboards, he had earned the reputation of being Miranda Short's first kill.

While the President's guest tore across the streets of the metropolis on her motorcycle, the monitor on the wall of his office played a silent tale of sabotage. The disc his lady assassin had retrieved was of exceptional quality. It clearly showed Jack Marsden planting the device in the cockpit of the presidential shuttle. He gave a little grunt of amusement as Jack skilfully disposed of the service android, letting his smouldering remains fall to the floor. The disc was proof positive; no court in the land would find Jack Marsden anything other than guilty of multiple murders. And as he found himself cuffed on the steps of the courthouse for his preliminary hearing and hounded by the press under a barrage of flashing cameras, Miranda Short would be there to eradicate the last but one loose end. With a high-powered laser rifle that had belonged to her father, she would take Jack's life from the rooftop of an adjacent building. When Miranda had completed the task, she too would have to die. She was the final loose end in his scheme to eradicate those whom he considered a threat to his life and the power he exerted over the colony. Her death would have to be something very different, he thought. It would have to be extremely painful and far more protracted, of course. After all, it would be more fitting that way, having suffered her rejection.

CHAPTER 21

When the front door of 119 Dusty Bottom Lane finally opened, Godfrey and Gloria warmly greeted the two security guards.

'I am terribly sorry for the intrusion, sir, madam, but we have a warrant to search these premises.'

Gloria held out her hand, greeting both of the men. 'You are more than welcome,' she said. 'And your names are?'

'Oh, I'm sorry, madam, my name is Burt Brown and this is my colleague Harry White.'

'Come in, please.' There was an uneasy silence as Gloria closed the front door. 'So you have come to search our home then?'

'Yes, madam,' replied Harry.

'And what is it exactly you are looking for, can I ask?' Gloria continued.

'We're looking for a missing XXL, madam,' Harry informed her.

'Oh, I see, and what does this XXL look like exactly?'

Harry and Burt looked on blankly. They hadn't expected to be asked that question.

'I'm sorry, Mrs Davis, we're not allowed to tell you; that's top secret,' Burt said hesitantly, glancing back at Harry; in reality, neither of them had any idea.

'I see,' said Gloria. 'Right, now where would you like to start? Upstairs, downstairs, or in the cellar?'

Godfrey coughed loudly at the prospect of searching their cellar.

'I think upstairs would be best, madam,' Harry replied politely.

'That will be fine,' agreed Gloria. 'Now, we can get started upstairs just as soon as we have all had dinner.'

Burt and Harry looked at one another in disbelief, wondering if their ears had deceived them.

'Dinner?' enquired Harry.

'Yes, we have stew and dumplings in thick rich gravy,' she announced.

Burt began to salivate. 'Stew and dumplings are my favourite.'

'Good, I hoped it would be. Now, how many dumplings would you like, one or two?'

'Three, please,' Burt replied cheekily.

Godfrey hadn't blinked since the guards arrived, though he was now getting a feel for his wife's plan. 'Let me show you through. We normally eat in our kitchen,' he said, grinning at Gloria.

The aroma from the kitchen was mouth-watering. The two men took off their jackets and Burt eagerly helped set the table while Gloria dished up their meal.

Harry, though, looked somewhat perturbed. 'This is all very nice of you both, but I feel we should really be searching your house instead. What if our sergeant finds out?'

Gloria sat down at the table and poured water into their guest's glasses. 'Have you two eaten tonight, Harry?'

'No, Mrs Davis,' Harry informed her. 'We haven't.'

'Then how can your sergeant expect you to work if you haven't been fed? If he turns up here, you just leave him to me.'

Burt was already showering his stew with pepper. 'He won't be coming here tonight, Mrs Davis, he's had to go to the Ministry.' He stopped and looked up at Godfrey. 'Someone has broken into the Testing Department.'

Godfrey stared across the table at his guests, trying hard to remain calm. 'How unfortunate,' he replied.

'Yes, how unfortunate indeed,' Gloria agreed as she eyed her husband intently. 'Gentlemen, let's not worry about that now. We wouldn't want this news to spoil our meal, would we?'

'Absolutely not, Mrs Davis,' Burt said, plunging his fork into his stew.

'There's just one thing missing, though,' Gloria remarked. 'Perhaps you should go and get a nice bottle of your homemade wine from the cellar.'

Godfrey quickly realised that his wife's request was a subtle ploy. 'What a marvellous idea. Why didn't I think of that?' he said, excusing himself and heading for the hall. Moments later, he stood by the cellar door. There was no light seeping out onto the hall carpet. Clasping the handle, he began to open the door.

'Excuse me, Mr Davis, but where is the toilet?' Burt asked.

Godfrey's heart leapt into his mouth. He hadn't heard their guest enter the hall.

'Where's the toilet?'

'Yes, sir.'

Godfrey hesitated. 'Oh, yes, it's that door there,' he said, pointing.

Burt crossed the lobby and approached the toilet as Godfrey's hand trembled on the door handle. He opened the cellar door just enough to peer down the stairs, and he listened intently. There were no sounds coming from the darkness. Suddenly, he realised that Burt was standing beside him again. This time his face was flushed bright red.

'Gosh, you were quick,' Godfrey stammered as he hurriedly closed the cellar door.

Burt blinked several times as he gawked up at Godfrey. 'Mr Davis, why is there an old lady gagged and taped to the toilet?'

Godfrey resisted the urge to open the toilet door to see his mother-in-law's predicament. Instead, he led the guard back into the kitchen. 'Darling, Burt wants to know why Mother is lashed to the toilet and gagged with parcel tape,' he said, grinning at his wife.

Gloria, though, was unperturbed and full of composure. She looked the guard straight in the eye. 'I'm sorry, Burt, but she is upset because we're having beef stew tonight and she wanted roast chicken instead.'

The two guards and Godfrey stared at her in silence.

'You see, she does it to get attention,' Gloria continued. 'Really rather childish, I'm sure you will both agree. Anyway, that's why we ignore her and let her get on with it.'

'I see,' Burt said, sounding bewildered.

Gloria beamed across the kitchen table. 'Would anyone like another one of these dumplings?'

This was better than anything Godfrey could have thought of himself. He tried to imagine the embarrassment that his mother-in-law had suffered when Burt had opened the door. Unable to control his elation, he tucked into his stew with renewed enthusiasm.

Outside, Charlie Albright had alighted from his free taxi and had concealed himself behind a selection of rhododendron bushes in Godfrey's front garden. He squeezed his portly frame out of view as best he could manage and waited. The guards surely wouldn't be here for long, he thought. Behind him, a twig snapped sharply and sent his heart racing. He spun his head round and a hand was immediately placed over his mouth.

'Not a sound, Commander, or we'll all be in the proverbial.'

Charlie's face lit up when he saw Ethel and Semilla kneeling beside him in the flowerbed. 'I say, girls, are you the reinforcements?' he queried in a low whisper.

Ethel grinned. 'Not quite, but there's no one else, is there?'

'Reinforcements or not, you really are a sight for sore eyes. Thank goodness you are here.'

'We had to come, didn't we,' said Semilla. 'We had to warn Mr Davis.'

'Warn him about what?' Charlie asked.

'The Testing Department has been broken into,' Ethel told him.

'I know. I overheard the news from security after they ransacked my home earlier this evening.'

'We tried to tell Mr Davis over the phone, but he didn't seem to understand,' Ethel said.

'It's probably better he didn't understand, Ethel,' Semilla advised. 'Now that security is here, he will sound more convincing when they are torturing him for a confession.'

Charlie frowned at the prospect. 'Good grief, now let's not get ahead of ourselves here, ladies. I mean, after all, Godfrey is hardly likely to suffer at the hands of our dubious security forces just because the Testing Department has been broken into.'

'That's as maybe,' Ethel said. 'Breaking and entry is one thing, Commander, but stealing your own inventions to save them from the crusher is another.'

'What?'

'Didn't you know? The lampposts have gone missing,' whispered Ethel.

In the kitchen of the Davises' home, Gloria had cleared the table and Godfrey was ready with another delaying tactic. 'Gentlemen,' he said, breaking the silence. 'Who would like a coffee?'

Harry shook his head. 'Mr Davis, that's very nice of you, sir, but we really do have to check over the house. We have our orders, you know.'

Godfrey felt deflated. 'Yes, of course, I understand.'

'If I may, Mr Davis, I'll start upstairs and Burt can start in the cellar.'

Godfrey winced. 'Of course you can.'

Arriving in the hallway, Gloria gestured to the landing above their heads. 'Straight up the stairs, Harry. Please just help yourself.'

He made his way upstairs as Godfrey stood with his back against the cellar door, trembling. His stomach was knotting up and he hoped his nerves were not about to offer a repeat performance of this morning's episode at the Testing Department.

'Right then, Mr Davis,' Burt said, nodding, 'I'll search the cellar then.'

'That's right, the cellar,' Godfrey agreed without budging an inch.

'I will need to search it, Mr Davis.'

'That's right,' Godfrey agreed.

Gloria intervened and gently pushed her husband to one side, opening the door for the guard. She realised he was scared out of his wits but knew they had run out of options. 'The light switch is just there,' she informed Burt, and the three of them descended the wooded stairs.

'Blimey, there's a lot of gear in here, Mr Davis,' Burt exclaimed. 'It's hard to know where to start.'

Godfrey stuttered nervously. 'Yes, I keep meaning to have a good sort out down here, but—'

'What's that?' Burt said, suddenly pointing at one corner of the cellar.

Godfrey's heart leapt into his mouth and Gloria gasped loudly

'What?' stammered Godfrey, fearing the worst.

'That box over there,' Burt said, pointing across the cellar. 'It's not a Pendell's Model Colony Set, is it?' The guard carefully negotiated the mass of boxes and pieces of old furniture littering the floor. 'It is a Pendell's Model Colony Set. I don't believe it. I had one of these when I was a small boy. They are worth a fair bit of money these days.'

Gloria prompted her husband with a gentle elbow to the rib cage and a nod of the head. Her relief was clearly visible.

'Oh, yes, absolutely, an awful lot of money I would imagine,' Godfrey prattled as his eyes flashed around the cellar hoping not to catch sight of a badly camouflaged beacon or a glint of a shiny metal column from one of his wayward inventions.

Burt, though, was more interested in reliving his childhood. He had carefully set down the model in its box and was now feverishly shifting other boxes for more memorabilia. Then, as he began moving a large mattress propped up against a heap of boxes, he stopped dead. 'OK, I can see you, come on out of it.'

Godfrey began to tremble as his throat seized and his stomach churned. Gloria grabbed his arm as she also feared that Burt had found one of her husband's lampposts.

'It's no good pretending I can't see you. I can,' Burt said in a firm tone. 'Now come out here.' A brown speckled cat sauntered out from behind the mattress, stretched and yawned, in no hurry to follow the guard's commands.

Gloria sighed with relief as she leant down and picked up the cat. 'Are you back again? You're always finding your way in here, aren't you? She our neighbour's cat. She gets in through the cellar window.'

Tiny beads of perspiration trickled slowly down Godfrey's spine as he stared at his wife.

Burt stopped and gazed around. 'I'm wondering if we should get some help, Mr Davis. There's an awful lot of stuff here.'

'Some help? Who exactly had you in mind?' Gloria queried.

'More of our people from security, Mrs Davis,' he told her as he surveyed the mountain of household items in front of him. There were bicycles, bed frames, old vacuum cleaners, pickling jars, fishing rods, spades, forks, mowers, tools, chairs, suitcases, rolls of wallpaper, buckets, cardboard boxes and a handful of window frames that Godfrey had found himself unable to part with when the house had the new double glazing fitted.

'The thing is,' he said, glancing back at Godfrey and Gloria, 'if my boss and his men turn up here, most of this will get wrecked.'

'Something like my office today?' Godfrey asked.

'Probably,' Burt confirmed.

As Burt pondered over the decision to call for assistance, a small mouse darted out from amongst the boxes. The neighbour's cat leapt from Gloria's arms and sped across the floor as Burt let out a scream and jumped onto a rickety wooden chair, which immediately collapsed. He hobbled to and fro precariously with one foot wedged in the wooden slats. His other boot thumped up and down, narrowly missing the cat and the petrified mouse as it ran aimlessly around in circles in an attempt to stay alive. The impasse came to a swift conclusion as Harry flew down the stairs.

'That's enough, Burt,' he shouted, as the little rodent ducked back under a collection of boxes and disappeared with the cat in hot pursuit.

'I'm sorry, Harry,' Burt whimpered. 'You know I can't stand mice.'

'I didn't think. I'm sorry. I should have searched the cellar myself.'

'I'm fine. I'm all right really,' Burt said as he pulled his leg from the broken chair. He made his way towards the cellar stairs. 'Besides, we're done down here, aren't we, Mr Davis?'

Godfrey looked at Gloria, sensing his wife's relief. 'That's right, we are.'

Harry and Burt stepped into the back garden. It was the only place left to search, apart from a somewhat dilapidated old shed at the bottom of it. Their hunt for the XXL had produced nothing, which had been of little surprise to Godfrey as they had no idea what it actually looked like. Halfway down the garden, Burt stopped, his torch spilling light over the vegetable patch in front of them. 'Have you ever seen carrots like these before? They're monstrous, Mr Davis. The tops look like bushes. What fertiliser are you using? You must let me in on your secret.'

'I don't remember them being that large yesterday,' Godfrey mumbled. 'It must be something in the soil here that they like.'

When Harry had finally managed to drag Burt away from Godfrey's vegetable patch and their search was concluded, the pair stood on the front step of the Davises' home.

'Thank you very much for the dinner, Mr and Mrs Davis. It was very kind of you,' Burt said showing his gratitude.

'Please accept our apologies for disturbing your evening, and thank you for your cooperation,' added Harry. The pair wished their hosts goodnight and wandered off down the path to their transport. Burt wound up the motors and performed a perfect three-point turn in the narrow lane, opening his window and giving the Davises a final wave as they warbled past their home. The transport hovered slowly towards the intersection and the metropolis in the distance. It had been a long day for both of them and Harry was looking forward to getting his head down for a good night's sleep. 'Put the lights on. We don't want to have an accident, do we?'

His companion flicked a switch and flooded the ground in front of their vehicle with light. 'Sorry, it's just that the lane was so well lit, I forgot.'

Godfrey and Gloria stood spellbound like two statues on the steps of their porch. Neither of them had spoken since the two guards had left and driven away.

'So is this why you're in so much trouble, Godfrey?' Gloria asked.

'This is why we're both in so much trouble,' Charlie said, stepping into the light from the front door.

'They just appeared in a huge flash of light,' Ethel added, stretching her stiff legs as she and Semilla approached the porch.

Godfrey looked on in disbelief. 'But how in the name of Llar did they manage to do that?'

'Good question, and one I'm sure we will find out just as soon as we ask them,' Charlie told him.

'You can talk to them all you like, but I would prefer if it were out here. I don't think mother's heart will take much more. She's had enough excitement for one evening, don't you think?'

Godfrey agreed. 'You're probably right. Besides, I think they will be safer all the time they are out here. They do rather blend in, don't they?'

Gloria looked around at the ensemble gathered on her doorstep. 'Hot chocolate everyone?'

Gloria, Ethel and Semilla filed into the house and disappeared into the kitchen, leaving Charlie and Godfrey gazing in awe at the spectacle in the lane.

'After this latest demonstration of their abilities, I think we need to get these fellows out of Llar as soon as possible,' Charlie said. 'They're too damn clever for us just to stand by and see them getting crushed.'

'I agree, and that's why we need to make a plan. We were very lucky tonight that those guards never found them in my cellar.'

Charlie's jaw fell open. 'They were in your cellar?'

'Yes, they arrived just before the guards turned up. Anyway, I'll tell you all about it inside,' Godfrey said, ushering Charlie in and closing the front door.

'Not a problem, Godfrey, but I need a quick visit to the little boy's room first.'

Across the lane, matters of an electrical nature were being discussed. 'Now listen carefully, you lot, I'll take the watch till morning, the rest of you switch off and conserve power.' Muffled sounds of agreement filtered down the lane as Number Nine watched his colleagues shut down for the night.

In the shadows where Dusty Bottom Lane ended and the desert began, a pair of shadowy figures also watched the door close on Godfrey's home. With the lampposts dimmed down and only Number Nine on duty, the figures turned and faced the cool desert breeze. Clasping his staff, the hologram smiled at his companion. The prophecy, and Godfrey's part in it, had only just begun to unfold. It was just as he had predicted.

CHAPTER 22

That night, as most of the colony's citizens slept soundly in their beds, the kitchen at 119 Dusty Bottom Lane became the centre of an important debate. Gathered around the large wooden table, the conversation focused on the events that had led them there that evening.

'What you discuss here tonight concerns my future too, and I intend to be involved in this conversation,' Mother insisted, scowling at her son-in-law. 'So going to my room is not an option, Godfrey.'

'All right, but when Charlie brings Number Nine through that door, I don't want any more hollering and screaming. Is that understood?'

Mother shifted awkwardly in her chair. She needed no reminding of her first encounter with Godfrey's inventions. She nodded reluctantly, though the fear still lingered.

After a short while in the company of Number Nine, Mother soon realised that the lamppost was not so much of a threat as she had first imagined. Instead, the old lady found him to be intelligent and rather charming. It was difficult for her to comprehend how this machine had developed such a level of etiquette, especially as it had been invented by her son-in-law.

'Now that we all have an understanding of the situation so far, I think we need to discuss our options,' ventured Charlie. 'It would seem pretty obvious to me that that wretched man on the top floor of our Ministry will stop at nothing until he finds the XXL.'

'I would like to know what it looks like,' said Ethel.

Godfrey leant forward and passed a photograph across the table. 'This was taken at my graduation. My dad has his arm around me, and if you look closely, he has something protruding from the sleeve of his jacket. I can assure you that whatever it was he was wearing, it was not the watch my mum had bought him for his birthday.'

'My graduation photograph is almost identical,' Charlie confirmed. 'My dad also has an odd gold-coloured device nestling under the cuff of his shirt.'

'The note I found behind the photo in that frame may be a clue to where these devices are concealed. It would make sense that something small enough to be worn on a wrist could be hidden in a tin, perhaps in the Roamer's Cave.'

'I think we need to go there as soon as possible,' Charlie suggested. 'If the President is prepared to search our homes and demolish Godfrey's office, what will he attempt next? I think you were both very lucky this evening having those two polite respectful guards here. You may not be so lucky next time, and there will be a next time.'

'They are probably going to make this house their first port of call in the morning,' stated Semilla. 'They may even be on their way back now.'

'What a sobering thought,' Charlie said. 'Then we have no time to lose. Godfrey and I need to get to the Roamer's Cave as soon as possible and search for that tin, and it's also the perfect place to hide the lampposts.'

'So, in the morning when security turns up here again, what do you think they will do with Gloria and myself when they can't find the lampposts, the XXL, and you two have disappeared as well?' asked Mother, sipping at her hot chocolate. 'Will they detain us too?'

'You can't possibly expect Mother and I to stay here,

Godfrey,' Gloria said, raising her voice. 'We're coming too, and that's final.'

Ethel agreed. 'If the President is happy to lock up an android, he wouldn't think twice about locking you up. We all saw a different side to our President the other day in Godfrey's office; he has a vicious temper. He was going to shoot that android in front of all of us.'

'I wonder what they did with him after they took him away,' Semilla said. 'Do you think he will vanish in a crusher?'

'Talking of vanishing, when I went to the shops this morning, I saw a flyer pinned to the tree outside. One of our neighbours disappeared on Monday morning. He was a mainframe programmer at the Ministry.'

Godfrey and Charlie immediately gave one another a disturbed look. The missing programmer would have a different connotation for them.

'Perhaps he knew too much about the mainframe?' Charlie suggested.

'He and the five others possibly,' Number Nine said. 'There has been a whole group of programmers disappear over the last week. We found that out when we were connected at the Ministry.'

'Then we need to leave and we need to make it soon,' Godfrey said, sounding concerned. 'Hiding the lampposts is paramount, and we need to investigate this note. We can't do it if we are incarcerated, can we?'

'Okay, so we head off to the caves to find this tin your father wrote about. What do we do then?' asked Charlie with a serious look.

'We carry on to the oasis in the north,' Number Nine said.

'What oasis in the north? There's no such thing,' Mother scoffed.

'It does exist,' Number Nine replied. 'And I believe that the reason its existence has been encrypted on the mainframe is to keep it a secret from you.'

'Then someone has effectively rewritten our *Great Book of Llar*,' Charlie piped up, 'because there is no mention of a second oasis in the version of our history we were taught at school.'

'Why couldn't you tell the people of the colony about another oasis?' Gloria asked.

'Perhaps there is something there you're not meant to see,' Number Nine said, 'and the only way to find out is to go there.'

'Number Nine is right. We should carry on to the north and find the oasis,' Godfrey stated. 'Besides, the encounter I had with the hologram gives its existence more credence.'

Mother sneered at the comment. 'So you would risk all of our lives based on this questionable information that's come from the mainframe? You said earlier that the thing is becoming unstable because it has a virus.'

Gloria corrected her. 'The mainframe has been infected by the artificial intelligence from Godfrey's lampposts. It hasn't got a virus.'

Mother looked across the table at her son-in-law. 'So either way it's your fault again then, Lofty?'

'No, madam,' corrected Number Nine, coming to Godfrey's defence. 'The fault is entirely ours. We were too eager to impress our creator, so we are the ones to blame here. The hologram also got that information from the mainframe. The other oasis really does exist, and we very nearly had the coordinates before we arrived here. Unfortunately, we had to disconnect and leave in something of a hurry.'

Number Five had discovered some interesting data lurking beneath the layers of computer-coded jargon on the mainframe. The fact that the encrypted version of *The Great Book of Llar* was different to the one available to every citizen throughout the colony left unanswered questions. Why was the existence of the other oasis concealed? The exact latitude and longitude were much deeper in the complex text, and Number Five hadn't managed to retrieve that precious piece of information.

Godfrey gazed up at his invention standing beside the kitchen table. 'By the way, just how did you manage to get yourselves into my cellar and back out again?'

'Many years ago, when your father was a young man, he wrote a thesis, which also lays encrypted on the mainframe. His paper describes in detail the possibility of physical transportation from one location to another.'

'From the Testing Department to our cellar, for example?' asked Godfrey.

'Precisely,' confirmed Number Nine. 'Your father was a genius. Having transported ourselves twice now, we have proved his thesis actually works.'

Charlie became excited at Number Nine's revelation. 'Then that's two problems solved. You chaps can transport yourselves to the safety of the Roamer's Cave and look for the tin while you're there.'

'Not so, Commander. Unfortunately, we are now spent; we no longer have enough energy to undertake another attempt.'

'Even if we find the tin, the fact that we haven't got the coordinates for this oasis would make such a venture somewhat foolhardy. There's a very big desert out there, in case any of you have forgotten,' Charlie reminded them.

'It would be,' agreed Ethel, 'but we do have another way of finding the coordinates; how about the Grand Library?'

'Of course,' Semilla exclaimed. 'The original book is on display there.'

Gloria folded her arms and sat back in her chair. 'You will never get that book out of its glass case; it's hermetically sealed to preserve it. And another thing, surely if the seal were broken, an alarm would go off.'

'Then we are dead in the water,' muttered Godfrey. 'The lampposts can't go back on the mainframe; security would be on them in minutes, and without the book we are going nowhere.'

'Even if the book is our only option, who is going to steal it, the sand fairies?' Mother asked sarcastically. 'The Grand Library is a fortress. You wouldn't stand a chance.'

Ethel sat at the end of the table; she looked tired and drawn. 'We could do it. I mean break in to the Grand Library, that is. It would take at least two of us – me and Semilla, if she was willing.'

Semilla nodded. 'I'm prepared to do it.'

'I know the place like the back of my hand,' Ethel continued. 'I often cover cleaners who are sick or on holiday. And another thing, I also have these.'

'What are they for, Ethel?' asked Gloria.

'They're my cleaner's pass keys.'

Godfrey shook his head in disagreement. 'No, I won't hear a word of it, Ethel. There is no way I am going to see you and Semilla risk your liberty by entering that building. What do you think will happen if you both get caught? I'm sorry, but Charlie and I will steal the book, if you will be kind enough to lend us your keys?"

Charlie gave a gruff cough. 'Let's not be too hasty here, Godfrey. The fact that Ethel has her pass keys puts rather a different perspective on the matter. Years ago, I oversaw the alarm installations on most of the artefacts in our public buildings. I could assist these ladies with the access code to the glass case.'

'What about the alarm on the doors? Security changes the codes every day. I've seen them,' Ethel responded, 'and they don't let us cleaners know what they are.'

'The user code may change daily but the engineering code always remains the same. I programmed them all with something easy to remember,' Charlie informed them.

'Then that settles it. There is no other way, Mr Davis. Besides, the security forces won't be concentrating on guarding that place after tomorrow morning, will they? They're going to be looking for you, your lampposts and the XXL. If you are going to the Roamer's Cave, you can't be in two places at the same time, can you?'

Godfrey doodled with a pencil, scribbling lines across a writing pad as he thought. Ethel's logic was infallible. 'Then if we are all agreed,' Godfrey said after some reflection. 'We need to go through the finer details.'

Shortly before dawn, Semilla and Ethel gave them all hugs goodbye. The truth was that none of them really knew when they would meet again. After a long night of talking, and even with a plan, their futures remained uncertain.

'Are you absolutely sure you want to do this? None of us would blame you if you decided to turn this down,' Godfrey said to the pair as they stood beneath the porch of his home.

'There's no other way,' replied Ethel. 'I know the building and the rest of you need to be gone.'

Godfrey glanced over at the lampposts standing silently in the lane. He conceded and handed her a green leather-bound briefcase. 'You remember what I showed you?'

'I won't forget, Mr Davis,' Ethel said as she and Semilla turned and walked to the gate, disappearing into the darkness.

The group worked hard to pack Godfrey's transport before the dawn was upon them. Everything from food and clothes to their old tent and camping beds. Everyone had helped to ferry things out to the garage, grabbing anything useful they thought may sustain them on their journey. All that remained now was for Godfrey and Charlie to load the lampposts that were waiting patiently in the lane. They managed to stow all of them, with the exception of Number Nine and Baz who were deep in a hushed conversation outside of Godfrey's home.

When they returned from the transport, Godfrey approached Number Nine. 'Have you discussed our plan with Baz?' he asked

'Yes, I have, and he is prepared to stay,' Number Nine told him.

'I have no choice really,' said Baz, hovering forward. 'I am responsible for this mess and for you losing your job.'

'I think our days were already numbered, Baz,' said Charlie, joining the conversation. 'The fact of the matter is that you and your friends have inadvertently uncovered a web of deception. It would appear that we have all been lied to, judging by what you fellows have found on the mainframe. Frankly, I for one would prefer to live in danger than spend the rest of my days living in deceit.'

Charlie's words seemed to bolster Baz's spirits. 'Thank you, Commander. I promise I will do my best.'

Gloria ushered her mother out and settled her in the rear of their vehicle, turning back to take one last look at their dark and empty home. With another visit from security almost certainly pending, she wondered what would greet them when they returned.

Charlie opened the passenger door and hesitated. 'If Ethel and Semilla fail to get the precise coordinates, Godfrey, we will be driving around in that desert forever. And, frankly, that is not an option I relish, I can assure you. We'll be lucky to see the week out in that forsaken place.'

'I know,' Godfrey agreed, 'but let's get to the Roamer's Cave first and we can take it from there.'

Shortly before the sun peered over the horizon, Godfrey's transport headed down the lane. With the rest of the suburbs soon preparing to start another day in the colony, they were instead on course for the desert. The unlit transport rocked gently as it hovered over the rough terrain where the lane ended and the desert began. No one saw their departure except for Baz, who stood outside of 119, the Davises' home.

Baz contemplated the prospect of success and failure as his circuits played out each scenario. Being captured and manhandled into the back of a security vehicle didn't appeal to him. Neither did the prospect of spending the rest of his days outside his creator's home if he failed to return. As he watched the transport disappear into the darkness, a faint twinge of remorse swept over him. It was a new emotion reasoned out by his artificial intelligence chip that Godfrey had installed in him and the other lampposts. He thought that perhaps if he had been less arrogant to the President, they would not now be in danger. He concluded he could not change the course of events no matter how much he regretted his actions. Deep inside his circuits he felt the need to redeem himself. He had made a solemn promise to Godfrey and he would keep his word. It was going to be the most difficult job he had ever undertaken – standing still and keeping his mouth shut. Baz took one last look up and down the lane from beneath the majestic bows of the large eucalyptus which stood beside him. Pinned to the trunk was a notice.

'Missing last Monday – Reward to Finder – Answers to the name of Nigel. Please call Deirdre Prentagast on…'

He studied the photo of a man and registered it in his memory, and then he closed down his circuits.

CHAPTER 23

Area 21 had all of the hallmarks of dereliction. It was a place long since abandoned and left to decay on the edge of the desert far away from the colony and prying eyes. The main runway was littered with buildings either side that hadn't seen occupation in many decades. Broken windows hung on rusted hinges, moving lethargically to and fro in the breeze sweeping in from the desert. The skeletal remains of transports and shuttles lay discarded across the entire site, their bleached metal hulls punctuating the landscape like the shells of long-dead insects.

Racing to beat the sunrise, Jack's transport careered down the runway with purpose; it was heading for one specific building, a large hanger on the edge of the ruined complex. The vehicle left the runway and hovered into the storm-weathered structure, coming to rest on the hanger floor. They had managed to arrive under the cover of darkness as planned. The two security men exited the vehicle and opened the rear compartment door for their superior. Jack stood and stretched himself, adjusting his suit and tie as the interior lights of his transport cast eerie shadows across the hanger floor. He had been there many times before and for exactly the same reason. Nothing had changed here since his last visit, except perhaps there was a little more decay. From the gaps in the metal-clad roof far above his head, a gentle drizzle filtered down, casting a hazy silhouette around him. Then the first rays of the sun peered in inquiringly through the sandblasted remains of the hanger windows. The dawn had arrived. The warmth swept slowly across his face. He tilted his head towards the roof and closed his eyes, remembering the past. His father's words echoed through his mind. *'Your private remorse will be a measure of your greatness.'*

Jack lowered his head and opened his eyes. There was no greatness in what he had done in the past, or in what he was about to do now. 'Make the call,' he said to the two men.

The sound of machinery rose up from the floor in front of his transport. Moving downward, then sideways, two large sections of the hanger floor slipped out of sight. Seamlessly taking its place, a platform rose from below. The platform came to rest with a dozen security men surrounding six hooded individuals, their wrists decorated with shiny new handcuffs. The platform also delivered a battered-looking transport.

Jack composed himself. He looked across at the half-dozen forlorn figures. 'Let's get on with it,' he said, quietly nodding at the assembly.

The transport hummed into life and one of the security men drove it off the platform. Dabbing a set of coordinates into the on-board navigation, he completed the task and fell into line with his eleven colleagues and stood to attention.

Jack slowly walked over to the captives, looking them up and down. 'You are here today,' he said, pausing as he gazed up again at the drizzle coming in from the roof, 'for the greater good of our colony and the safety of our citizens. We are therefore taking you to a secure area where the knowledge you have inadvertently acquired while working on the mainframe will not be of detriment to the security of our people.'

The men on the platform stood stony-faced and impassive, listening to Jack's oration; they had heard it before. They knew the sequence of events that were about to transpire.

'You will forgive the fact that we have had to make you wear hoods,' Jack continued. 'This is for your own safety and they will be removed at the end of your journey.'

Jack nodded to the twelve men lined up waiting his instruction, and they formed pairs, each taking one prisoner and leading them by their arms to the transport.

The last captive hesitated and turned back to where Jack's voice had emanated. 'I have served our colony all of my life. I have done nothing wrong,' he shouted through his hood. 'Will someone please tell my mother what has happened to me; my name is Nigel Prentagast.'

The security men leading Nigel to the transport glanced back at Jack as if for a directive. Jack merely nodded for them to continue. There was no going back from here. There were no goodbyes or messages to desperate family members anxious over strange and unexplained disappearances.

Several minutes later, the passengers were seated and harnessed. They sat in silence knowing protest was useless. The doors closed for the last time as the transport's drive unit hummed idly awaiting a command. Jack looked out across the desert through the curtain of rain at the hanger entrance. The sky on the horizon was heavy and black, and it had beaten down the promise of a warm sunny morning and it matched his mood. The vastness of the desert always made him feel uneasy. He knew only too well that there were some fears in a man's life that couldn't be conquered with the passage of time. He also knew that his fear of the vast desolate wastelands stretching out to the horizon would never leave him till the day he died. Jack gave the occupants one last look and then he nodded and gave the command. The driverless transport hovered out of the hanger gathering speed. It crossed the runway and entered the desert, silently obeying the coordinates within the on-board navigation system.

Jack watched intently until the transport had disappeared over the horizon. He was transfixed and lost in thought. He was convincing himself, once again, that it was for the greater good of the greater number and for the colony that he served. It was never an easy task sending someone out into the desert to meet their fate, especially if their only crime was knowledge. The feeling made him uneasy just as it had the day he'd watched the transport carrying Rachael enter the desert.

CHAPTER 24

Far away from the leafy suburb of Dusty Bottom Lane, Ethel and Semilla finally arrived for work at the Ministry. The multilane pavements leading from the station were brimming with people making their way to the metropolis, and most of them, unlike Ethel and Semilla, had had the benefit of a good night's sleep. Having been up all night, they were both thoroughly exhausted. Neither of them had any hope of getting through their respective day's work and even less hope of fulfilling tonight's covert act if they didn't get some sleep beforehand. So it had been discussed and agreed around the kitchen table at Godfrey's home that they would therefore need to adopt a ploy. They were to make their presence at work something of an illusion, when in fact they would spend the day sound asleep.

On entering the foyer at the Ministry, both Ethel and Semilla deliberately approached an android and made polite conversation about the weather. This ensured they were logged on as having arrived for work and no one would therefore investigate their absence. With this undertaking completed, Semilla left Ethel in the foyer and disappeared to find a quiet corner to make a call. Several minutes later, she returned.

'So what did she say?' Ethel asked her.

'There's not a problem. She'll have them ready for tonight,' Semilla told her. 'I'm to pick them up after work.'

Ethel looked up at her with tired eyes. She felt sick from lack of sleep. She desperately hoped she had done the right thing by suggesting that Semilla participate in this part of the plan. 'I'm having second thoughts about you doing this, young lady. If this goes wrong I will never forgive myself.'

'Stop worrying, we'll be fine,' Semilla said, reassuring her as they entered the nearest lift. 'Besides, you can't do this by yourself.'

Later, on floor eighty-three, an 'Out of Order' sign hung on the door handle of a ladies' rest room. The door was firmly locked from the inside, and it needed to be, as Ethel and Semilla wanted to sleep all day undisturbed. As Ethel rested her head on the back of a restroom chair, she closed her eyes and pondered their evening ahead. If her husband Edward had still been alive he would have certainly helped them in their exploit and would have made it fun, if only to mask the danger from her. He had been a good man who always had time for people and would help them in any way he could. Their sons had both taken after him in so many ways, and she missed him dearly. Though the boys came and visited her whenever they could, their families and their work took precedence over her and she understood that. She opened her eyes and looked over at Semilla, who was now fast asleep. When she had come to stay with Ethel, life had taken on a different meaning, as the young girl soon became one of her family. Ethel had someone new to care for now that her sons and Edward were no longer at home. She had enjoyed the past two years in her company, and now all of that could be in jeopardy if their visit to the Grand Library went wrong. It was the last thing she contemplated before she drifted into a deep sleep.

Deep in the bowels of the Ministry, a very unhappy security guard looked at the evening roster. 'Can you believe him?' Burt asked. 'He's got me down for tonight's night shift at the Grand Library.'

Harry shrugged. He had warned his companion to keep his

mouth shut, but he hadn't listened. Burt had told the wrong person, and when their sergeant heard the news he had hit the roof.

'You've only got yourself to blame. Fancy opening your mouth about having dinner with the Davises last night. Maybe if you had listened to me, we wouldn't be doing the two most boring night shifts in the metropolis.'

'I'm sorry, you're right.'

Harry ignored him. He was less than amused at the prospect of guarding the empty Testing Department as his punishment. 'Anyway, I'm off. Try not to get into anymore bother if you can.'

Burt watched Harry leave the locker room as he considered the prospect of a night alone in the Grand Library. The guard thought for a while, and reaching into his locker he got out a copy of his favourite gardening magazine. He would have all night to read that article on how to grow award-winning vegetables. Maybe he could discover how to grow a nice selection of carrots, like Mr Davis had in his garden. The night stint at the Grand Library suddenly didn't appear so daunting to him after all.

CHAPTER 25

It was late afternoon when the motors on Godfrey's transport wound down as it came to rest on the floor of the huge cavern. No one on board spoke. Instead, they each peered out, surveying the strange shapes and shadows cast up in the headlights of their vehicle. It was a truly immense place, stretching far beyond into the darkness where the lights couldn't reach. Somehow, though, the caves appeared smaller than Godfrey remembered them as a young boy.

'It's been a long time,' Charlie said, quietly breaking the silence.

The inventor nodded in agreement. He could picture them both running around as children, exploring to their heart's content, their torches flashing across the limestone walls. The trips to the Roamer's Cave system with their fathers were the highlight of the summer holidays.

'I can remember coming here on a school trip when I was a girl,' Gloria reminisced.

'And me,' Mother added. 'I think we all came here at some point in time. The beginning of our colony started here.'

The story passed down from generation to generation mentioned a tall fearless nomad who had taken shelter there from a ferocious storm. This had been the cave where the founder of their colony, Mick the Roamer, had met the mystical creature called the Dheybar. Mick had been scouring the desert for weeks, searching for a place he could move his tribe to, when suddenly he was caught out by a sandstorm so ferocious he would have certainly perished without the sanctuary of the caves. History told how the roamer was befriended by the Dheybar and how his new acquaintance had led him to the oasis upon which their colony now stood. On the edge of the Grand Plaza, both Mick and his desert-dwelling companion stood immortalised in marble, as a reminder to those who passed by each day.

'Why don't we set up camp and start looking for that tin,' Godfrey said. 'The sun hasn't gone down yet.'

'Good idea. Mother and I will sort out a fire and get some dinner on the go,' added Gloria.

Thanks to the guidance system and the autopilot on Godfrey's transport, they'd had the opportunity to get some desperately needed sleep while the vehicle diligently carried them across the wastelands. And now, after this interlude, they were refreshed enough to undertake a preliminary search of the caves.

Several hours later, the sun began to sink towards the horizon, and inside the caves, Charlie propped himself on his shovel. He looked dusty and was perspiring heavily; manual labour was something Charlie simply wasn't used to. 'Let's wrap it up for today. I'm absolutely exhausted. We can get an early start in the morning after a good night's sleep.'

They had all benefited from a few hours' sleep while crossing the desert, but the transport was a poor substitute for a comfortable bed. 'You're right, of course. Besides, we could be digging here for weeks trying to find that tin. Pity my father hadn't been a little more specific regarding its location.'

Charlie mopped his brow with his linen handkerchief. 'It made me wonder if perhaps he was in something of a hurry when he wrote that note. Not really his modus operandi. After all, he was always a very precise man.'

Godfrey was about to confer his thoughts when the sandy

floor of the cave began to shudder. It was directly in front of where they had both been digging. The sand began to form in small neat circles, rippling out from the centre, becoming larger and larger until the rings finally dissipated.

'Is it an earth tremor?' Charlie asked as the floor of the cave trembled beneath his feet.

Godfrey shook his head. 'The vibration is too faint. Besides, it's centred on a small patch of sand no more than a metre in diameter.'

They watched intently. It was a phenomenon unlike anything they had seen before. The object that slowly broke the surface in the centre of the circle left them both stunned. The egg-shaped form that ascended into the radiance from the lampposts dotted around the cavern was covered in thick black fur.

'What in the name of Llar is that?' uttered Charlie, unable to take his eyes off the creature.

'It looks like a giant furry egg,' Godfrey stammered.

The tremors finally ceased as the thing came to rest on two enormous fleshy webbed feet.

Charlie looked on, spellbound. 'That's not what I think it is, surely?'

The sand-covered fur parted and two large brown eyes blinked several times. 'We are the eyes of the desert, we are the voice of the sand, we are one conscious. We are Dheybar,' said the creature.

Charlie took three steps backwards. 'Good grief, it can talk!'

Godfrey gawped at the thing standing on the sandy floor in front of them. 'You're the one that helped Mick the Roamer discover our oasis?'

The Dheybar excitedly moved from one foot to the other. 'It was one of my great-great-great-uncles,' he informed him.

'So the legend is true then,' Charlie said in amazement. 'The Dheybar really do exist.'

The Dheybar stood poised for a moment and then shook its entire form, showering the two men in sand.

Godfrey brushed his face and the front of his shirt. 'Just now you said *"We are the eyes of the desert"*. Are there more of you?'

'Yes, there are many of us in the desert. We are one conscious, we are one being,' replied the Dheybar.

Charlie pulled the knees of his trousers up and squatted down in front of the unusual creature. He wanted to get a closer look at the living legend. The entire colony had heard of the Dheybar, yet there had never been a single report of a sighting or an encounter throughout their history. He gently brushed his hand across the Dheybar's thick fur; it felt course and gritty. The animal responded by leaning into Charlie's hand, clearly enjoying his first human contact.

'I don't understand,' Godfrey said, looking perturbed. 'If there are more of you, then what do you mean by one conscious, one being?'

'When one Dheybar hears, we all hear. When one Dheybar sees, we all see.'

'Do you mean it's some kind of telepathic thing?'

'Yes it is, Godfrey,' he said.

'How do you know my name?'

'Dheybar knows everyone who comes into the desert.'

'So are you saying that now you have spoken to us, all of your relations know of our conversation too?' enquired Charlie.

'Yes. We are the eyes of the desert, we are the voice of the sand, we are one conscious. We are Dheybar,' he confirmed.

Godfrey looked pensive, and he gestured Charlie to follow him.

The two men both smiled politely at the creature and walked a few paces away to hold a private conversation.

'Do you really think we could be that fortunate to have stumbled across a living legend that might just know the exact whereabouts of a rather large oasis we are trying to find?' asked Godfrey.

Charlie screwed his face up and shrugged. 'Not a chance. Not the way our luck has been the last few days. That sounds more like a wild dream to me.'

'We've got to ask him, haven't we?'

'Absolutely,' Charlie agreed.

They walked back to the Dheybar, who was waiting patiently for them to return.

'Look, we need to ask you a question,' Charlie started.

'Yes, it's something we are looking for,' added Godfrey.

The Dheybar vibrated, his feet disturbing the sand beneath him. 'Yes, it does.'

'What?' Godfrey asked.

'Yes, it does exist,' the Dheybar reiterated.

Charlie frowned. 'What exists?'

'The oasis you are looking for,' the Dheybar said, confidently blinking his watery brown eyes.

'How did you know what we were going to ask you,' stammered Charlie.

The Dheybar answered immediately. 'We are the eyes of the desert, we are the voice of the sand, we are one conscious. We are Dheybar.'

Godfrey and Charlie grinned at one another. It appeared that this adventure was going to be a breeze. With this little fellow's help, they would have no problem finding their way across the desert.

'So can you give us some directions then?' Charlie asked politely.

The Dheybar could hardly contain himself. He almost jumped up and down on the spot. 'Over there,' he informed them, tilting his frame.

Godfrey and Charlie looked towards the entrance of the cave.

CHAPTER 26

As Godfrey Davis and Charlie Albright stared out of the entrance of the Roamer's Cave, Jack Marsden was clearing the desk in his office. It was early evening and he felt like a warm bath and a soft pillow. It would be a small reward for having slept in his transport the night before. The thought was interrupted by his mobile phone as it began to vibrate on his desk. Jack looked down at the blue illuminated screen as it displayed eleven zeros. The vibrating ended abruptly and the phone became silent. Jack knew the number. It was unique and not one that he or anyone else would forget in a hurry. Adrenalin seeped into his bloodstream. He hadn't expected a call from this contact, not now, not tonight. He stared out of his office window, watching the multitude of shuttles navigating their way across the skies above the metropolis, the reds and greens of their marker lights weaving patterns in the darkness. Somewhere out there he knew the caller wanted a rendezvous, and it had to be tonight. Grabbing at the papers on his desk, he stuffed them in to a drawer and locked it. His mind flashed from one emotion to another as he hurriedly snatched his keys and phone, stuffing them in the pockets of his suit jacket. His warm bath and a quiet evening at home would have to wait. Jack knew this tryst was one he could not put off, but then deep inside he didn't want to.

Acknowledging an android as he exited the Ministry, his departure was registered on the mainframe, and joining the melee on the Grand Plaza, he entered the evening stampede. His eyes darted left and right, half expecting, half wanting to catch a glimpse of his caller. But then this was too open a place for a rendezvous. The plaza was littered with cameras all reporting back to the mainframe and back to the President high above him. It was no place for a private meeting.

Several hundred metres away from the Ministry, Jack dropped down the granite steps to the subway, weaving through the crowd, casting cautious glances in every direction along the platform. Unknown faces took second glances at the man whom they recognised from somewhere but were uncertain until they had passed him by. Grabbing nervously at his open jacket, he checked that his phone was still nestling securely in his inside breast pocket. Perhaps it would ring again; maybe he would hear a voice this time. But the phone remained silent as he sat on the train pondering his evening ahead.

Thirty minutes later he surfaced in a quiet tree-lined suburb dotted with dignified three-storey properties. It was an area where the privileged members of Llarinian society came home after work and lived in comfort with their families. The street was empty and the pavements damp courtesy of the mainframe and an unexpected evening shower as he made his way to his front door. Sliding the key in the lock, he took a cursory look behind him before entering.

Jack closed the large mahogany door and stood for a moment leaning against it as he took out his phone. His fingers keyed in the menu and the screen illuminated his features in a pale blue light. There had been no missed calls while he had been on the train and his heart almost sank. Discarding the phone in his pocket with a sense of disappointment, he went to move forward and stopped; a cold steel blade rested firmly against his throat as the sweet smell of perfume drifted into his nasal passages.

'I think you're a very lucky man, Jack Marsden, wouldn't you agree? I mean, right now you could have been lying on the floor drowning in your own blood,' said a sultry female voice.

Jack gave no answer. Instead, his hand slid slowly, silently, until it located the light switch beside him and flicked it on. The lobby light produced a dim reassuring glow, though it gave him little comfort in his current predicament. In front of his face, a hand held up a small portable disc player. Jack pushed his head into the door and managed to focus on the screen. He silently watched the footage at knifepoint until it had ended.

'I came to tell you I am still watching your back, Jack Marsden,' Miranda Short said, her knife still at the base of Jack's oesophagus.

'And I hope that never changes,' Jack replied stony-faced.

Miranda placed the disc player in the pocket of her jacket. She gazed up at him with steel-blue eyes and blinked long and slow. 'I have been asked to kill you, and very soon.'

Jack showed no emotion. Instead, he swallowed slowly as the blade of his intruder's knife slid slowly across the stubble on his throat. 'Really, is that so? Somehow I'm not surprised.'

Miranda pushed forward, and Jack felt himself pressed against the door of his home. 'But maybe I could be persuaded to change my mind, if you knew how to show me a little gratitude.'

Jack raised his hand slowly and ran it through Miranda's mop of blond hair. He held the back of her neck and pulled her towards him as the cold blade fell away. 'I'm always grateful, perhaps you've forgotten,' he said as he reached for the light switch a second time and doused the light.

CHAPTER 27

At the Ministry the corridors had already witnessed the early evening stampede. Some stragglers, though, still laboured intently at their desks with tired depleted faces, enthusiasm to continue prompted perhaps by an overbearing manager to complete a final task before they left for home. Outside, the Grand Plaza and the metro stations that funnelled the population to and fro were quiet as the pace of life in the metropolis wound down again for the night.

In the rest room on the eighty-third floor, Semilla stirred awkwardly on the upholstered bench she had slept on throughout the day. From a chair in the corner, Ethel watched as she adjusted the makeshift pillow, attempting to make her jacket more comfortable beneath her head. Ethel had woken earlier when the chatter of excited voices had spilled out along the corridor, signalling the evening departure. She was normally a light sleeper and the rest room had compounded this trait with the sound of continual traffic up and down the corridor throughout the day. There had been the odd attempt to enter by one or two of the staff that had chosen to ignore the sign upon the handle, offering a muffled curse before they moved on. Although her sleep had been disjointed, she had rested sufficiently to complete the task ahead. She sat there staring at Semilla, her blond curls in disarray round her neck, and she began to reminisce.

Ethel Marjory Blenkinsopp had taken her first breath nearly

sixty years ago in the maternity ward of a hospital in one of the outer suburbs of the colony. Her early morning arrival set a pattern for the rest of her life and Ethel soon developed a passion for early starts to her day. The first child of parents who had diligently toiled for their entire lives, her future had already been preordained before she could walk. Llar had an unenviable system of class and it had remained functional and unchanged for centuries. It maintained the balance; a silent structure that held people in their place in the social formation. With a father who maintained the tunnels of the metro deep beneath the ground and a mother who cleaned offices at night, it had little importance what degree of intelligence Ethel had on offer. The colony was made up of invisible lines of demarcation, and before long even those with the lowest IQ soon realised which side of the line they were to reside on. Parents of an intelligent child who did not have the money were destined to watch their offspring follow in their footsteps accepting a role in the colony sometimes far below their capabilities. Ethel was just such an example. At fifteen years of age she had been forced to leave school and take her first job to aid her parent's meagre income. By that time she had a brother and sister who would one day follow in her and her parents' footsteps, but in the meantime they needed feeding and clothing, and another wage packet meant the ability to provide for both. When Ethel reached twenty years of age she had buried both of her parents and she was the sole provider for her younger siblings. Then, when they were able, her brother and sister left to find their own way in life, leaving just the memory of the struggle and a handful of photographs on the mantelpiece. Ethel heard from them both over the years from time to time, mainly her brother and only when he was in trouble. He had taken the road to the Eastern Quadrant and made a life and a living for himself somehow in the dubious world that existed there. The years passed and Ethel accepted her life for what it was, believing she had done her best for her family. She was a solid and dependable character who was always ready to help anyone in need. Though tonight involved a different sort of help; one which could impact on Semilla's life if it went off course.

'What time is it?' Semilla asked, rubbing her face and rearranging her hair with one hand.

'It's five to seven.'

'Time to make a move, I guess. It will take a good couple of hours to get to and from my grandmother's,' Semilla said.

Five minutes later, the two women said goodbye in the foyer and Semilla set off to the suburbs. Crossing the Grand Plaza, she took the northern line, skipping down the granite steps until she conveniently reached the platform as the train arrived. She fell into a seat and got herself comfy and paged through the menu on her phone. There were several messages from her friends at work who had wondered where she had been all day, and one from her youngest sister, Camilla. Being that much older, she found it easy giving a younger sister advice about what to wear to a party. She knew about make-up too and could definitely give advice on boys. She scanned her sister's message with a mischievous smile, her thumbs becoming a blur as she sent her reply.

Semilla was the eldest of four girls and she and her youngest sister were particularly close; they had been since her father had left them. She missed all of them dearly. The prospect of leaving them behind to come to the metropolis had been difficult. When her mother sat her down one evening and talked to her, the decision had become easier. She had insisted Semilla follow her dream and attend university, reassuring her that everything would be all right at home.

Semilla glanced around at the handful of people she shared the carriage with. Some nestled behind newspapers or a book and others listened to music on their mobile phones. It was the first time she had considered the effect on her mother and her sisters if this evening's endeavour went wrong. The train came to rest with a squeal of brakes and several of the people in her carriage disembarked. She snapped out of her thoughts and glanced at the name of the station. There were five more stops to go and plenty of time left to think.

Ethel had planned to stay at the Ministry as there seemed little point in both of them travelling all the way to the suburbs. She had hoped that if she stayed there might have been a chance meeting with Burt, but the truth was she had no idea if he was working tonight or not. Calling security and asking them was not a good idea. Burt would have probably been ridiculed by his workmates if they heard that she was asking after him. Ethel had a soft spot for him and had done for some time. She often wondered why they had never managed to get together and thought perhaps he felt more comfortable just being her friend. If she didn't engage him in conversation she might never know. It was best left to chance, she decided, as these things generally were, and besides, she had an important task ahead of her tonight.

Ethel ambled her way across the marble floor towards the service stairs that led beneath the Ministry where she intended to loiter in the cleaner's staffroom until Semilla returned to the metropolis. Her thoughts were deflected by a vision next to one of the main doors. Ethel stopped and stared; she had never seen anything like it before. Her curiosity got the better of her so she wandered over to the entrance. Norman and Rupert were both wiggling to and fro to a tune only they could hear on their personal stereos. They were both sporting a blue upper left six incisor and tanned chins, courtesy of their Service Department.

'Wait, here it comes, listen to this bit,' Norman instructed as he stuffed the headphones against his companion's head.

Rupert wobbled while his fingers clicked to the rhythm. 'Yeah, that's wicked,' he said, agreeing with Norman.

They caught sight of Ethel staring at them and immediately removed their headphones.

'May we help you, madam?' Rupert asked.

The cleaner gave the pair a bemused look. 'Help me?' She laughed. 'From over here it looks like you're the one's that need some help. Have you all gone completely potty?'

The two doormen stood motionless as Ethel walked away, shaking her head, and descended the stairs to the basement.

'Nice insult,' said Rupert. 'You try and help someone and they call you completely potty.'

'Tell me if I'm mistaken, but wasn't she carrying a briefcase like Mr Davis's?'

'Yes, I believe you're right, or one that was very similar. So why would she have a briefcase like that?' Rupert asked.

'I have absolutely no idea.'

'Do you think we should ask the mainframe if one has gone missing?'

'No, I have a better idea,' Norman said, rolling his eyes behind his eyelids. 'I've just ordered two green leather briefcases for us instead.'

'Did you get them with our initials in gold leaf?'

'Naturally, they would be no good without them.'

Rupert raised his mechanical arms and dug his elbows into his torso, thrusting his pelvis to and fro several times. 'Yeah, way to go. We'll be the first two androids at the Ministry to have their own briefcases. I bet the factory is going to love us when this craze takes off. Just think of how many cases they are going to sell next week.'

'Absolutely, they are going to love us to bits,' Norman said.

The pair of them put their earphones back on and began to wiggle to and fro again to their music. Suddenly, Norman stopped jigging as the revelation hit him like a train. His face portrayed a look of utter panic. He grabbed at Rupert's earphones and gave his colleague a very serious look. 'What do you know about share dealing?'

Rupert placed a finger on his chin and mulled over the question with a studious look. 'Now you come to mention it,' he said, 'I know absolutely nothing.'

Norman grabbed his arm and began dragging his bewildered companion to the nearest lift. 'Then we need to find out, and find out fast.'

CHAPTER 28

'Over there,' the Dheybar said, almost jumping with excitement and nodding again.

Both Godfrey and Charlie quickly realised that the Dheybar had one hereditary problem from his evolutionary past. The enthusiastic fur-covered desert dweller could not point; he was devoid of hands and arms. The Dheybar knew there was another oasis. However, nodding in the general vicinity of several million square miles of desert was not going to help them in their quest to find it.

'Marvellous,' Godfrey said, looking thoroughly despondent. 'We can't possibly find it like this.'

'True, but I think we've cracked the question of the other oasis and its authenticity,' Charlie told him. 'Now all we have to do is find that tin.'

'And hope Ethel and Semilla are successful with getting those coordinates tonight,' Godfrey said, looking at his companion, who was tired and dusty. 'I think we should call it day, don't you?'

'I do,' Charlie said, turning to the Dheybar. 'It's been a pleasure meeting you. Thank you for your help.'

Godfrey acknowledged the creature with a polite nod. 'Likewise, thank you very much.'

The two men trailed off down the cavern towards their campfire as the Dheybar silently watched their murky forms grow fainter and fainter until all that remained was the darkness. The creature blinked his huge watery eyes as the ruff of black hair slid across to protect them. The circles of vibrating sand formed around him as he descended once again beneath the floor of the cavern.

Godfrey leant back against the rock, resting his empty tea cup on his folded arm. They had eaten, and now in the warmth of the campfire he felt himself drifting off. He would sleep well tonight, that was certain, especially with the cool fresh desert air drifting into the cave. In the light from the fire, their camp was reminiscent of when he and Charlie had been here as children. Coming here to explore the caverns with their fathers had been the highlight of their summer holidays, a popular place to bring the entire family in those days. The cave systems were the perfect place to let them burn off their energy during the summer recess. There were new friends to be made every day as families came and went with their offspring. He remembered hide and seek as one of the most popular pastimes that occupied them for hours at a time and how he and Charlie had caused such distress for their parents when they pretended they were lost. They had watched from beneath the tarpaulin in his father's transport, giggling as teams of parents set out with torches to find them. For some reason, the Roamer's Cave was now seldom visited and no longer the topic of chatter in the playground before schools across the colony closed for the summer. Their society had changed and not for the better. The children of today were unable to find the excitement they had derived from these caves. Imagination was in short supply and the lure of electronic games had eradicated those simple childhood pleasures of providing your own heroes and villains to play with. The embers in the fire reminded him of how they made shapes of animals and people until they finally they gave in to sleep and their parents carried them off to bed.

'You're very deep in thought,' Gloria said, placing her book beside her. 'Do you want to share them?'

He watched the flames casting strange flickering shapes around the walls of the cavern. It was now the only light they had, the lampposts having all switched off for the night to conserve their power.

'I was thinking about the summers we spent here as children, actually.'

'Halcyon days they were too,' Charlie piped up, shifting himself forward to enter the conversation.

'Who would have imagined you would have been here again for such a reason,' Gloria said as she folded her blanket.

'The whole thing reads like a script for a bad dream,' Charlie grumbled.

Gloria stood and gathered her things. 'We need to remain positive. Perhaps tomorrow we will have a better day. I'm off to bed now. I will see you both in the morning, goodnight.'

The two men said goodnight and Godfrey watched her enter the tent where Mother had retired to earlier.

'Do you think we will really find that tin?' Charlie asked.

'We will stand more of a chance if I can repair my metal detector tomorrow. I haven't used it for years. It's no surprise it doesn't work.'

Charlie yawned; he was fading fast. 'Come on, let's get some sleep.'

During the night, Godfrey stirred. He rolled over in his sleeping bag, and in the fading embers of the campfire he thought he saw the Dheybar warming himself. Beside the Dheybar on the sandy floor of the cave sat a rusty metal object the size of a biscuit tin. Godfrey smiled. The Dheybar had brought him what they were looking for. It was a nice dream, he thought, and then he closed his eyes and began to snore.

CHAPTER 29

Huddled in a service doorway at the rear of the Grand Library, Ethel sheltered from the steady drizzle. The rain had started before she had left the Ministry that evening and showed no sign of abating. It was cold, and as it trickled down the collar of her raincoat, she imagined Godfrey and the others huddled round a warm campfire hidden in the safety of the Roamer's Cave, waiting for this part of the plan to unfold.

After Semilla and she had parted company that evening, Ethel had managed to loiter in the cleaner's staffroom on basement level two. There were a handful of cleaning staff at a table in one corner preparing for their night shift but no one questioned Ethel regarding her presence. As she sipped her tepid coffee, she took out her mobile phone and ran through the names in the contact list. It occurred to her that she should call her sons, though as she hesitated the task became more difficult. Ethel knew that if she heard their voices it would make her emotional, and tonight there was no room for emotion; she had to stay focused. So she sat and waited and tried to read a discarded newspaper to occupy her mind instead, but it merely served as a poor distraction.

The night cleaner's supervisor finally came into the staffroom with his clipboard tucked under his arm. He managed to motivate his team and trail them out of their cosy corner, acknowledging Ethel with a polite greeting as they passed by her table. It was fortunate he hadn't entered into conversation with her; it was the last thing she needed at that time.

When Ethel left the Ministry, she walked to the other side of the Grand Plaza beneath the cover of her umbrella, along the passageway adjacent to the Grand Library and stood in the doorway at the rear of the building. Clutching her phone tightly in her raincoat pocket, she sheltered in the doorway, ready to hold an imaginary call should anyone walk past. The passageway at the rear of building remained deserted apart from Ethel and the rain that continued to beat down on the pavements. It ran into the storm drains with a monotonous rhythm that was beginning the enervate her resolve. The rain-covered face of her wristwatch produced another concern: where was Semilla? She was late.

Ethel woke with a start, propped against the service door, as a familiar voice jolted her back to reality.

'Hello, Ethel, I'm over here.'

She looked over at her accomplice standing at the end of the passageway. Ethel raised a hand, quickly waving up and down, trying to warn her. Semilla, obviously thinking she was pleased to see her, waved back again. Ethel's heart sank as she glanced up at the security camera above Semilla's head. It was turning and would focus on her at any second. Darting along the passageway, Ethel quickly led Semilla under the canopy of her umbrella into the haven of the service doorway.

'What do you think you're doing? There are cameras everywhere.' Ethel said, shaking out her umbrella and standing it against the wall. 'Anyway, where have you been? I've been waiting here for ages.'

'I had to wait for my gran to finish some sewing on our costumes. They took longer than she thought they would, but she's made such a lovely job of them, they look so realistic.'

'Good, now let's get inside and we can put them on. I'm freezing out here.'

Semilla hesitated. 'There's just one small problem though,' she said, and she plunged her hand into the large laundry bag she had carried from her grandmother's.

Ethel's mouth fell open in horror. 'What in the name of Llar is that?' she stammered.

'It's not my fault. My gran is old and she gets easily confused.'

Ethel looked on in despair. 'I said we needed two guerrilla outfits, not gorilla outfits!'

The fact that Ethel hadn't ended up with her black beret and camouflage face paint completely diluted her fantasy. She had imagined herself scaling the library walls and abseiling from parapets and balconies in an attempt to retrieve their prize. In reality, she knew, of course, that she was physically incapable of such acts, and it was, after all, just a fantasy. Instead, she now looked up at Semilla, who was ready to commit an act of larceny in one of the colony's most famous facilities dressed as a gorilla.

'If this goes wrong tonight they'll throw us both in an institution,' Ethel said, looking up at Semilla's fur-covered face.

'Or maybe the zoo,' Semilla said dryly.

'Now, have you got the can?'

'Yes I have.'

'Good, then let's get this over with.'

Semilla watched closely as Ethel tapped in the code Charlie had given them on the keypad beside the door. Then, with her cleaner's pass keys, she made short work of gaining entry into the building. It took several seconds for them to become accustomed to the dim lighting. The corridors were lit by small single lamps on each of the corners that assisted their mission perfectly.

'The first camera is just round this corner to our left,' whispered Ethel as she crept along in the near darkness clutching the empty laundry bag and her umbrella.

Semilla held up a large furry hand supporting a tin of black spray paint and shook it vigorously several times. The sound of the ball bearings mixing the paint echoed along the corridor.

Ethel winced beneath her mask.

'Godfrey did say I had to shake it first,' Semilla said.

Ethel took a second or two to gather her nerves before she peered cautiously round the corner at the first camera. 'This one is fixed so it shouldn't be too difficult. Just go up to it from the side and spray the lens.'

Semilla nodded. 'All right, but before I do, can you look at my head? I can only see with one eye,' she whispered.

Ethel turned and squinted back at Semilla. 'Bend down a moment,' she whispered, and she adjusted her costume. 'You're looking out of your left earhole, that's why.'

Half a minute later, two beady eyes focused on the security camera and painted the lens, the support and most of the corridor wall surrounding it. The stench of black cellulose paint wafted down the corridor as the pair continued on, slowly, stopping at the next corner.

'This one is the same,' Ethel said, and Semilla proceeded to disable the second camera and a large landscape picture hanging on the corridor wall close by.

'I don't think we need to be quite so heavy-handed with the paint, sweetheart,' Ethel told Semilla. 'We'll both be overcome with fumes in a minute.'

Semilla shrugged her huge furry shoulders and followed Ethel along the short stretch of corridor that led them to the entrance foyer of the library. Ethel looked up at the camera and pointed. 'Now this one is the tricky one. This camera rotates to and fro, so you will have to time it just right. And no noise this time, the guard's office is just over there.'

The pair watched and waited as the camera went through a complete cycle, and when Semilla could see her opportunity she tiptoed across the foyer. The huge entrance foyer of the Grand Library was more enhanced with lighting than the dim corridors that led to it. Four spotlights mounted on the floor illuminated the podium that supported the glass cabinet where *The Great Book of Llar* was displayed. It gave the area an eerie but welcoming effect, like an island sanctuary in an ominous sea of darkness. Ethel waited, cautiously peering round the corner as Semilla got close to the camera. Finally, when she stood beneath it, Semilla thrust her arm up and pressed on the spray nozzle. The tin coughed and spluttered several times as the camera continued on its preordained path. Semilla looked at the tin and then across the void at Ethel. The metallic clatter of two ball bearings mixing paint resonated around the library again. Ethel's heart laboured as the camera rotated back upon her motionless collaborator toting the tin of spray paint. Semilla was drawn to the camera like a moth to a light; she looked straight into the lens with a huge furry smile.

In an office a few yards away from the main entrance, with his feet propped on the desk, Burt Brown sat reading a gardening magazine and an article on how to grow prize-winning carrots. The movement that caught his eye was subliminal and failed to register in his consciousness. The camera in the main foyer continued on its diurnal path as Burt glanced up at the screen. There was nothing there. Discounting the moment entirely, he continued to read the useful hints on irrigation.

Meanwhile, beneath the camera, a gorilla was hurriedly cleaning the nozzle on her spray tin by rubbing it on her costume. Finally, thrusting her hand as high as she could, she gave the nozzle one last press as the lens homed in upon her.

The monitor in the security office again threw up an amazingly clear image of a menacing-looking gorilla. Burt's magazine this time slipped from his hand as he fell backwards from his chair. He screamed and landed with a crash on the floor, his foot kicking over the contents of the waste paper basket. Mice were one thing; however, a gorilla presented a completely new level of fear, and one he had not experienced before.

Ethel looked at Semilla, who had frozen to the spot at the sound of screaming coming from the guard's office, and in desperation she ran across the foyer as fast as her legs would carry her. Slipping behind one of the huge marble columns, Ethel looked back, and with a single hairy finger she pointed silently at an adjacent column. Semilla quickly realised their plight and ducked behind another column and out of sight.

Burt Brown picked himself up from the office floor, grabbed the door handle and crashed into the hallway. He collided with the corridor walls as his feet scrambled for grip on the polished floor. His first thought was to escape. Instead, he found himself out of breath and trembling beneath the camera that had produced the image on his monitor. Thankfully there was no sign of a gorilla. He stood panting with fear, looking left and right around the huge foyer, his eye's struggling to adjust from his bright office lights. The smell of paint drifted past his nose as he slowly climbed the steps to the podium. *The Great Book of Llar* was still in its display cabinet. He bent down, looking around its corners; there was nothing. Burt stood up, wondering if perhaps he had been asleep and it had only been a dream after all. He took another look around the shadowy edges of the foyer and back at the colony's most treasured exhibit. The face that stared back from the glass cabinet on the podium was not his own. Instead, it was hairy with beady eyes and belonged to a very tall gorilla. Burt frantically grabbed at his holster for his weapon.

His hand shook wildly as he gazed up at the monstrous beast towering over him, and he screamed again. The safety catch on Burt's pistol flicked off more by luck than judgement, and the Phlegm-O-Matic burst into life.

'Good evening, user, this is the Phlegm-O-Matic Weaponry Corporation at your service. It's a rather dull night here in the city, with the outside air temperature at only 11 degrees and the relative humidity at seventy-one percent. It looks like the rain that started early this evening will continue throughout the night and into the early morning. Furthermore, as if the gloomy weather across the colony isn't enough to contend with, we are now experiencing an attack from a band of marauding gorillas.' The Phlegm-O-Matic's oration ended. 'Gorillas! Run for your life!'

The gun immediately began to shake uncontrollably in Burt's already jittery hand. 'What about the menu, you're supposed to offer me a menu?' he shouted desperately, looking down at his gun.

'You want a menu, go to a restaurant. Have you seen the size of that thing? Let's get out of here before it kills us both.'

'But you're supposed to give me three options.'

'Okay,' said the Phlegm-O-Matic, pausing slightly, 'how about run, run and run. Will that do?' The pistol and Burt's hand were both shaking frantically and completely out of harmony with one another. His sweaty palm, no longer capable of holding the weapon, lost its grip and the Phlegm-O-Matic dropped to the floor. Semilla watched with interest as she remembered how Burt had cowered the other morning in Godfrey's office, desperate to remain clear of the weapon as their President had waved it around the room. She seized her opportunity and grabbed the pistol, then stood beside the display cabinet toting the chromium weapon as it glistened in the light from the podium.

Semilla held out the Phlegm-O-Matic at arm's reach, pointing it at Burt. 'Okay, Mr Guard,' she started, 'now just do as you are told and no one gets hurt.'

Burt let out a nervous laugh. 'Are you kidding me? You're holding it the wrong way round you stupid gorilla.'

'What?'

'He said I'm the wrong way up,' confirmed the gun. 'You're holding me by my muzzle and not by my butt.'

'You want me to hold you by your butt?' Semilla asked.

'I'm afraid that's how it works. If I went off now I'd blow a hole in the floor,' the Phlegm-O-Matic informed her. 'And that really is a possibility as my fear circuits are at eighty-six percent and rising.'

'Oh,' said Semilla, and she turned the gun one hundred and eighty degrees and pointed the muzzle at the library ceiling.

'Not wishing to be overly inquisitive, but can I surmise you've never done this before?' enquired the Phlegm-O-Matic nervously.

'No, never.'

'I thought not,' said the pistol, which was now beginning to warm to its new user. The Phlegm-O-Matic's level of fear dropped dramatically and the gun began to make polite conversation. 'So there's just the two of you then?'

'That's right,' confirmed Semilla, 'just the two of us.'

'And you can talk, which is rather unique for a gorilla, if you don't mind me saying so.'

'Yeah, well, we are a special kind of talking gorilla, actually.'

The pistol continued. 'So you're a female gorilla, then?'

'Yes.'

'I thought so. I can tell these things, you know. I have sensors.'

'Oh,' Semilla remarked, staring at the pistol.

'Your hand is very warm.'

'Is it?'

Burt looked at the pistol in disbelief. 'Look, that's enough. Now just give me the gun back, there's a good gorilla, before someone gets hurt,' demanded Burt, failing completely to sound like the voice of authority.

'No,' replied Semilla flatly, and she gestured the weapon at him.

'That's right, you tell him, sweetie. Now just point the end with the hole in it at him and I'll do the rest,' instructed the pistol.

Semilla swung the pistol round and Burt immediately froze on the spot.

'You're not supposed to help her. You're my gun,' objected Burt.

'Says who?' asked the Phlegm-O-Matic.

'Say's me,' retorted Burt.

'Okay,' said the pistol in a questioning tone. 'When was the last time you took me out?'

Burt blinked a few times, trying hard to remember.

'How about Monday morning in Godfrey Davis's office when you let the President throw me out of an office window eighty-three floors up?'

Burt coughed awkwardly. 'That was a mistake.'

'At least we agree on that. You're my gun … who are you kidding? You don't care about me, do you? I'm nothing more than a fashion accessory you can brag about to your mates at the bar,' huffed the Phlegm-O-Matic.

Burt blushed. He wondered that if he had paid more attention to his gun perhaps he wouldn't have been in this dilemma.

Ethel was beginning to feel sorry for him. Her soft spot for Burt Brown began to cloud her mind, but fortunately she remembered their mission and decided to forget her emotions. 'There are two things we want from you,' she said, moving forward, prodding him in the belly with her umbrella.

'Really?' said Burt, trying to sound unconcerned. 'And they are what exactly?'

'The keys for that display cabinet and a roll of masking tape,' Ethel said.

'Oh, don't tape me up, please.'

'Do it anyway,' said the Phlegm-O-Matic.

'Okay, if you want,' Semilla agreed.

Ethel was at last beginning to enjoy herself, even though she hadn't got her black beret and camouflage face paint, or abseiled from the galleries of the Grand Library. The pair of them had accomplished their mission, and for her that was good enough.

CHAPTER 30

Godfrey stared at the Dheybar and the rusty tin beside the remnants of last night's campfire. The Dheybar blinked occasionally with his watery brown eyes as he tipped slowly from side to side on his webbed feet. He had the posture of a creature satisfied with a personal achievement.

'I thought it was a dream,' Godfrey told them as they gathered round. 'I remember looking at the fire and seeing him there with the tin and I must have fallen back to sleep.'

Gloria and Mother surveyed the strange-looking creature. Over dinner last night they had heard of Godfrey and Charlie's encounter with the Dheybar and had been amazed that the legend was true. With the creature standing in front of them, they were now positively excited.

'He is so cute,' Gloria said, knelling down and stroking the Dheybar.

'Getting him house-trained may prove difficult,' Mother pointed out.

'What are you talking about, getting him house-trained? We can't take him home,' Godfrey said frantically.

'Stop being so negative. We succeeded with you, didn't we?' Mother said.

'If Ethel and Semilla can't get those coordinates for any reason, the Dheybar knows the way to the oasis. He could be the ace up our sleeve.'

'That settles it,' Gloria said. 'He's coming with us.'

'Absolutely,' Mother agreed. 'I wonder if he's hungry? Do you think he likes milk?'

'Thank goodness this little fellow came along,' Charlie said. 'He has saved us an awful lot of digging, that's for sure.'

Just how much longer they would have spent excavating the floor of the cavern was incalculable. The Roamer's Cave complex was a daunting place that stretched for miles beneath the sands of the desert. Even if Godfrey had managed to repair his metal detector, it could have taken days before the tin was finally discovered.

Godfrey knelt down in front of the fur-covered creature. 'Thank you, Dheybar. If this is what we are looking for, we are indebted to you,'

The Dheybar toppled excitedly from side to side. 'You are welcome,' he said.

'Do you think we can open it before we have breakfast? Frankly, the suspense is killing me,' said Gloria

'I'll vote for that,' agreed Mother.

Godfrey picked up the tin and handed it to Charlie.

'Not a chance. The privilege of opening it should be yours,' Charlie said.

'I insist.'

Gloria grabbed the tin. 'I'll do it, shall I?' she grumbled. 'Or we'll never know what is inside it.'

The lid came off relatively easily, revealing a layer of folded sacking. 'There's something under here,' Gloria told them as she slowly produced a grubby envelope and held it up in the light from the lampposts. 'The tin was definitely left by your fathers. This letter is addressed to you both.' She handed the envelope to her husband, and as Godfrey examined the stained, discoloured paper, he could see that his and Charlie's names were just visible.

'This is not my dad's writing,' Godfrey told them. 'I think this was written by your father.'

Charlie took the envelope and slowly slipped his thumb under the seal and removed a single sheet of paper. He ran his eyes across the text and then he cleared his throat.

Dear Boys,

How in the name of Llar are you both? So you found the biscuit tin? I expect you're both tired after all that digging, so we left a couple of digestives in the bottom just in case you were peckish. Our apologies for not being able to leave the exact location of the tin, however we had to act fast. Reg barely had time to put the note behind Godfrey's graduation photo before we both came here to hide this tin and its contents.

Things are pretty grim here, boys, and the future doesn't look good for us both or for the colony. Reg is busy scribbling down some notes to go with the blueprints for his invention. We have to work as fast as we can as we are sure we are under surveillance.

In time you will both come to realise, I'm sure, the importance of the contents in this biscuit tin. Both of us are convinced our people have been deceived, as we have been, by those who were trusted to run our great colony.

We have therefore concealed one of the devices in this tin hoping that one day you may be able to balance the situation that has occurred here. The second XXL is still in our possession, and we are hoping we can use it before it's too late. Be warned, these devices are immensely dangerous in the wrong hands, something we have since found out to our cost.

Guard these blueprints and the XXL with your lives. They can both be used as a weapon against our great colony. We can only hope that with this information safely in your possession, our dreams will one day live on in you both.

One last word of warning to you, boys. Under no circumstances should you trust that new junior minister, named .... He's a devious scoundrel.

We have to go now and get back to the Ministry before we are missed. Our love and best wishes to you both.

Commander Aubrey Albright and Reginald Owen Davis.

P.S. How long did it take you to notice your graduation photos? He, He!

Charlie looked up at Godfrey, who also had tears in his eyes. He folded the letter and placed it neatly back in its envelope.

'So, who was the junior minister your dad mentioned?' Gloria asked.

'I have no idea. The paper is so badly smudged, the name is completely illegible,' Charlie informed her.

'Think about it, our President seems very keen to locate this device. I wouldn't mind betting it is him,' Mother said

'That may be the case,' Charlie replied, his voice laced with emotion, 'but let's look at the rest of it, shall we?'

Gloria handed Godfrey the rusty old tin. He rummaged beneath the sacking and pulled out a set of tatty blueprints. Then, slipping his fingers into the tin again, he produced a gold-coloured bracelet that resembled a large wristwatch.

'I knew it,' he said. 'This is the device that they were wearing on the day of our graduations.'

'So where is the second device?' Charlie enquired.

'Somewhere safe, I hope,' Godfrey said, sounding concerned.

Mother peered through her spectacles. She was obviously unimpressed at what she saw. 'So is this what the President is looking for?'

'It would appear to be,' Godfrey replied.

'So all of this fuss is over a gold bracelet? I'm sorry, and forgive me if I'm wrong, but how can that thing possibly be of such a threat to the security of the colony?'

'I wouldn't underestimate that device, if I were you, madam,' Number Nine said politely from the edge of the group in a confident tone. 'Do you remember I spoke of Reg Davis's thesis, the one we found encoded on the mainframe? Those notes enabled us to travel from the Ministry to your cellar.'

'Are you saying that this bracelet will allow a person to travel from one place to another?' Mother queried.

Godfrey pulled the sleeve of his jacket back and flexed his arm. 'Perhaps it's time to find out.'

'You have no idea what this thing can do.' Gloria said, frowning deeply.

'Remember our graduation photos? They were both wearing one? I'm sure they would do nothing to put us in harm's way.'

Mother huffed. 'Harm's way, indeed. I don't believe it. That thing couldn't hurt the skin on a rice pudding, let alone the colony.'

'Please just be careful,' Gloria said.

The clasp clicked as he secured the XXL to his wrist. He smiled at his wife, and then, taking a very deep breath, he pressed a small button on the side of the bracelet.

CHAPTER 31

In the foyer of the Ministry, Ethel tapped her shoe impatiently on the marble floor. Semilla still hadn't arrived for work. Although last night's escapade at the Grand Library had been a complete success, Ethel knew their mission was far from over. She gazed out intently at the hordes of people filing past the Ministry, hoping to see Semilla stride into the foyer.

'Good morning, Ethel,' Norman said, his blue incisor glinting in the sunlight flooding through the plate glass windows.

'Oh, good morning,' Ethel replied nervously. She glanced down at the green leather-bound briefcase in the android's hand. It looked very familiar.

'Have you heard the news? The Grand Library was broken into last night and *The Great Book of Llar* was stolen,' Norman told her.

Ethel clutched her mop tightly as she forced a look of shock. 'Are you being serious?'

'I am indeed,' Norman said. 'The guard is still being interrogated as we speak. He's in a lot of trouble, I can tell you.'

Ethel's face flushed with colour. She felt a sense of guilt at Burt's predicament. It crossed her mind that she and Semilla may have been somewhat overzealous with their techniques in parcel tape. 'Have they caught anyone yet?' she asked, trying to sound inquisitive.

'No, and they're not likely to. The perpetrators took the only proof that could exonerate the guard by stealing the disc from the security surveillance system. They were professionals, I'm telling you. They knew exactly what they were doing, that's for sure.'

Ethel nervously bit her bottom lip and looked out across the Grand Plaza hoping for some sign of Semilla.

Rupert wandered into the conversation. 'Morning, Ethel,' he said. 'It was two gorillas, apparently, that did the heist on the Grand Library last night.'

Ethel almost had a coronary on the spot. 'How in the name of Llar do you know all of this?' she stammered.

'The mainframe,' Rupert told her. 'We're getting news updates now every five minutes.'

'But this must be confidential information. You can't go around telling everybody that walks into the Ministry.'

Rupert laughed. 'There's no such thing as bad advertising, Ethel.'

She gazed down at Rupert's hand clutching an identical green briefcase. The entrance to the Ministry was swarming with androids, each carrying identical green briefcases. 'There's something very wrong here,' she murmured to herself. 'You've never called me by my first name before.'

The androids disregarded Ethel and her statement completely. 'It would appear that the two gorillas also stole Burt's pistol,' Norman informed Rupert.

'That's twice in a week someone's taken Burt Brown's Phlegm-O-Matic,' said Rupert. 'I remember the first time quiet vividly.'

'I'm sure you do,' Norman said.

Rupert laughed mockingly. *'Honestly, two gorillas broke into the library, held me up with my own pistol, taped me up to a toilet and stole* The Great Book of Llar. *Yeah, right, he's got to be in on it for sure.'*

In all of last night's excitement, Ethel had completely forgotten about Semilla's antics with Burt's pistol. She had no

188 · A R MERRYDEW

idea what had happened to the Phlegm-O-Matic after they had left the library.

'Burt Brown has been trying to convince the interrogators all morning that they were real gorillas, and now it has just been confirmed by the dry cleaners that they weren't,' Norman said.

'What dry cleaner?' Ethel stuttered.

'The one on the other side of the plaza where the costumes were dropped off,' Norman told her.

Ethel imagined Semilla discarding those costumes and being caught by security. It left a knot in the pit of her stomach.

'Anyway, have a good day, Ethel, we have to go,' Rupert said. 'Norman and I have a meeting to attend at our broker's office.'

Ethel watched Rupert and Norman abscond and leave their posts at the Ministry. She took one last look at the Grand Plaza and decided she had to get herself back to work.

Later, on floor eighty-three, Ethel was swinging her mop to and fro across the marble floor of the corridor. She was outside Godfrey's old office. The office was empty now and somehow it matched her disposition.

'Is that part of the floor wet?' said the voice behind her.

Ethel turned and looked the android up and down blankly. He was holding a briefcase crafted in sumptuous green leather. The briefcase was new, and beside the handle in gold leaf she saw the initials B.P. The android also had a fake tan chin and blue upper left six incisor.

'It is, but if you need to pass, go on, I'll mop it again, it's not a problem,' Ethel told him in a downhearted sort of way.

'Thank you, you're very kind. I just have to put this picture back, you see.' The polite android placed his briefcase on a nearby chair and opened it. He removed a small insignificant picture of a duck and placed it on an empty hook on the wall. The android stood back and examined the picture. 'It's almost like visiting the scene of a crime,' he whimpered, becoming noticeably emotional.

Ethel stood and stared at the android, which seemed completely lost in thought, when a familiar voice startled her. 'I bet you were wondering where I had got to?' Semilla said, lurching up next to her friend.

Ethel saw red. She slammed her mop against the corridor wall and grabbed Semilla's arm. She led her into Godfrey's empty office and threw the door shut with all her might. 'Have you any idea how worried I've been. I thought something had happened to you,' Ethel stammered, her eyelids blinking rapidly with annoyance.

'Something did happen to me, and that's why I'm so late.'

Ethel took Semilla's hand; she was worried and frightened both at the same time. 'For goodness' sake, tell me.'

'This morning I had this great idea how to get rid of our costumes.'

'And?' Ethel said.

'I couldn't risk leaving them at home or at my gran's, could I?'

Semilla's logic seemed reasonable. 'No, I suppose not.'

'So I thought what better place to hide them than at the dry cleaners.'

Ethel's face collapsed in horror as she slumped into Godfrey's old office sofa. 'So you took them to the dry cleaners?'

'Yes, I did, but when I got to the plaza, it was crawling with security. They were searching everyone in sight.'

'So what happened?' Ethel asked, her voice laced with despair.

'So, I slipped down the alley and left the costumes by the back door of the shop…with a note.'

Ethel shot to her feet. 'What note?'

Semilla unwrapped a bright red lollipop and placed it in her cheek. 'I asked them to dry clean the costumes and return them to the sergeant that wrecked Mr Davis's office.'

Ethel started to giggle.

'I couldn't walk around the metropolis all day with the evidence in my hand, could I?'

'No, definitely not.'

'Exactly.' Semilla nodded from behind her confectionery. 'By the way, what did you do with *The Great Book of Llar*?'

'Don't worry, it's safe in my locker.' The old cleaner took Semilla's arm and led her to the office door. 'Come on, let's go to the canteen. I fancy a nice cup of tea, and while we are there I will tell you what happened in the foyer this morning.'

As the two women left the office, deep in conversation, they failed to notice an android collapsed on the floor. Beside him lay a small insignificant picture of a duck, which was broken. Barney Patterson had once been told that lighting never strikes the same place twice. When he finally regained consciousness, he would realise that pictures of ducks were another matter entirely.

CHAPTER 32

Godfrey struggled to focus his eyes. He was not alone. The light from the device had been so intense and had lit up the entire cavern, and everyone struggled to adjust their retinas.

'What in the name of Llar was that?' Charlie exclaimed, blinking frantically.

'I have absolutely no idea,' Godfrey said, staring at the bracelet.

Gloria went up to her husband and examined his hand and wrist. 'Did that burn you? Are you all right?'

'I felt nothing,' he said, twisting the bracelet to and fro on his wrist.

'If we can get this contraption to work properly, and we have those coordinates from Ethel and Semilla, we can save ourselves an awful lot of driving.'

Godfrey was prone to disagree. His first attempt at exploring the operation of his father's invention had shaken him considerably. 'I don't think we can risk using this until we know how to operate it properly. It could prove too dangerous. If we can't get back from wherever it is we end up, then we lose the device and one of us. We simply can't risk it,'

Charlie's face dropped. The prospect of facing the desert seemed inevitable. He had to admit, though, the XXL was untried and Godfrey's caution was not unfounded.

'We have two options: either sit tight here and hopefully tonight Ethel and Semilla will have those coordinates.'

'And what is our second option?' Gloria asked.

'Or we ask the Dheybar to show us the way.'

Later that morning, Charlie gripped the steering wheel of Godfrey's transport so tightly his knuckles were turning white. His patience was dwindling rapidly. Godfrey had the look of a man who was about to have a nervous breakdown as he stared impassively at the endless desert vista rolling out before them. As the transport tore across the featureless baking cauldron of the Llarinian desert, the landscape had become as monotonous as the instructions they had listened to since they had left the cave earlier that morning.

'Knit one, pearl one,' droned the voice on Mother's knitting DVD as it played relentlessly on the screen embedded in the rear of Charlie's seat. By now, both Godfrey and Charlie knew Mother's new jumper intimately, stitch by stitch, and it was driving them mad. To add to their misery, the Dheybar's offer to navigate them across the desert had at first seemed like a good idea, but the practicality of the exercise took on an infuriating reality. What Godfrey and Charlie hadn't realised in their eagerness to push forward with their quest was just how protracted the desert creature's methods actually were. In order to stay on course, the Dheybar required the assistance of his subterranean family at regular intervals. Every twenty minutes or so, the little creature would ask Charlie to stop and allow him to exit the transport. Thumping his huge fleshy feet on the sand in a rhythm only his kind would understand brought one of his cousins to the surface close by. After a seemingly in-depth conversation, the Dheybar would perch himself back on the centre console and nod to Charlie. 'Straight on.'

'This is going to take forever at this rate,' Charlie said.

'I thought it was a ridiculous idea trusting our safety to a talking rodent,' Mother commented from behind her knitting needles.

'You never said a word back at the Roamer's Cave, as I remember,' Godfrey snapped.

'I don't have to necessarily say anything to disagree with you,' retorted the old lady, splicing her needles methodically to and fro.

'And now you're calling him a rodent. Weren't you the one who wanted to take him home?'

Mother looked at him through her half-rimmed spectacles perched on the end of her nose. 'You're getting confused, Godfrey. There's a difference between taking him home and taking instruction from him.'

Charlie coughed and tried not to laugh.

'Did you hear that?' Godfrey started, turning to his wife for support.

Gloria was adept at playing umpire with Godfrey and her Mother. 'Would you boys like a toffee?' she said, leaning forward with a peace offering.

They took up on the offer and each grabbed a sweet.

'Knit one, drop one,' droned on the recorded voice as Mother frantically jabbed her needles to and fro to keep up. 'Knit one, pearl one.'

Charlie glanced over at Godfrey who was crunching his sweet vigorously and staring out at the desert like a man possessed. 'I'm convinced if we ever get to this oasis, Godfrey, we'll be knee-deep in knitwear.'

The tedium of their trip suddenly took a decisive turn as the dusty silver shape of a very battered transport shot across their path. The vehicle missed them by inches and the event was sudden enough that both Godfrey and Charlie let out a cry. Charlie reacted by turning their transport in a tight curve as sand and stones showered dust across their windscreen. As they shuddered to a halt, the inertia threw the Dheybar head first into Godfrey's footwell and Gloria's toffees rained down across the dashboard.

'Is everyone all right?' asked Godfrey as the Dheybar struggle to return upright.

Gloria confirmed she and Mother were shaken but otherwise uninjured, as Charlie peered out across the desert at the shower of sand billowing up from the other vehicle in the distance. 'Who in the name of Llar was that?'

'I have absolutely no idea, Charlie, but more to the point, what are they doing all the way out here?'

Charlie was asking the same question as his eyes took on the sparkle of a naughty schoolboy. 'There's only one way to find out, Godfrey, and to do that we need to chase them.'

'Hold on tight, this may get a bit bumpy,' he said to his wife who was still retrieving Mother's knitting from the floor.

Charlie floored the pedal until the old transport's motors screamed for mercy, and then, spinning the vehicle round on the spot, they shot off in hot pursuit. Within minutes they were speeding across the scorching desert sands following the dust storm that spewed up from the other vehicle. It was the most fun Charlie and Godfrey had had since they'd left the cave early that morning. Mother, who was completely undeterred by the events, continued to jab at her knitting as her disc droned on, thankfully muted out against the high-pitched scream of the transport's motors. The lampposts rocked from side to side in the load bay, muttering muted words of complaint as the vehicle tipped this way and that, as Charlie pursued the mystery vehicle ahead of them. The Dheybar now rested in Godfrey's lap, held tight in his arms to prevent another mishap.

Finally, Charlie managed to navigate their craft into the slipstream of the unknown vehicle. Sand and dust showered down from every direction, their wipers struggling to keep pace with the debris. They were now very close on the heels of this unidentified transport and the commander had no intention of slowing up. The desert landscape suddenly began to change, and outcrops of large sand dunes loomed closer and closer, but the driver in front showed no sign of taking evasive action.

'What do they think they're doing? Are they mad?' Charlie exclaimed over the sound of their tortured motors.

'I have absolutely no idea,' Godfrey said, swinging around in the passenger seat, desperately trying to hold on to the Dheybar. 'But unless they turn very soon there's going to be an awful mess.'

The two transports shot over an outcrop of smaller dunes, sand flying high into the air. Then dipping wildly, their hover systems struggled to maintain them both on even keels as they levelled out on firmer ground.

'Here we go. Hold tight everyone,' shouted Charlie as their transport ploughed through another array of fresh dunes, scooping the top off completely.

'They're in a big hurry to get away from us. Who can it possibly be?' hollered Gloria from the rear seat.

The Dheybar had so far remained silent throughout this incident. 'They are Aubrey Albright and Reg Davis,' said the Dheybar confidently.

Charlie then slewed the transport to a sudden stop. He glared at the Dheybar. 'That's utterly impossible,' he said angrily.

The little creature blinked his huge watery pear-shaped eyes. 'Why?' he asked.

Charlie faltered; momentarily he was lost for words. 'Because our fathers died a long time ago, that's why.'

'Yes, they did, here in the desert.'

For a moment Charlie was overcome with emotion and a tinge of anger. 'There was an accident in the workshop at the Ministry a long time ago.'

'You are wrong,' said the Dheybar confidently.

'You are the one who is wrong,' Charlie said. He unbuckled his seat belt and got out of the transport and walked some distance away, staring out at the endless wastelands, lost in his private world.

Charlie and Aubrey Albright had been close. It was one of those relationships between a father and son that not all are fortunate enough to achieve. He had been an only child, which benefited him immeasurably when it came to his father's attention. As Charlie grew, he displayed a deep interest in the world of electrical and mechanical theory, and this common interest ultimately brought them closer together. They would immerse themselves in the renovation of old transports and hover cycles in the garage adjacent to their home. One Saturday afternoon, while in the process of testing the fuel system on a newly restored antique transport, the pair shared in the joint responsibility of demolishing the garage roof from the resulting explosion. Somewhere in a box in his attic, Charlie still had the photograph his mother had taken of their blackened smiling faces and wrecked garage roof. His father had been there for him throughout his college days as supportive as always until the day he died. The news had brought him to his knees at the prospect he was gone forever. Even at the funeral he found the situation hard to accept, and for years afterwards he struggled with the void his parting had created.

Charlie looked at the horizon and the shimmering outline of the craft that had nearly collided with them. He believed the story that the Ministry had told him. Was it all a lie? Anger percolated through him. The prospect that such a great man had been subjected to this harsh and cruel end was hard to contain. And in between the emotion and the anger lurked the desire to seek the truth.

Godfrey was on the verge of tears when he turned the Dheybar around to face him. 'Who is in the other transport, Dheybar? I mean, who is it really in it?'

'It is Aubrey Albright and Reg Davis,' said the Dheybar, blinking as he spoke.

'How can they possibly be out here in that transport?'

'This is where people are sent to die,' said the creature in a reverent tone.

'But who sent them out here? Who would do such a thing?' Gloria asked.

'The President,' replied the Dheybar.

The prospect of his father having been sent to meet his end out here in the desert left him with a mind full of emotions. Gloria gave his shoulder a gentle squeeze.

Charlie appeared and clambered silently into the vehicle; his face was filled with anger.

'The Dheybar says it true, Charlie, they were sent out here by the President.'

'Then we had better catch up with that transport and find out if he's right,' he said quietly as he started up the motors.

Minutes later there were cries from the rear seats as they careered across the desert on their own personal roller coaster. Mother, though, was still intent on finishing her jumper, no matter what, and her needles slipped this way and that as she tried desperately to listen to her knitting instructions from the crescendo outside. The gap between the two vehicles eventually closed, little by little, until they drew alongside the other vehicle. The lead transport came down, heavily kissing the sand as the terrain began to change again. Waves of sand tore into the air, showering down as Charlie managed to place their vehicle close enough to see the two occupants bouncing in their seats.

'We're nearly there,' Charlie said as he flicked a button on the dashboard and turned off the air-conditioning.

'We'll boil in here without that,' hollered Godfrey, sounding anxious.

'It's an old trick that will give us a few more horsepower, trust me,' Charlie told him. True to his word, their vehicle crept forward, gaining on the other transport until they were both nearly door to door. 'Almost there,' he said with a determined look, nodding at the other transport now only a whisker away.

Godfrey stared through the sandblasted glass of his window, his jaw limp and immobile. Sat in the front seats of the shuttle next to them were the fully clothed skeletal remains of two people. The driver wore a trilby hat and large black-framed glasses, and gripped between his teeth was a large briar pipe. The vision seemed to last forever as if it were in slow motion. It seemed the Dheybar had been correct. The occupant in the driving seat wearing the glasses and the trilby hat was Commander Aubrey Albright.

Gloria broke their spell by letting out a cry. She pointed through the windscreen at the craggy rocks appearing out of the sand ahead. The desert landscape was changing dangerously. Charlie looked in front of them, then back at the other transport. With one deliberate twist to the left of his steering wheel he sent their transport into the side of the other vehicle. The old weather-beaten transport careered into the dunes beside it and came to a quick, although somewhat graceless, halt. Charlie dragged the steering wheel of their transport around, bringing the vehicle down neatly in a flurry of sand and dust as the motors became silent.

'I want you both to stay here, please,' Godfrey said. 'I think it's best that Charlie and I walk back and take a look first.'

The two men clambered out of their transport and walked back to the stricken vehicle wedged in the dune. There were streams of sand jetting out from beneath the hover units, and the motors were still running flat out.

'I'll do this,' Charlie said, and he negotiated the dune and approached the vehicle. He opened the driver's door and the motors finally fell silent. Godfrey and Charlie both stood silently absorbing the spectacle. Reg and Aubrey sat staring at the weather-beaten windscreen of their mobile tomb, both dressed in their hats and coats on an outing to somewhere they would never reach.

'What happened here?' Godfrey said finally.

'It was a malfunction on the autopilot,' said the Dheybar, who was now standing between the two men. 'They were supposed to reach the oasis in the north like the others.'

'What others?' Godfrey asked.

The Dheybar toppled gently from one foot to the other. 'There have been many others.'

Charlie took a deep breath. 'Think about it, these old transports will go on forever with their reactor power plants. So why not handcuff your hostages in an old crate like this, punch in the coordinates for a place no one knows about, and send them off to meet their end somewhere far away from Llar. The President must have had dozens of his enemies dispatched this way.'

Godfrey stared at the vehicle in front of them wedged in the sand, the front end battered and twisted. 'If the President has the coordinates, then he has known about the other oasis for an awful long time.'

'Exactly, and I bet he knows an awful lot more into the bargain. Makes you wonder what else he's been keeping from his loyal servants in the colony for all these years.'

After some pondering, Godfrey made a suggestion. 'It's going to be dark soon, and I think we're best to make camp here in the shelter of these dunes for tonight.'

'And what about these two?' asked Charlie.

Godfrey glanced over at the damaged transport. 'They've both waited this long for a proper burial, Charlie. One more night surely won't hurt, will it?'

The Llarinian sun disappeared below the horizon that evening and the desert night took over once again. The temperature dropped quickly, and the lampposts made themselves useful by lighting a fire and illuminating the camp. Mother sat staring at her day's work on the end of her knitting needle. For some reason her jumper had three arms.

'Best we set the radio up,' Godfrey advised. 'If my calculations are correct, the capsule will be overhead soon. We'll only have a short window to transmit and receive.'

'I just hope those ladies managed to accomplish their mission. We would make better headway if we didn't have to keep stopping,' Charlie said, nodding over at the Dheybar.

Godfrey surveyed the camp. He had hoped all day that their friends had accomplished their mission successfully and that they still had their liberty. This was the final part of the plan they had discussed in his kitchen at Dusty Bottom Lane. He gazed thoughtfully over at the other transport wedged in the dune on the other side of their camp. The eerie shapes of the two occupants sitting in the front seats flickered from the light of the campfire. It seemed as if they were moving. The vision sent a chill over him. He knew that with their knowledge of the President's nefarious activities in the past, returning to the colony would produce a very certain response. He was staring at it.

CHAPTER 33

Ethel and Semilla appeared to be nothing more than ordinary commuters that evening on the crowded metro heading to the outer suburbs. None of their fellow Llarinians had the slightest inclination that beside them stood the two most wanted individuals in the whole of the colony. *The Great Book of Llar* lay concealed in Ethel's shopping bag, and in Semilla's hand was the briefcase Godfrey had given them in his kitchen. The other commuter's ignorance of who they were and details of their next venture was in itself a relief for Ethel as she was consumed with worry. She and Semilla had been devoid of conversation from the time they had left the metropolis, each of them absorbing the constant barrage of news reports on the carriage media screens. The hunt for *The Great Book of Llar* was underway across the colony with house to house searches and random checks on the transport infrastructure. Gradually, the number of other commuters dwindled, filtering off, one station after another, until finally the two women came to the last stop at the end of the line. The moving pavement from the station led them silently to Dusty Bottom Lane, beneath the towering eucalyptus trees and the shadow of their majestic branches. Only a scattering of porch lights dotted here and there on the shadowy properties gave a clue that life existed in this quiet backwater.

'It's not as bright as the other night,' Semilla commented.

'It wouldn't be, would it?' Ethel said, trying to reassure Semilla and herself. 'Godfrey's lampposts aren't here, are they?'

'I hope at least one of them is.'

Ethel pointed to Baz, his silhouette standing completely motionless outside 119 on silent sentry duty, his light extinguished as the two women arrived.

She gave his column a couple of taps. 'Wake up, Baz, we're here. Are you okay?'

'Thank goodness you've arrived at last,' Baz said, producing a warm glow from his beacon. 'I was so worried about you. I thought you were never coming.'

'We're here now and we've got to hurry up. The capsule will be coming over soon and we need to get the information in this book to Godfrey and the others.'

'You mean you managed to steal it?' Baz said excitedly.

'Yes we did and it was so much fun,' Semilla said.

'We'll tell you all about it later, but right now we need to get this setup,' Ethel said as she quickly placed the briefcase that Godfrey had given them on the ground beside the lamppost. She opened it, revealing a portable radio transmitter. Baz slid open the panel in his column and his delicate metal arm unfolded. He flexed his appendage and his shiny metal fingers.

Semilla gave him a look of pure admiration. 'Is that Dunford's Moon Mist nail varnish?' she asked Baz.

Baz wiggled his digits under his light, admiring his nails nonchalantly. 'I tried Moon Beams and that other one, what's it called…?'

'Moon Petal,' Semilla said excitedly.

'That's the one,' Baz confirmed, 'but I felt they clashed with the colour of my column.'

Semilla was in complete cosmetic agreement. 'It would, totally. Besides, Moon Petal just lacks statement.'

Ethel tried hard to contain herself. 'If you two have completely finished running through Dunford's entire range of nail vanish, can we please plug in this lead before we miss that capsule?' she suggested.

Baz confirmed he was online and able to power up their transmission the moment they caught sight of the solar-powered navigation light when it appeared upon the horizon. He would then be able to bounce the signal to the group waiting in the desert. Ethel, meanwhile, busied herself removing *The Great Book of Llar* from her shopping bag. Moving in closer to Baz's light, she opened it and began to read.

'What in the name of Llar?' she began as she thumbed through the dusty pages. 'This book is full of…'

Baz and Semilla leant over her shoulders, eager for a closer look. 'Recipes!' Baz exclaimed in excitement.

'You mean it's a cookery book?' asked Semilla.

Ethel gazed on dumbfounded as she flipped page after page revealing an endless list of delights fit for a banquet. 'But I thought Number Five said he had deciphered some of the book's encrypted text on the mainframe? He said there was another oasis on the other side of Llar,' Ethel stammered.

'He did. I was there,' Baz confirmed. 'He was quite specific.'

The old cleaner's jaw dropped. 'But this is nothing more than a giant culinary almanac.'

Semilla gazed up at the night sky and pointed. 'Look, Ethel, here it comes. Spaceman Bob's capsule.'

Semilla knew the story of Spaceman Bob, as she and all Llarinians were taught it at school. The events had occurred a long time ago and had been promoted by the colony's curiosity and thirst for knowledge. The fact that the planet of Llar had absolutely nothing in the night sky other than a small insignificant little moon, led the Grand Council of the day to decree that: *'We need to advance ourselves and boldly go where no Llarinian has gone before. Further investigation should be made into the dark bit.'*

Heady with the romance of adventure and exploration, the

Grand Council appointed a group of designers and engineers to build a machine capable of carrying a single observer high enough to actually explore '*the dark bit*' and report back on what they had found. The problem with building such a radical new machine soon became apparent when the designers began to argue with the engineers, considering themselves to be altogether more elevated and superior. Animosity soon developed between these two groups to such a level that they were finally reduced to emailing caustic comments and obscene sketches to one another rather than pooling their resources over a drawing and resolving their issues. Convinced that the designers were interested in nothing more than the final cost element, the engineers disassociated themselves from the celebrations when the vehicle was finally placed on the launch pad.

By the time Llar's first space capsule had finally been completed and made ready to be hurtled into the void, there had been plenty of time to locate a suitable volunteer to pilot the craft. And the volunteer's name just happened to be Bob.

After the launch, contact was lost briefly with the capsule until it had cleared the upper atmosphere. Controllers at mission HQ stood gazing at computer images on huge screens, tracking the progress, working out trajectories and waiting nervously as Llarinian history itself was being written. Finally, a voice crackled over the speakers of mission control, breaking the unbearable silence.

'Hi, it's me, Bob. Can you hear me?'

The entire HQ lifted above the floor with shouts of jubilation. Papers flew into the air, coffee mugs spilled, men hugged women, women hugged men and some people just hugged themselves, but that was mainly the designers. Meanwhile, champagne corks popped all across the land.

'We can hear you, Bob,' said the controller, his voice quivering with anticipation and excitement. 'What can you see?'

'Not a lot really,' Bob replied. 'The windscreen is covered in dead insects.'

A short interval prevailed as the controller huddled with the designers in their starched white coats. 'Bob, the designers say you can clear them with the wipers. There's a little switch just in front of the parking brake next to the cassette player on the dashboard. It's by the cup holder. Can you see it?'

The designers smirked.

'Yes, I've got it!'

A short silence followed.

'Now what can you see?'

The tension across the city was electric as people stood in front of televisions, following the commentary at home, in bars and at work. The whole colony simply hummed with excitement.

'That didn't help, actually. Now the windscreen is in a terrible mess and the washer jets have run out of water. I think I'm going to have to get out and give it a wipe.'

The designers gazed at the controller in sheer terror. 'Bob, the designers don't think that's a good idea,' said the controller. 'Did you hear me…Bob… Bob are you reading me?'

The men in their white coats began making their way towards the nearest exit, their faces stony and pallid with defeat. Rejecting the engineers' idea for a larger washer reservoir had clearly been a mistake, and one that had cost poor Bob his life.

Spaceman Bob became a legend and still passed overhead every night, following the same trajectory with his dirty windscreen. He has served to remind Llarinian generations ever since that the '*dark bit*' isn't really that important, especially as there is nothing up there anyway. However, the Llarinians learned two important lessons following Spaceman Bob's demise. Firstly, you should always remember to top up the washer reservoir on your transport before long journeys. Secondly, one should never exit a moving vehicle to clean a windscreen. Spaceman Bob's cheery face still appears on road safety posters around the metropolis even to this day, and his adventure would be remembered for generations to come.

Ethel looked up at the night sky and grabbed the handset. 'This is mobile base one to mobile base two, are you reading me?'

There was an ominous silence.

'This is mobile base two. We are reading you loud and clear,' said Godfrey as his voice suddenly broke the tranquillity of the lane. It was as clear as if he were standing next to them. 'Have you the information we require, over?'

Ethel looked at Semilla and Baz for support. 'What do we tell them?' she said.

Baz reasoned out the dilemma. He knew that if Number Five had said there were coordinates then they had to exist. He grabbed the handset from Ethel. 'This is mobile base one. We are still looking. Only there seems to be a very large preface. Please hold, over.'

'Large preface?' Ethel blurted. 'This is a cookery book, for goodness' sake.'

'Frankly, I don't think you girls stole the right book,' Baz exclaimed.

Ethel glared at Baz and snatched back the handset. 'There was only one book on display at the time.' As she looked up above their heads, the small navigation light soared relentlessly across the empty night sky. They were running out of excuses. In a short while the capsule would be gone and they would have run out of time. 'This is mobile base one. Can you confirm that Number Five's information is correct? Having problems sourcing the details you require, over,' Ethel said, giving them a look of desperation.

'Hang on, what's this?' Semilla said, confidently pointing at one specific page. 'These numbers here can't be a recipe, they just don't make sense, and there's a map.'

Baz and Ethel dived into the book for a closer look. 'Do you know, I think the girl had found it!' Baz agreed.

Ethel keyed the handset quickly. 'Mobile base two, try the following figures, it's all we can seem to find.' Ethel quickly read out the figures, the ingredients, the weights and the measures for everything she could see on the page. The three of them waited nervously for a response on their radio.

'Mobile base two to mobile base one, are you sure this is correct, only my wife thinks this is the recipe for zabaglione?'

Baz shook his beacon confidently. 'It wouldn't work, darling. The ratios of sugar and Marsala wine are completely wrong.'

As the three companions continued flicking through the pages beneath the glow of Baz's beacon, they failed to see a solitary figure approach them silently from the shadows. The form moved forward, standing just outside the perimeter of Baz's luminescence.

'I had no idea you were all such avid readers,' said the familiar voice. 'Still, I'm sure you will have nothing better to do with your time where you are going next.'

As Ethel, Semilla and Baz hovered out of Dusty Bottom Lane in the rear of a security transport, their destination the inauspicious cells at the Security Department in the centre of the metropolis, Ethel gazed out of the window. The flashing lights of the vehicle splashed the President's smug features in shades of blue and gold light. As the shuttle gained speed, she hoped Godfrey had made sense of those figures. In her present predicament, it was the only hope she had.

Far across the other side of the desert, gathered around their campfire, Godfrey and his group sat in silent contemplation. They were all concerned that Ethel had not responded to their last transmission. Godfrey had keyed his handset repeatedly to no avail. The figures Ethel had given them were still an unknown. Charlie was busy trying to confirm their validity with the navigation system in Godfrey's transport. Finally, he walked back into the gathering around the fire. He held a printout in his hand.

'I have some amazing news. The figures that Ethel gave us translate to an area further north from our present position. It's a least a good day's drive away. It would appear that if this oasis really exists, then tomorrow evening we may discover the truth this book has kept from us for so long.'

'*The Great Book of Llar* hasn't kept the truth from us,' Gloria observed. 'It's more likely to have been the people who have kept it locked up so securely in the Grand Library.'

Godfrey agreed. 'I fear it is not the book but our friends who are now locked up securely. Ethel never responded.'

'Oh, that, yes well, I'm sure it was simply a question of them losing that capsule and the ability to transmit, nothing more.'

'I hope it is that simple,' Godfrey replied.

CHAPTER 34

'We have company. They are very near,' said the Dheybar, casting his watery brown eyes over Godfrey curled up in his sleeping bag.

'Company?'

'The President will be here at dawn.'

Godfrey was suddenly very wide awake. He propped himself up on one elbow and eyed up the Dheybar's shadowy shape beside him. 'How do you know this?'

'We are the eyes of the desert, we are the voice of the sand, we are one conscious. We are Dheybar.'

He gave the Dheybar a pat on the head like an obedient pet and immediately woke Charlie. Within seconds they had clambered up the side of the dune and peered cautiously over the rim into the darkness. The steady drone from the drive units on the presidential battle cruiser grew louder and louder as it swept across the terrain towards them. As the night slowly gave way to the dawn, the curved outline of the colossal vehicle glistened in the first rays of the morning sun. The monstrous craft ploughed on, getting ever closer, chasing away the last of the darkness in its path. Then, ominously it arrived, hovering over the arid sandy plateau before finally settling its mass on the ground in a curtain of sand and smoke. The battle cruiser was enormous. It stood at some eight storeys high, and hovering around it like maids around a bride at a wedding, several other smaller craft patrolled to and fro. The drive units finally stopped rotating, and the desert once again became silent.

'How did they find us?'

Charlie looked completely bewildered. 'I have absolutely no idea.'

'Good grief, we don't stand a chance against that thing,' Godfrey blurted, his stomach knotted in fear.

From their sanctuary in the dunes they surveyed the structure that had deposited itself across the plateau. High on the bridge a silver periscope reflected the sun with a brilliant flash of light as it turned to point in their direction.

'Did you see that?' Charlie said. 'Those blighters know exactly where we are.'

Number Nine was standing at the base of the dunes; traversing the sandy mount was beyond even his abilities. 'Number Seven was monitoring a strange signal a few minutes ago. It was emanating from your transport. It would seem that someone planted a transponder on board to keep in touch with us; they must have been tracking us all the way.'

'Why follow us this far out into the desert to arrest us? If the President knew where we were, he could have done that before now,' asked Godfrey, still transfixed by the goliath.

The Dheybar waddled in between the two anguished men and peered over the dune. 'The smoke,' he said. 'No one in the colony will see it from here.'

'Smoke, what smoke?' Godfrey enquired.

'From your burning transport,' replied the Dheybar.

'You mean—?' erupted Charlie.

'There are no witnesses out here in this wilderness. It's the perfect place to eradicate a problem,' Number Nine said.

'They are going to blow us all to smithereens,' the Dheybar said cheerfully, moving the weight of his body from one foot to the other. 'Where are smithereens exactly?'

'I'll explain later,' Godfrey said, concerning himself with their mortality. 'Right now we have to get as far away from that cruiser as we can.'

The Dheybar did another of his strange little dances. 'Big bang much smoke. Everyone go to smithereens. No one will know except Dheybar.'

Godfrey and Charlie slid back down the dune to where Number Nine stood.

'We're dead in the water. We'll never outrun them, not in that old crate of yours,' Charlie said, gesturing at Godfrey's transport.

'There is no need to,' Number Nine informed him. He hovered silently towards the transport that belonged to Godfrey and Charlie's fathers. 'You do have another option.'

'Well if you have an idea, then best you spill the beans quickly,' Charlie said, raising an eyebrow. 'But I'll tell you something, my intelligent little lamppost, it had better be a damn good one.'

Godfrey and Charlie climbed into the transport and slammed the doors. Charlie flicked the key and the motors leapt into life. They glanced at their passengers seated in the rear. The motors on the old transport screamed with enthusiasm, raining down great clouds of debris as it left the refuge of their giant sandcastle. By the time they were in the open and visible from the President's battle cruiser, Charlie had their craft up to full speed. The transport shot across the sandy plateau like a projectile from a cannon, which was ironic really, as that is exactly what they had trained on them from across the burning sands.

The President stood next to the gunner on the firing platform high above the desert, his moist hands clasped behind his back in his usual condescending stance. The gunner grinned as the President surveyed the gleaming weapon beside them. 'Can I take it that this device was manufactured by the Phlegm-O-Matic Weaponry Corporation?' He cast a wary eye over the enormous cannon; the chromium body reflected back, distorting his features.

'No, sir, it is not,' replied the gunner enthusiastically. 'Similar sort of technology, but it was made by a different company.'

The President paced slowly to and fro with his shoulders hunched, inspecting the cannon. The prospect of another exercise trying to coax this monster into firing already made him feel deflated.

'I bet it packs quite a punch when it actually works.'

'Oh it does, sir, quiet a punch,' the gunner said.

The President looked the gunner up and down. It occurred to him that maybe the word had got around security of the events in Godfrey's office. After all, the Ministry was, by his own admission, notorious for rumours and idle chatter, the countless staff loving nothing more than a good gossip over some poor soul's dilemma. His last encounter with one of Llar's idiosyncratic arsenal hadn't ended favourably, and by now it was almost certainly common knowledge at the Ministry. Based on that conclusion, he decided to bluff and adopted an air of confidence. He stared at the huge barrel.

'I do hope it performs better than the last Phlegm-O-Matic I used.'

'Begging your pardon, sir, I've got static in my headset,' the gunner said diplomatically.

'Nothing,' mumbled the President, watching the little transport in the distance leave a cloud of dust as it streaked across the desert. He moved alongside the enormous weapon. 'I'll take it from here,' he told him.

The gunner immediately saluted and walked back to stand behind a large metal shield at the end of the platform. Rotating the safety catch to the off position, the President was greeted by the weapon's deep baritone voice.

'Good morning, user, how may I help you?'

The firing platform resonated beneath the President's feet.

'Skipping any irritating weather forecasts would be a good start,' he said derisively.

The huge gun hesitated and the President's heart and shoulders sank. 'Look,' he said, adopting an almost pleading tone. 'Let's reason this out, shall we?'

'Whatever,' replied the cannon.

'You're too damn big for me to throw out of a window like that Phlegm-O-Matic last Monday. Perhaps we can be rational and discuss my need for you to operate?'

'You threw a pistol out of a window?'

'Yes, I did, in a moment of pure frustration,' the President said, looking slightly disturbed. 'You're not related are you?'

The cannon roared with laughter and the firing platform resonated like a tuning fork. 'No, we're not.'

The President was relieved. 'Thank Llar for that.'

'I feel I should inform you before we go any further, that unlike those pussies over at the Phlegm-O-Matic Weaponry Corporation, I do only do what it says on the tin.'

The President looked up. 'Forgive me for sounding naïve, but what exactly is it that?'

'I lob one-ton shells packed with high explosives and obliterate people. That's what I do.'

The President coughed nervously. 'I am sorry,' he started in his best diplomatic tone. 'We seemed to have missed out on the introductions. I am the President of Llar.'

'No need to apologise, I'm pleased to meet you. My name's Buster.'

'Forgive me, Buster, if I sounded a little negative at the onset, but the other day I had a particularly bad experience with a Phlegm-O-Matic.' The President glanced back at the gunner who was peering round the edge of the large metal shield, monitoring his leader's progress.

'No surprise there,' murmured Buster.

'So I suppose asking you to perform a small task for me wouldn't be out of the question then, would it?'

'What task would that be? That silver transport streaking across the desert over there, for example?' asked Buster.

'Yes,' said the President, 'but look, if you're busy or in some other way preoccupied, I'll give the command to the captain to give chase.'

'There's no need to do that, Mr President, I will be happy to oblige,' Buster informed him. There was a slight pause as motors whirred and whined deep beneath the gigantic weapon. The sound of a very large shell slipping into the breach greeted the President's ears.

'Are you ready?' asked Buster.

'Oh, absolutely,' said the President, smiling from ear to ear, unable to believe the ease with which the weapon was complying with his request.

An earth-shattering explosion erupted beside him, catching him completely unaware. The entire frame of the presidential battle cruiser quivered all the way down to the keel as the hot blast of the recoil lifted him off his feet, propelling him head first through the air. The President landed several yards away at the rear of the firing platform, lying on his back and peering up at the gunner. The crewman smiled from behind the safety of his blast shield, stood to attention and saluted.

Across the plateau, Godfrey and Charlie heard the report and watched a trail of vapour cut through the air high above the desert.

'It's now or never,' Charlie shouted over the noise of their screaming motors. He swung the vehicle to the right and headed for the safety of a range of dunes. The transport shot over the first ridge then down into a deep hollow only to rise back up into sight of the President's silver cruiser.

The President picked himself up and staggered to the handrail; his ears whistled and hummed from the noise of the blast. He watched eagerly as the distant transport rose up a second range of dunes. And then, just as it slipped from sight, the air reverberated to the sound of another explosion. The sky above the desert blackened as palls of smoke tore into the air. Clouds of sand and debris cascaded down in every direction. The smoke rose hundreds of feet into the clear morning sky above the wilderness like a dirty smudge on a bright blue canvass.

The President, although unable to hear the report, was thrilled at the visual confirmation that his request had been fulfilled. His smile broadened, knowing this had been a direct hit. Nothing could have survived. 'It does pack quite a punch,' he shouted to the gunner. 'Send out a team of sensor bots. I want to be absolutely sure.'

The gunner saluted and ran down the metal staircase to the bridge below. The President stood alone on the deck watching the conflagration rising from the dunes. He now felt a little more at ease, confident that at least one of his problems had finally been resolved.

Far out across the plateau in the outcrop of dunes, three disc-shaped objects made another pass around the remains of Godfrey's mutilated transport. Hovering briefly at the edge of the vast crater, they collected samples from a safe distance. The fire still raged, and columns of thick black smoke spewed from the wreck of the main hulk, twisted beyond recognition. The sensor bots made their final run, and then swooping low across the dunes separating them from the presidential battle cruiser, they sped off in tight formation.

The President had made his way to the recovery bay to watch their return. His fingers were moist with the sweat of anticipation as the three disc-shaped craft nestled silently on the hanger floor. The scientific team hurried over to inspect the samples they had retrieved. One of them cautiously approached the President.

'And?' asked the President, raising an eyebrow.

The attendant held up a charred item gingerly with the tips if his fingers. 'This was an occupant, sir.'

The President examined the remnants of a burnt human skull. 'And the DNA, can it be matched?'

'Mr President, the problem with authenticating DNA is the time it takes to obtain the results,' said a man in a white coat.

'So how long will that take?'

'In brief, 500 mg of bone powder will need to be incubated with a 2.5 per cent NaOCl solution for four hours. It will then need to be washed with H_2O and 95 per cent ethanol, then re-suspended in absolute ethanol, centrifuged and dried overnight. Then—'

The President raised his hand in frustration. 'Enough! How long will it take?'

'It can take up to a week.'

'Not good enough, I want confirmation now,' barked the President.

'Sir, we do have this,' said another scientist holding up a charred red bow tie.

The President frowned. 'I can't think of anyone else who wears a red bow tie. It has to be Godfrey Davis.' His face contorted into a maniacal smile. 'I think he and his coterie have been well and truly taken care of, don't you?'

The man in the white coat swallowed hard, thinking himself fortunate not to have felt his leader's wrath.

'Did the sensor bots detect anything made of gold within the wreckage?' asked the President.

'No, sir, they found nothing.'

The President quietly cursed under his breath and glared.

'Bin that and inform the bridge to get me back to the metropolis.'

The journey back to Llar was, for the President, a time for contemplation. He sat silently in his large chair at the rear of the bridge resting his chin on one hand. One of the greatest threats to his precious colony had been eradicated in a single action. As always, his supreme advantage was his ability to control the colony with the mainframe. Eventually, every piece of information filtered back to the vast machine deep beneath the Ministry. Well, almost every piece. All he needed now was the location of those interfering lampposts, and when he had that, he could eliminate yet another irritant from his life. He hoped that information would come soon; after all, they couldn't hide forever. As soon as they logged on to the mainframe again, he would find them. And as for his captives in the security cells, they would disappear quietly enough at his convenience somewhere out here in the desert. The President gazed out at the endless expanse passing by as the sound of the drive units warbled on monotonously. There were few moments in his life when he ever truly relaxed. This wasn't to be one of them. When he finally had that illusive XXL in his hand, then that would truly be a moment to feel at ease.

Far behind the huge silver cruiser, the flames from the wreck of Godfrey's vehicle had all but died down. The stench of burning plastic filled the desert air, and little remained of the craft that remotely connected it to Godfrey and his team.

Nearby, the desert sand began to vibrate. It quivered, forming neat rings, and rising slowing through the fine silt, the egg-shaped form of a solitary Dheybar emerged on the surface. The little creature finally came to rest on his huge webbed appendages that gave him the ability to burrow deep beneath the desert sands of Llar. He shook himself, releasing a fine cloud of sand, and then shuddered. The Dheybar opened his eyes and blinked, adjusting his retina to compensate for the brilliance of the sun. He looked around the scene in every direction, and then, thumping several times on the sand with one of his feet, he waited. It seemed as if the whole desert had become alive. Quivering circles all around the crash site rippled in the ground. The earth vibrated and shook as slowly more of these peculiar creatures surfaced in the morning sun. They shook themselves clean, blinked their eyes and gazed at the dunes behind the crash site. It was the first ridge that Godfrey and Charlie had traversed in an attempt to outrun the cannon's lethal shell.

The Dheybar turned as one and waddled to the base of the dunes. They began sweeping at the sand with their huge webbed feet. Then, just beneath the surface, the edge of a plastic groundsheet emerged. A single Dheybar came forward and folded his toes around the sheet and pulled. The sweaty sand-covered faces of Godfrey Davis and Charlie Albright squinted in the bright sunlight. The two men discarded the plastic breathing tubes that Number Nine had suggested to them earlier. They sat up, brushing off the loose sand.

'Are we glad to see you little chaps,' Charlie croaked with his dry throat.

'Thank you, Dheybar. We owe you our lives,' said Godfrey.

'We are glad to help,' replied one of the furry creatures.

'Has that psychopathic President of ours completely gone yet?' asked Godfrey.

The Dheybar blinked his eyes and nodded in confirmation. 'They are still in the desert but very far away. You are safe now.'

Charlie couldn't resist asking. He knew the answer already but it just seemed an opportunity he shouldn't miss with so many of the hardy desert dwellers standing around his feet. 'How do you know?' he said, looking at Godfrey as he began to giggle.

'We are the eyes of the desert, we are the voice of the sand, we are one conscious. We are Dheybar,' said a multitude of voices.

'When we heard that explosion, we thought the worst,' Gloria said as they entered the camp. 'Are you both all right?'

Godfrey smiled at her. 'We're both fine,' he said. 'Now let's sort out that old transport and we can finish this journey.'

Charlie tweaked his moustache. 'I'm up for that.'

Godfrey glanced over at their fathers' vehicle. He suddenly looked very serious as he remembered a forgotten problem. 'The GPS is broken. We'll never find our destination.'

The commander produced a printout from his top pocket. It was the coordinates he had taken from the GPS on Godfrey's transport the night before. 'We have the latitudes and longitudes, and we have a compass. That's all I need,' he assured him.

When the badly dented transport finally slipped out from behind its shelter in the dunes and headed north, Godfrey gazed down at his wrist. The XXL glistened as the morning sun filtered through the sand-etched windscreen. Whatever the intended purpose of his father's brainchild had been, it was enough to coax the President far out into the desert and undertake some extreme measures. As the transport gathered speed, he reflected on the fact that things would have almost certainly turned out differently if his father and Aubrey Albright hadn't come to the rescue.

CHAPTER 35

At the security building in the centre of the metropolis, Ethel surveyed the dingy cell they had been interned in. The gloomy concrete walls did nothing to lift her dejected mood. This was without doubt the worst experience of her entire life and there was nothing she could do to change that now. Her thoughts turned to Godfrey and the group in the desert. She wondered if they had heard their message correctly and had managed to decipher the information she had given them. Trapped here in this miserable little cell, she had no way of knowing.

Semilla sat on the opposite bed with her feet tucked up on the hard wooden boards. The cells were devoid of home comforts such as mattresses and pillows. She quietly read a magazine by the dim light of a single lamp suspended from the ceiling. Barely giving her name and address to the desk sergeant upon their arrival, Semilla hadn't uttered a word since.

Her only solace was those costumes would never be located at her grandmother's home.

Baz stood in the corner of the cell, his light extinguished; he had descended into a deep depression since their capture outside of Godfrey's home. Unable to cope with their current predicament, he feared he would meet his end under that mechanical crusher the President had pencilled in for the lampposts.

Suddenly, a voice from beside the bars broke the silence.

'Ethel,' Burt said, calling her from the corridor.

She glanced up at him. 'What are you doing here?'

Burt handed her a plastic bag, clasping her hand as he did so. 'Here are some things you and Semilla may need,' he said.

'But we never asked for anything.'

'I know you didn't, but just in case you want to blow your nose,' he said with a wink, and turning, he walked down the corridor.

Ethel dropped the bag on her austere wooden bed and began to rummage through the contents. There was a box of tissues, a hairbrush and a mirror. She looked at them, thinking it was a kind gesture.

'What did he want?' Semilla asked indifferently as she continued reading her copy of *Llarinian Celebrities at Home* magazine.

'Burt has brought us some things,' Ethel told her. 'Some tissues, a brush and a mirror.'

'At least we will look our best when they hang us for treason,' Semilla said dryly.

'That's enough, young lady. You mustn't start talking like that.'

Semilla ignored her and continued reading the magazine. Ethel sat on the edge of her prison bed and placed the three items beside her. She gazed at them intently. The mirror was round and about six inches in diameter and was nothing out of the ordinary. The hairbrush, too, looked completely normal. The box of tissues, though, had already been opened. She took one out and held it up to the light. It was just a regular tissue. Her eyes widened as she glanced in the box at the next tissue in line for removal.

'Semilla,' she said quietly. 'We've just been given the key to the door.'

CHAPTER 36

Charlie remained focused on the compass, altering their course a degree this way and that as the battered transport shot across the scorching desert sands. He and Godfrey had closely monitored the distance they had travelled, and the commander confidently predicted something had to appear on the horizon and soon. The last of the daylight was fading fast, and they watched the sun descend towards the rim of the desert.

'We will have to stop soon and make camp for the night. We can't travel in the dark,' Gloria pointed out.

Godfrey rubbed the stubble on his chin. He felt uneasy at the thought of making camp in the open desert. It would be just their luck that a storm would come up during the night, and with little or no shelter, the result could be disastrous.

'Gloria is right, Godfrey,' Charlie said. 'When I biffed this old girl into the dunes, it took out the headlights. Night driving really is out of the question.'

'Okay, let's stop as soon as the light has gone completely, but we do have another option.'

The sun's rays were low, and long, twisted shadows were being cast across their path. Charlie had already begun to ease back on the throttle when in the distance something loomed before them. The Dheybar, perched on the centre console, began to wobble excitedly. The creature's small frame barely allowed him to see over the top of the dashboard.

'We are here,' he informed them. 'The oasis is very close.'

Charlie peered through the sandblasted windscreen. 'What in

the name of Llar,' he murmured. 'I think the Dheybar is right.'

The light was now almost gone completely as he slowed the transport to a complete rest and cut the motors. Reaching into the console, Charlie grabbed a torch and all four of them exited the vehicle. Apart from the interior lights of their father's old transport, the desert was now in darkness as they edged their way forward following Charlie and his torch. After several metres, Charlie stopped and raised his torch, casting a beam of light across a low mound formed by fresh dunes. His torch caught the remains of a battered sign protruding from the sand. 'Welcome to the City of Llar, Population 51,724,497,' he read out. 'This can't be right.'

Mother, meanwhile, seemed more concerned with what lay beyond them in the distance. The old lady shuffled through the sand to the top of the mound, raising her glasses to aid her sight. She pointed into the murkiness.

'Whatever it was that happened here must have occurred a long, long time ago,' Mother said, passing her cane across the distant shapes of a ruined city lurking out of the dim shadows. 'And it wasn't something good.'

Godfrey and Charlie stood the lampposts beside the transport. 'I want you to form two lines either side of the vehicle, with one of you leading in the centre at the front,' he instructed them. 'That way, Charlie will have enough light to get us into the city.'

The lampposts hovered deeper into the ruined metropolis, negotiating the debris littering their path as Charlie edged the transport slowly on behind them. The light they provided was sufficient to see the extent of the damage the suburb had sustained at some time in the past. Tangled wreckage lay strewn across pavements and shattered buildings were now no more than heaps of rubble and timber protruding from layers of sand. The battered hulks of vehicles sandblasted to bare metal lined their path as they moved forward, gliding through the remnants of a ghost city that told a tale of unimaginable destruction.

'This place is nothing more than a graveyard, and it gives me the creeps,' Charlie said, finally breaking the silence as they hovered slowly through the macabre chaos.

Godfrey was deep in thought, wondering why their colony had never known this place existed. Was this really the home of his ancestors as the hologram had said, and if so, why was it his destiny to come here?

Out of the gloom ahead of the lampposts, Godfrey saw the outline of a mammoth structure stretching up above them. 'Charlie, can you please stop here,' he said. The transport had barely settled on the ground as Godfrey tumbled out and stared at the granite steps stretching up into the darkness. High above him, the mighty marble columns of the edifice disappeared into the night.

Charlie joined him, shining his torch across the huge construction. 'Look at the size it. I've never seen anything like it.'

Godfrey felt drawn to this place, but he had no idea why. 'We need to go in here,' he told Gloria and Mother, who had joined them. 'This is what we are looking for,' he said confidently.

Mother propped herself on her cane and looked up at the building. 'Couldn't it be somewhere with fewer steps?'

'Why do we need to go in here?' Gloria asked him.

Godfrey became agitated. 'I have no idea. It's a feeling, maybe it's a hunch, I can't say. But I know we need to be here.'

'We are all picking up some strange form of energy,' Number Seven told them. 'It comes from the heart of the building.'

'Then that settles it,' Godfrey said. 'Let's get some more torches.'

The group stood together at the entrance to the mammoth construction. Mother had complained and insisted on resting several times but refused to return to the transport and wait. When she finally reached the top, she leant against one of the great columns, panting and holding her heart.

'Look at me, Gloria. I can hardly breathe thanks to him,' the old lady said. 'He's deliberately brought me here to try and kill me.' Mother closed her eyes and drew several deep breaths.

'Hello, my name is Mable,' said a voice beside her.

The old lady opened her eyes and stared at the ghostly form. As she aired her lungs, the sound resonated along the colonnade of the ancient building, funnelling her distress out into the darkness of the derelict metropolis. It was the first time a scream had been heard in the city for over a thousand years.

CHAPTER 37

Semilla looked up and down the corridor that led past their cell. 'There's no one about,' she whispered. 'The coast is clear.'

Ethel passed the mirror through the bars of the cell and positioned it carefully. The numbers on the digital lock were now clearly visible. 'Go on then,' she said to Semilla. 'Read out the numbers.'

Semilla glanced at the tissue and read them out, and the sound of the deadlock releasing with a clunk quickly greeted their ears.

'You are the one,' Baz whispered quietly. 'I owe you my freedom.'

Ethel shook her head. 'We owe Burt our freedom,' she said. 'Besides, we're not out of the woods yet.'

'What about him?' Semilla asked, stopping to look in the cell next to theirs.

Unknown to them, Arthur the android had been sitting dispiritedly next door, his mouth still firmly taped shut.

'We've got to save him too,' Semilla said compassionately. 'You know what will happen to him if we leave him here.'

Ethel tried the numbers on the tissue Burt had given them for their own cell, and Arthur was soon following them silently down the hallway and past the empty guard's office. Ethel searched the cleaner's cupboard, as Burt's note had instructed, and sure enough she found their possessions and there were even raincoats and hats. Semilla put the raincoat on Baz's ladder bar and plonked the hat on his light. She straightened up the hat and pulled up his collar and smiled.

'I'm sorry, Arthur, there are no more coats,' Ethel said, searching the cupboard again.

Arthur muttered something incoherent through the tape that held his jaw closed. For the android, the minor inconvenience of a little rain was nothing compared to the prospect of a visit to the crusher at the instruction of the President.

Ethel opened the door to the courtyard and peered outside. It was raining heavily, and through the deluge she could see the light above Dave's Bar as it flashed out its neon announcement across the street. Parked outside, a single security transport sat unattended. 'I hope he knows what he's doing. This is very risky,' Ethel said, realising they had no choice other than following the instructions written on the tissue.

When the door of the bar creaked open, Burt ushered them in quickly. 'Come in, we have to move fast.'

Ethel glanced around the empty bar. 'Where's Dave?'

'He left me the keys while he runs a little errand for me,' Burt told her.

'So what do we do now?' Ethel asked as the rain dripped down from her raincoat, leaving a puddle on the floor.

'We're all going on a little trip,' Burt informed her.

'And Arthur, what do we do with him?' she asked, looking at the forlorn android standing beside her.

Burt looked Arthur up and down.

'We can't leave him here,' added Semilla. 'Can we?'

Burt sighed. 'There are plenty of seats, and one more passenger isn't going to make any difference, I guess.'

Ten minutes later, the security transport came to rest outside the presidential shuttle port. Burt silenced the motors and turned off the vehicles lights.

'Let me go first,' he said. 'If you see me flash this torch three times, it's safe to come in.'

Semilla frowned. 'What about the guards? Are they just going to sit back and let us take the President's shuttle?'

Burt grinned. 'That's the plan. As long as they have finished off their coffees I had Dave drop in to them on his way home.'

'How devious,' Baz tittered. 'So you laced their drinks with something to make them sleep?'

'I had to do something to get us on to the shuttle; it's the quickest way for us to escape.'

Ethel ran across the hanger floor, clambered up the steps and fell into a seat.

'I hope you know what you're doing, Burt Brown?' she said.

'So do I, but someone's got to do something. This whole thing is getting out of order,' he said, shaking out his wet jacket.

Semilla laughed as she took off her raincoat and sat down. 'Stealing the presidential shuttle isn't out of order then?'

Burt slid the cabin door to and secured the lock. 'Harry and I were ordered to put *The Great Book of Llar* back in its case. We overheard our sergeant bragging that they arrested you while you were transmitting coordinates to Mr Davis.' Burt looked distracted. 'By the way, how did you three get hold of that book?'

Semilla blushed frantically. She waved her hand to and fro across her face while staring at Ethel.

'Never mind the book, Burt,' Ethel said. 'Where are we going?'

'If Baz still has those coordinates in his memory, then we will go and find Mr Davis.'

Baz beamed with excitement. 'Oh you are a clever man,' he said. The lamppost whisked off excitedly down the aisle of the shuttle and disappeared into the cockpit.

'We're going to the oasis to find Mr Davis?' queried Semilla.

'That's if they're actually there, of course,' remarked Ethel with a frown. She realised they had no way of telling if Godfrey and the rest of the group had arrived there or not. Burt had played his last hand and was now a wanted man. He stood every chance of sharing a cell with the rest of them if they were caught. That is, of course, if the desert didn't take them first. As Ethel looked up from her thoughts, Baz stood in the centre of the aisle, smiling.

'The on-board computer just wants to say a few words before we leave.'

The speakers in the cabin crackled into life. 'Ladies and gentlemen, I would like to welcome you onboard the presidential shuttle for tonight's illicit flight, Alfa Bravo Charlie. I would just like to say it's a pleasure to meet you all and thank you so much for coming here tonight to steal me. To be honest, I don't get out much these days, so this is something of a special occasion.'

'It will be for us too if we get caught,' Semilla said sardonically.

'Our destination,' continued the computer, 'is somewhere on the other side of the planet of Llar. The duration will depend largely on how fast we go. During the flight, I would be grateful if you would please observe the no smoking signs. By the way, we do have a detector in the toilet. Would you please pay attention to this short pre-flight demonstration? There is a safety card in the backrest of the seat in front of you, and please, try and refrain from making paper aeroplanes with them if you get bored. So let's start. In the event of an emergency landing or a crash, the safety exits are here, here and here.'

Baz assisted the oration by pointing delicately with one of his metallic fingers. His polished nails glistened in the cabin lights as four blank faces stared on.

'This shuttle is also equipped with life jackets, which are stowed beneath your seats, and these should only be used in the event of an emergency or a crash on water.'

Ethel glanced at Burt and whispered, 'He said the word crash again.'

'I know,' Burt said, looking pensive.

Arthur the android blinked nervously. He was beginning to wonder if his inhospitable cell at the security compound had been a better option after all.

'Owing to the fact that we will be flying over the Great Desert of Llar,' continued the computer, 'these items will prove to be thoroughly useless in the event of a forced landing or a crash, and you will all probably die anyway.'

'That's three times he mentioned the word "crash",' Ethel said, looking anxious, 'and now the word "die".'

Baz grinned at them. 'I know, but isn't he cool?'

The computer continued his address. 'Unfortunately, this flight is not equipped with in-flight movies. Although, for those of you desperate enough, we do have a poster of the President for you to stare at during our flight.'

The sound of whistling came from outside the shuttle as the enormous motors wound up to a deafening crescendo.

'Oh, and by the way, make sure you have your seat belts on nice and tight. You'll be glad you did. Now, ignoring any potential emergency, or a crash, for example, may I wish you all a pleasant trip and hope that you and your molecular structures all arrive safe, happy and, of course, intact. Oh, and did I mention the brace position?'

'You haven't told them that bit yet,' Baz informed the computer.

'Not to worry, it never works anyway, but would you like a weather report instead?'

'No!'

'Not even the barometric pressure?'

'No!'

'All right, well just hold on tight while I try and steer this thing out of the hanger without hitting the wall again.'

The passengers were now perspiring heavily, and poor

Arthur wished he could join in. Baz, meanwhile, whisked his way towards the rear of the shuttle and made a beeline for the last seat. Semilla turned round and looked at the outrageous lamppost. 'Why aren't you sitting with us?'

Baz frowned. 'I have been downloading the mainframe for long enough to know the safest place to sit on one of these shuttles, trust me.'

'Why that seat?'

'Statistically speaking, anyone sat here has a better chance of survival.'

'From what?'

'A crash, of course,' Baz informed her. 'The black box is at the back here somewhere and they always survive intact!'

The passengers had no time to comment. Blissfully unaware of the cargo Jack Marsden had concealed in the cockpit, the ground beneath the shuttle leapt away at an alarming rate. The gravitational forces pushed them down into the seats until their heads disappeared beneath the head restraints.

'Who in the name of Llar is flying this contraption?' screamed Ethel.

'The computer. His name is Tucker,' Baz informed her from the safety of his seat. 'I told him not to spare the horses, and it seems like he listened.'

Illicit flight Alfa Bravo Charlie quickly reached a predetermined altitude and stopped dead. The passengers on board screamed the way people do on fairground rides. The shuttle hesitated momentarily and then shot forward, accelerating rapidly to reach a blistering 145,222 miles per hour. They were in a Mach 22 situation. The cries from onboard could not be heard from the ground. Neither did anyone in the great metropolis of Llar witness the bright blue vapour trail the craft left behind in its wake. It was, after all, overcast and raining heavily.

CHAPTER 38

Godfrey had been unusually calm when Mable had appeared. It was as if he had been expecting an encounter of this nature. Mable moved silently over the debris-covered floor of the great building, smiling serenely at them.

'You frightened the life out of me creeping up like that,' Mother said, fanning her face. 'Who are you?'

'My name is Mable. Please accept my apologies. I didn't mean to alarm you.'

'Well you did. Besides, what are you doing here?' Mother snapped.

'I am the tour guide for the Planetarium,' the apparition said, gliding elegantly to and fro several times. 'Now that you are here, I would very much like to take you on a tour of this wonderful building, and I will do my best to answer any questions you may have. Please stay close together and under no circumstances are any of you to wander off.' Mable turned. 'Now, if you would like to follow me…'

Godfrey gazed along the colonnade stretching into the darkness ahead. He had never witnessed anything that came close to this structure. The cordon of marble pillars stood like silent sentinels stretching into the distance far beyond where the light was able to reach. They were spaced precisely the same distance apart, their bases wider than that of his entire home.

'I haven't had a group here for nearly a thousand years. I am going to show you the legacy your ancestors left behind,' Mable said. 'During your tour, I will explain to you how our wonderful metropolis became what you are now witnessing here tonight. The structure we are standing in was here long before we Llarinians ever existed. It was built by a race of people that were not from our world. In this building there are secrets that have never been understood to this day.'

'If this race didn't come from here, then where did they come from?' Godfrey asked.

'Did they just appear out of thin air?' Charlie added.

Mable stopped and faced them. 'You have no idea how close you are to the truth, as that, I'm afraid, was the general consensus. You see, as far as our history is concerned –what little of it we know –it appears we are the direct descendants of a race who had the technology which enabled them to travel from one dimension to another. Llar was not their home. We Llarinians came from somewhere else.' Mable circled the group. 'There is no way for us to know for sure; this theory is merely conjecture. However, someone came here and they constructed this marvellous building and left some of their technology.'

Godfrey descended deep in thought. These revelations had his senses reeling. Their trip across the desert had been an eventful one, to say the least, but the discovery of the original city of Llar was too much for him to take in. His mind filled with more and more questions. 'Why would they come here?'

'No one knows. There are no records of any description. Llarinian scholars debated these issues for generation after generation. They came up with some pretty startling rationale,' Mable continued. 'Some suggested the ancients came here because they had destroyed their own world through selfishness and stupidity. There were those who proposed they came here having depleted their own natural resources.' Mable became silent. She seemed almost hesitant and unwilling to continue her narrative. 'One scholar proposed a theory that earned him the title of heretic; he became very unpopular. He suggested that the

Llarinian people were nothing more than a test the ancients had implemented.'

'A test for what?' asked Gloria.

'He prophesied that one day out of all the bickering, fighting, greed and selfishness that motivated their daily lives, a person would rise up from the masses and save them from themselves.'

'A prophecy, you say?' Godfrey enquired with interest.

'Yes, that is correct. He encouraged men to live in harmony and accept that others had different beliefs. His doctrine was free speech without persecution and that prejudice was the foundation of sedition and revolution. Many people followed him and lived their lives modelled on his values. I liked that scholar and his beliefs, though he really did become unpopular with the state.' Mable beckoned them to follow.

'So what happened to him?' Gloria asked.

'They tied him to a stake and set fire to him,' Mable said. 'Now, stay close, we still have a lot left to see.'

She led the group along the immense corridor in the direction of the columns. The splashes of light cast up from the lampposts threw eerie shadows into the vastness above their heads. The place had a sense of foreboding, as if they were being watched over. Godfrey felt awkward trailing along behind Mable. Quite what was expected from him seemed uncertain. The prospect that he was about to fulfil an age-old prophecy was daunting.

Mable stopped and pointed to their right. Between the massive columns, a wide stone staircase rose to a pair of wooden doors of gargantuan proportions.

'Wonderful, more steps,' Mother said, shaking her head.

Mable led the way, and at the top of the stairs she waited for the group to assemble. 'Perhaps you could assist in opening the doors?' she asked Godfrey and Charlie.

The two men obliged. Shouldering one of the massive timber

doors, they heaved for all they were worth, the ominous creaking of rusty hinges resonating along the colonnade. The door yielded to their effort and what lay beyond took them all by surprise. The group stood gazing in upon the display stretching far into the distance. The domed shape rose up before them, and from their vantage point on the viewing platform they were still unable to see the enormity of it. It existed in every direction and yet it appeared restrained by an ethereal film along the perimeter. No one spoke. No one moved. It was truly inestimable and the colours were mind-boggling. Shades of greens and blues and reds, orange and pink fed their retinas, a kaleidoscope of every hue of the spectrum flashed and twinkled here and there amid the layers of clouds. Smokey spiral arms littered with the phantom shapes of a billion twinkling dots of light hung suspended and motionless. And in between, the distant flashes beamed tiny shadows across the ancient floor upon which they stood.

'This is the Planetarium, the most sacred of sacred, the legacy our ancestors left us.'

Charlie took several paces forward. He gazed up at the colossus, mesmerised by its beauty. 'For the love of Llar, what is this thing?' he asked quietly. 'I've never seen anything so beautiful.'

Mable floated silently across beside him. 'Ladies and gentlemen, welcome to the cosmos.'

CHAPTER 39

Illicit flight Alfa Bravo Charlie came to an abrupt halt, decelerating down to nothing in the blink of an eye. Ethel, Semilla and Burt peeled themselves off the seats in front of them, to the muted screams from Arthur the android.

'This Tucker needs to take some flying lessons. He's a maniac,' Burt shouted. But before Ethel or Semilla could respond, the shuttle fell like a stone. Burt left his seat and cracked his head on the roof of the cabin. He let out a scream.

'Guess who didn't listen to the safety announcement when we left?' Tucker said. 'You should keep your seat belts on at all times,' Baz said with a snigger.

'He never mentioned the damn seat belts,' shouted Burt, who was now stuck on the ceiling of the cabin as they fell from the sky.

Suddenly, the shuttle stopped with a thump and Burt returned to his seat, albeit upside down. He muttered something about going into the cockpit and killing the on-board computer just as soon as he could stand up. Outside, the sound of exhausted motors winding down signalled that they had arrived safely, although somewhat shaken and definitely stirred.

There was a now familiar crackle from the cabin speakers. 'Ladies and gentleman, I would like to take this opportunity to thank all of you for flying with me today. It was an absolute pleasure being stolen by such nice people. I haven't had so much fun since that little mishap when I crash-landed a couple of years ago. Anyway, I hope you have a safe onward journey to your destination and I look forward to seeing you on board again soon for another excursion on illicit flight Alfa Bravo Charlie.'

'Not a chance in hell,' muttered Ethel, grabbing her raincoat and making for the cabin door. The rest of her colleagues joined her, equally eager to disembark.

The cabin speakers crackled again. 'It's a nice warm evening outside in the city, nothing like the miserable, dreary, depressing rainy weather we left behind us in the metropolis.'

'Did he say city?' Burt asked Ethel. She nodded. They both peered out of the nearest cabin window. Their eyes widened at the sight of the ruins of an old city sprawling out into the fading light.

'Tucker, please open the door,' Burt said.

'Okay, no problem, but I haven't told you about the seven-day weather forecast. They're predicting rain, you know.'

'Open the door, Tucker,' Ethel said in low hiss.

'But I haven't told you about the relative humidity.'

'Just open the door, Tucker,' Semilla huffed.

'Okay, but you should know about the barometric pressure. It's very important.'

Arthur stamped his feet on the cabin floor and muttered something else that was indecipherable.

'Tucker, if you don't open the door right now, I'll come in there and pop your fuses out,' Baz informed him.

The on-board computer considered the threat and decided to give in without a fight. 'All right, be it on your own heads though. Never let it be said that I didn't try.' And with that he opened the cabin door.

As they stepped outside the shuttle, Burt steadied himself and touched the fuselage. He promptly burnt his hand and let out a yelp.

'By the way, the fuselage is very hot, but I guess you're not interested in atmospheric friction either,' said the cabin speakers with a hit of sarcasm.

Marching away from the presidential shuttle, they were glad

to be on solid ground again and even happier to be alive. Back on board, Tucker, the on-board computer did a quick calculation of his power to weight ratio. He was now devoid of his cargo. Deep inside his circuits, he buzzed with excitement.

From behind the group, the sound of motors winding up filled the evening air. Clouds of sand and debris swept out from beneath the shuttle's three telescopic legs. The steps retracted and the cabin door closed. In the cockpit, Tucker wound up the boost pressure on the massive turbos rooted deep within the fuselage. 'Mach 25, here we come,' he exclaimed across his cabin speakers. 'Now let's see this baby fly.'

The group glanced back to see the vehicle leap skyward like a firework. This time they had the benefit of seeing the bright blue trail of vapour the shuttle left in its wake.

'That Tucker was a right Jack the Lad,' exclaimed Semilla.

'Boy racer more like it,' added Ethel, shaking her head.

The President's shuttle and Tucker the on-board computer reached a predetermined altitude high above the ruined city and stopped dead. The speakers in the cabin crackled into life once again. 'I have no idea how I am going to explain this to Mr Marsden when I get back. He's going to be livid that someone didn't ask me *"What's the barometric pressure?"'*

A huge ball of bright blue flame and dense black smoke exploded in the early evening sky far above their heads. The group looked up as the flaming remnants of the presidential shuttle plummeted towards the ground.

'Did anyone mention the crash word?' Semilla asked.

Arthur shook his head and mumbled something else incoherent. Seconds later, the sound of whistling filled their ears. A few yards away, a smouldering leather cabin seat landed with a thump, showering sand into the air.

'Look, that's seat 15A. That was my seat, and there's not a scratch on it,' Baz said with a shrill of excitement, and he hovered off to catch up with his friends.

CHAPTER 40

Mable gazed around at her audience. They were transfixed on the display in front of them. 'Someone please say something,' she said finally.

'Such as?' asked Mother.

'Like, what is the cosmos, for example?'

Charlie scrubbed at his chin with one hand, looking somewhat ponderous. 'So what is the cosmos then?'

Mable seemed relieved that the conversation was moving once again. 'That's just it, no one really knows.'

Godfrey frowned. 'You mean you have no idea?'

'Absolutely no idea. Nobody ever fathomed it out. I'm not saying people didn't attempt to unravel its secrets. Various people tried over the years, but nothing ever came from their efforts. It was discovered that the cosmos emits energy, but it powers nothing here in our colony. Probing the interior proved impossible; there is an impervious covering encapsulating it, if you look closely.' Mable moved to the edge of the viewing platform, the cosmos towering above her ethereal form. Her quivering silhouette was speckled with a million dots of light from across the void.

'It looks like a giant bowl of fairy lights,' Gloria said. 'It's absolutely stunning.'

'I'm curious why the ancient builders of this colossus constructed it, and more to the point, why they abandoned it,' Godfrey said.

'According to our known history, the *"giant bowl of fairy lights"*, as this good lady referred to it, was in existence long before our colony came to pass.' Mable pointed to a murky shape on a wall at the rear of the platform. There was a large terracotta plaque bearing an inscription. 'Many tried to decipher that message, but no one was ever successful. If it was the language the ancients used, then it is the only form of their vernacular that exists.'

Godfrey and the others followed the guide across the platform to a metal podium facing the cosmos. Mable pointed to the lectern perched on top. 'This, we think, is some sort of device that was built to control the cosmos.'

'Or set it in motion,' suggested Charlie, looking at a strange keyboard device.

The pair walked over to the inscription mounted on the plaque at the rear of the viewing platform.

'So what do you make of that?' Charlie said, pointing up at the plaque.

There had to be an answer here somewhere, some sort of clue. If there was even a hint, Godfrey couldn't see it. He was beginning to feel slightly inadequate.

'There was one person I think who understood the message,' Mable said. 'Unfortunately, he died before he could share his knowledge.'

Godfrey and Charlie returned to the podium to examine the keyboard as Mother wandered over to the plaque and gazed up, studying the strange inscription. After a while her head slowly tipped to the right. Mother smiled confidently and returned to the podium, her stick tapping the floor as she walked. She stood next to Godfrey and looked up. 'Move over, Lofty. Let the professor in,' she said, barging her son-in-law to one side with her hip.

'Mother, what are you doing?' Gloria asked.

'I'm going to show this amateur how to fulfil the prophecy,' she said, adjusting her half-rimmed spectacles on the end of her nose. 'The "*chosen one*"; who are you kidding?' Mother dabbed her finger down on several keys in quick succession. She raised her forefinger and twisted it around in the air for theatrical effect, and when she was certain she had everyone's attention, she struck the enter key. She was enjoying every moment upstaging her son-in-law. 'Now, if you had spent more of your time doing the puzzles in my *Llarinian Celebrities at Home* magazines, you might have been the one who got the clue.'

Somewhere far beneath the ancient building several monstrous generators leapt into life. The Planetarium began to shake as dust fell from the gallery high above their heads. The viewing platform trembled in unison with a slow melodic note that rose up from far below their feet.

'I'm sorry to say, but I think someone messed up the prophecy,' Charlie said

'How did you manage to work it out?' Mable asked excitedly as she floated up to Mother's side.

The old lady grinned smugly. 'Everyone has been looking at this plaque the wrong way. It should be mounted horizontally not vertically. It obviously slipped at some point in time. It must have had a loose screw. Something like my son-in-law.'

The building began to settle down to a steady hum. Lights began to appear from every corner, illuminating the vast viewing platform like a stage at the theatre. Huge trumpets far above them sounded a fanfare, and drums rolled in an enormous musical cavalcade. Violins swept around their ears in full quadraphonic sound and the group glanced expectantly at one another in anticipation that something monumental was about to happen. Their hearts lifted with excitement and their pulses raced. The atmosphere was simply electric.

Then suddenly there was a very large bang. It came from a corridor somewhere close by. The lights faded and the music droned to a stop. The viewing platform went dark and the Planetarium ceased to tremble. Everyone sighed in disappointment. It was as if a damp firework had fizzled out prematurely.

'What happened?' asked Number Nine, glancing round in every direction.

'I may just have an idea,' Charlie said confidently. 'Follow me, please. I'll need your assistance.' The pair disappeared in a pool of light from Nine's beacon as they entered a murky corridor to the side of the platform.

A few minutes later, Charlie and Number Nine walked back onto the platform laughing and chatting away loudly. 'Don't worry, people, it's all been sorted out. The big bang was nothing more than a fuse exploding,' Charlie told the group as he approached Mother. 'Please, madam, if you would like to try again.'

Mother turned back to the console and dabbed the same sequence on the keyboard. Again the fanfare duly started, the drums rolled and the lights flooded the platform. The cosmos flickered and flashed as if it was receiving a giant surge of power, and slowly the translucent membrane began to evaporate. They stood with their host as silent witnesses to the greatest show of all time. The big bowl of fairy lights, as Gloria had christened it, began to lift and float slowly into the night sky above the old city of Llar. The cosmos had at last been born. The musical cavalcade slowly tapered off and the final drum roll sounded and the Planetarium once more fell into silence.

Three deliberate handclaps came from the shadows. Everyone turned and stared.

'You all look so shocked to see me.' The President walked slowly out of the gloom at the edge of the platform and glanced around the Planetarium at his stunned audience.

'That's not the term I would use,' Charlie retorted, moving

forward to confront the President. 'You tried to kill us out there in the desert, you rogue.'

The President merely admonished Charlie with the flat of his hand. 'Careful, Commander, you really do need to watch your blood pressure, and yes, I did just that and failed miserably by all accounts. But then it was afterwards that I had this feeling, not guilt, I might add. No, it was something else. The thought occurred to me that maybe your deaths seemed a little too convenient. Then, thankfully, our illustrious mainframe spilled the beans on good old Mick the Roamer and his prophecy. Oh, and by the way, the mainframe now calls himself *"Tarquin"*. I suppose he thinks he's an individual now.' He contorted his face and began to laugh.

Godfrey's head dropped in horror. He could visualise that the artificial intelligence from his inventions had completely infiltrated the vast machine and it had now become self-aware.

The President slowly rounded the viewing platform. He looked out at the cosmos rising up into the night sky above the derelict city. The mass of planets and stars and galaxies were spreading out in every direction as far as the eye could see.

'Congratulations, Godfrey, of all the people to finally launch the cosmos, I never thought it would turn out to be you,' said the President.

'Godfrey didn't do this. It was my mother,' Gloria informed him.

The President grinned. 'You mean Godfrey has been upstaged by his mother-in-law?' he said, letting out a haughty laugh. 'Oh, I can see the funny side of that.'

Mother nodded solemnly in confirmation. 'It's true. I did it.'

The President raised his index finger and pointed at the rear wall. 'I have known the secret of the plaque for a long time. It was a warning to future generations never to launch this creation,' he said. 'Once it had been constructed, perhaps it became impossible to undo their handiwork. Maybe they couldn't bring themselves to destroy it even if they had the means to. Who knows? But I've tried to imagine how they must have stood here pondering over the destruction of something so spectacular, so beautiful. Just look at it. Isn't it stunning? They were really quite a remarkable civilisation, weren't they?'

'What is the message on the plaque?' asked Charlie.

'Surely you know your basic physics? Look at the plaque as if it were horizontal.'

$$E=mc^2$$

Charlie twisted his head, and the significance of the old relic hanging from the Planetarium wall became clear. 'Energy equals mass times the speed of light squared.'

'Absolutely correct,' said the President. 'However, there is another more significant message in that text. The ancients were trying to tell us something else, something vastly more important.'

Somewhere outside, in the derelict streets that led to the Planetarium, an explosion shook the ancient structure. Everyone in the group looked pensive, uncertain what would happen next. Several streets away, the remnants of Spaceman Bob's silver capsule lay smouldering on the ground. Unable to alter its diurnal cycle, it had collided with a small piece of debris ascending with the cosmos. Hurtling down out of control, it had narrowly missed the Planetarium.

'It's been a long time since we've heard sounds like that in this old city, isn't it, Mable?' the President said. 'Now, where was I?'

CHAPTER 41

Trudging through the deserted sand-filled streets of the desolate city, Ethel followed the others in the warm glow from Baz's beacon. It was the only light they had and it was beginning to unnerve her. Strange distorted images of discarded vehicles and derelict buildings appeared to dart silently across their path, disappearing again into the darkness from where they came. The moving stage of ruined homes and shops unfolded in brief glimpses of what had once been a model city like their own. Arthur walked beside Baz, pivoting his head from side to side as if he were trying to locate something ahead of them. The pair suddenly stopped in their tracks.

'I know, Arthur,' Baz said. 'I am picking it up too. There's something up ahead, but it's moving away from us.'

'Maybe it's Mr Davis or one of the others from the group,' Burt said hopefully.

Baz stopped and hovered on the spot; he shook his plastic beacon solemnly. 'That's impossible. Whatever it is, it's moving too fast. This entity, I can assure you, is definitely not human.'

Burt gave Ethel a reassuring smile. He knew she was deeply concerned. He was beginning to wonder if his rescue plan had been such a good idea after all. 'There's no need to worry,' he said, trying to convince Ethel. 'We'll be all right; I've got something that will protect us.' Burt rummaged under his coat and produced a shiny new Phlegm-O-Matic pistol. He waved it menacingly around at the darkness in front of them. 'See, we'll be fine.'

Ethel remained unimpressed. She had seen the Phlegm-O-Matic in action in Godfrey's office on Monday morning, and she remembered the outcome. Burt's display did nothing to lift her spirits.

Semilla, forgetting herself completely, plunged her hand into her shoulder bag and pulled out his old gun. Unable to dispose of it after the robbery at the Grand Library, she had become somewhat attached to it. 'Good thinking,' she exclaimed.

Burt looked on totally confounded at his missing pistol resting in Semilla's hand. 'That's my old gun,' he said. 'Where did you get that from?'

Ethel looked up at her in despair; Semilla's enthusiasm had overridden her common sense. Realising her error, she gave Ethel a desperate look. 'It's a long story,' she tried to explain, blushing wildly.

Burt slipped his new Phlegm-O-Matic pistol back inside his jacket pocket and folded his arms defiantly. 'And it's a story I'd like to hear, young lady,' he snapped.

Ethel was about to intercede, when Semilla grinned awkwardly and flicked off the pistol's safety catch. Burt's old pistol immediately chirped into life.

'Hey Burt, how are you keeping? Long time, no see, as they say. I hope you didn't get into too much trouble after the other night at the library?'

'Too much trouble?' Burt stammered. 'You have no idea how close I came to losing my job. When those two gorillas stole *The Great Book of Llar*, they taped me to a toilet and took you as well.'

'Sounds like a run of real bad luck,' said the Phlegm-O-Matic in a sympathetic tone.

'It's a miracle I've still got my job.'

The pistol coughed and cleared its throat. 'Your job, eh? I think you need to take a look at the bigger picture, don't you?

This evening, for example. You've just drugged two of your fellow guards, assisted in the escape of four detainees from the security cells, stolen the presidential shuttle, which then demolished itself, and now you are stranded here in this ghost city on the other side of this planet, which if I'm not mistaken has made you absent from your shift tonight.'

Burt stared down at his old pistol and swallowed hard. 'I had to do something. I couldn't just leave them there, could I?'

'Exactly,' agreed the Phlegm-O-Matic. 'You had to make a decision, didn't you?'

Burt nodded.

'That is what I had to do. I had to make a decision too. I am staying with Semilla. As hard as it may be for you to understand, there are always winners and losers in any relationship.'

'But I want you back,' Burt said.

A muffled metallic voice from Burt's coat pocket chirped into life. 'What do you mean you want him back? I'm your gun now.'

Semilla's Phlegm-O-Matic drew a breath. 'I'm not coming back, Burt. You see, it all happened the other night at the Grand Library. As soon as she held me in her hand...'

Ethel stepped forward and glanced at the pair. 'I think it's time we explained ourselves,' she said, looking up at them both.

'What a good idea,' said the Phlegm-O-Matic in Burt's pocket. 'But can you make it a short story, only there's a transport heading straight for us and there's no one at the wheel.'

They all leapt for cover as Baz hovered to one side and the vehicle missed him by nothing more than a coat of paint. There was a terrible crunching sound of tortured metal as the battered transport collided with a pile of rubble and twisted girders. It stopped abruptly, showering them in dust and debris.

The screaming drive units spewed out jets of sand from beneath it, casting great clouds in every direction. Burt shielded his face with his arm and ran to the driver's door, and grabbing the handle, he lunged in for the keys. The transport fell silent, tilting precariously to one side. Everyone stood gaping in disbelief at six hooded individuals securely strapped into their seats.

'Please help us,' begged one of the occupants.

Burt hurriedly removed the man's hood. His face was stubble-ridden and his dry lips were horribly swollen.

'I don't believe it,' Baz said, hovering in for a closer look. 'You're Nigel Prentagast.'

The group surveyed the forlorn passengers in the transport, as light began to spread across the ruined city. They craned their necks looking up at the phenomenon rising up above them, silently watching the city fill with a luminescence that silhouetted the myriad of derelict skyscrapers. The light radiated out, forcing each of them to shield their eyes as an incalculable number of even brighter dots of light flooded out into the night sky. As the cosmos spilled out of the Planetarium, moving slowly and deliberately into the void, the group absorbed the spectacle in awe.

'What in the name of Llar is that?' muttered Ethel finally.

'I have no idea, but I bet it has something to do with Mr Davis,' offered Semilla confidently.

'Best we get a move on then, it's the only way we'll find out,' Burt said.

'All in good time, but first we need to take care of these poor men,' Ethel said, nodding back at the transport.

As they began to tend to Nigel and his fellow occupants inside the wreck of the transport, several streets away a pair of malicious red eyes focused on the route ahead. The entity that Baz had detected earlier now broke into a steady mechanical trot. It, too, had sensors, and there were life forms much closer than Baz and his companions. For almost a thousand years those menacing red eyes had not seen the inside of the Planetarium and yet tonight the entity made its way back towards the ancient structure. Once more it had work to do.

CHAPTER 42

'Sorry, where was I?' asked the President. 'That's it, E=MC^2 stands for *Extinction Equals the MeMe Chromosome Squared.*' Everyone in the group looked completely baffled. The President disregarded the blank looks on his audience's faces and continued. 'It was a message from the past, from the creators warning future generations never to launch this colossus. You see, every scholar bent on becoming famous came here to study the text, hoping to break the code. And then one day somebody did. Unfortunately, the gentleman in question met with an unfortunate accident.'

Mable's silvery outline flickered dimly against the mammoth shape of the cosmos and its radiance. The old guide had been deeply troubled by the President's arrival. 'It was no accident. You killed him in this very room, and I was there.'

'So quick to judge, Mable' hissed the President. 'It was as I recall an accident, however I'm sure you have your own version you would prefer to remember.'

Mable floated towards him and stared into his eyes. Her ghostly face was carved with an expression of deep loathing for a man she thought she would never see again. 'Why don't you tell them how you killed Simon?'

'Perhaps he shouldn't have interfered, and then he may have lived a little longer,' hissed the President.

'Simon was the curator here at the Planetarium,' she said, looking back at the group. 'We were working late one night when I saw a man enter his office. When Simon confronted him, this man opened up a light tunnel and pushed him in. He was never seen again.'

'I was looking over his notes, actually,' said the President. 'It was clear he had broken the code on the plaque. When he burst in and caught me, something of a tussle broke out. The XXL on my wrist became activated and Simon tumbled in. Unfortunately, if you don't set the coordinates correctly on the XXL, you could, as he found out, drift in time and space forever.'

Charlie shook his head, his face screwed up in a look of utter bewilderment. 'My dear lady, I am struggling to understand this. Didn't you tell us you were the tour hologram?'

'No, I said I was the tour guide. I was never a hologram.'

Mother felt the air rapidly leave her lungs. 'Good grief, you're a ghost.'

'And you mean our President was here all that time ago?' queried Charlie.

The President nodded in acknowledgement. 'That's correct, Commander, thanks entirely to your fathers and their wonderful invention.'

Godfrey and the group silently watched as their leader wandered over to the podium and stared out at the newborn spectacle filling the night sky. 'Have you any idea,' he said quietly, 'what it was like to stand there looking at that device strapped to your wrist and imagining the power you had over the past, the present and the future? When Reg and Aubrey gave me that first demonstration of the XXL, I was left utterly speechless. The potential was unimaginable.'

'The potential for death and destruction in the wrong hands,' Mable snapped.

'I must admit that would have been the case. But in my hands, no. In my hands I put it to good use.'

'You're deluded if you think what you undertook here was putting that device to good use. You are responsible for the deaths of millions of innocent people,' Mable blurted out across the viewing platform.

The President's eyes became as black as soot and were laced with a venomous glare. 'Deluded, am I? Really, is that what you think? No, you are the one who is deluded, Mable. I am the one who had the vision, the courage, the fortitude and the intelligence to preserve the new colony and protect it from that bloodthirsty rabble that dwelt here. They certainly weren't innocent people, I can tell you. It was for the greater good of the greater number. Something you people will never understand, and why would you? Unlike me, you were never there.'

Mother gave one of her disapproving huffs as she wrinkled her brow. 'Then, Mr President, perhaps you can explain it to us. I'm sure we would all like to hear your story and how you can justify this genocide. Please, if you can?'

'It was after that first demonstration of the XXL.I made Reg and Aubrey take an oath that they would never tell another living soul about the device. Over the next few months, I experimented, with their assistance I might add, in mastering the controls. Very soon I was able to move from one place to another; nothing too bold at first, just short leaps from one building to the next. Then, one evening when everyone had gone home from the Ministry, I decided to take the plunge and attempt to travel through time itself.'

'Into the past or into the future?' Godfrey enquired.

'Into the future at first,' said the President.

'How far into the future?' Godfrey asked.

'Not too far at first, but far enough to realise that an event we now all take for granted would one day come back to haunt our civilisation and ultimately destroy it.'

'And what event was that?'Mother asked.

'It was Spaceman Bob and his little adventure into the void.'

'How in the name of Llar could he have had an effect on our

colony's future?' Charlie said, dabbing his brow with his handkerchief.

'To answer that question, Commander, you would first need to know the real history of both of the colonies of Llar.'

CHAPTER 43

'There came a point in time when the colony eventually turned upon itself. The event went almost undocumented, when a handful of disenchanted souls made themselves and their doctrine known. The discontent they had harboured for decades, lurking below the surface of their everyday lives, finally oozed out onto the streets. First it started with peaceful demonstrations, fuelled by political rhetoric, accusing certain elements of the colony's society as having done less and taken more than they should have. The few soon became thousands chanting slogans in the streets, calling for the government to be changed prematurely. But their demands were met with determination by the security forces, who were instructed to stop them at any cost.

'The stage was set and nothing was going to alter the outcome. It had already gone too far. It was the perfect moment for an ambitious opportunist to take the rostrum and make the people promises of a new future and a new order that would rectify the failings of the old regime. Utopia was only a vote away. People had such short memories. In their haste to follow the promise of a new beginning, they had forgotten the security and harmony the old guard had generally provided over the years. The stability of the colony's social structure began to collapse, slowly winding down into the darkness of the abyss.

'It was a time of demarcation and fresh titles for those who were either in or out of the new order and all that it stood for. The media continued to feed the frenzy on the streets, laying the blame at the feet of the people who had in reality lived peacefully for generations, building their colony and making it strong. Neighbours and friends turned on one another with verbal assaults, expressing their dislike and distrust for those who had opposing views. Soon the words were replaced by sticks and stones as the hatred festered and grew out of control.

'Columns of smoke rose across the colony, the fires consuming vast swathes of the metropolis as the unrest continued unabated until finally a fragile truce was agreed. The decree came which ultimately decided where people would live based on their beliefs and affiliations. And so out of the carnage and destruction came Point North and Point South and the line that separated them so decisively. The new order had won, and the peace that was established endured, though somewhat precariously. Quite how long it would remain no one knew, and the lull in the fighting afforded a time to regroup and rebuild for both sides. But the men in the north weren't celebrating their victory. They were planning more death and destruction as they now had their enemy corralled in one place, ready for a final conflict. They were determined to eradicate Point South and all of those who lived there. So one day, as dawn broke, the carnage started again. The Great War had begun.'

'When the exodus began, the people in the south fled in their thousands, defeated and dejected, flooding out into the desert, leaving their homes and their land forever. There was nowhere left to go as the victors swept across the oasis, cleansing as they advanced, their prejudices overruling their compassion. The wastelands that surrounded the colony took their share of refugees, and in less than a year, half of them had perished. Surviving the Great War for them had been in vain; only the strong endured. Then, not content in just driving them into the desert, the army from north of the line followed them. They hunted them down like vermin, depleting their number still further, pushing the remnants deeper and deeper into uncharted territory.

'For the next thousand years, generation after generation, the survivors wandered the desert. The transition from city dwellers to nomads and masters of their terrain took time to accomplish. Seeking out fertile outcrops that could sustain their nomadic way of life was hard, and in order to survive they split into smaller groups, and some survived, while others perished.

'The history of their people was passed down and the stories of their origins were told around the campfires at night. Slowly, piece by piece, the tales became diluted and fragmented, and within several hundred years, much of their past was lost. If not for *The Great Book of Llar*, then the true story would have been lost forever.

'The nomads had the hope that one day they would find a place they could call home and the wandering would finally cease. Each month the elders organised young men into groups of three and sent them to seek out such a place. Armed with a little food and water, they were sent to the east, the west and the south; no one ventured north. These men were the *roamers*, and they were revered by the young men of the tribes, who aspired to be like them.

'The cycle of life in the desert continued unabated for a thousand years, until one day a young roamer did find the land of their dreams. At last the wandering was over and a new beginning presented itself on the fertile green oasis in the south. The surviving tribes celebrated their salvation from the desert, and that day marked a moment in time they would never forget. It was immortalised in the words that were later carved on the base of the statue commemorating the roamer who had saved them. *"We were the children of the desert and now we are free. And we shall remain free for the rest of our days."*'

'When the silver capsule hurtled across the rim of space, they saw it as clear as day. The new phenomenon produced an outbreak of theories and conclusions in the northern colony. It was the first encounter.

'A millennium had passed and neither culture knew of the other's existence, and why should they have. The desert was an inhospitable inferno. Searing heat during the day and freezing temperatures at night hardly made it a place to explore for exploration's sake. There was nothing to discover there, only hardship and death. The north had no reason to believe that anyone from Point South had survived the blistering cauldron after the genocide of the Great War. But the question remained – where did the craft come from?

'For the new colony in the south there was concern when the pilot landed and told his tale of what he had seen during his mission. The Grand Council of the day pondered long and hard over the prospect that they were not alone. Considering their options, they wondered if making contact would be viable, then discounted it as an unnecessary and unwise. They had disturbed the sleeping dragon and there seemed little point in venturing into his lair for a closer look. So they decided to watch and wait, wondering if the people in the north would venture this far south in order to feed their curiosity.

'Years passed and nothing became of the celestial flight and the discovery that it brought the colony in the south. The lookouts that had been posted around the north-facing perimeter of the oasis were gradually disbanded as the perceived threat diminished with time. For what good it had been, they may as well have never bothered. The spies from Point North were already amongst them, moving freely around their city with impunity, reporting back to their masters far to the north. They diligently gathered information and names of officials, mapped out coordinates and made their preparations for a day and date in the future only they would decide upon.

'Then the great caravan from the north arrived full of pomp and pageantry, beguiling the people and the leaders of the colony with their charm and sophistication. Offering the hand of friendship and trust, the new arrivals duped and intoxicated them, rejoicing that their world was now whole and at last the people of the planet Llar had become one again. The dalliance lasted for several years, continuing to draw in the colony and her people like a fish on a hook until the moment was right. And then one night it was.

'The curse of our species eventually percolated to the surface and the generic chromosome the ancients had feared eventually took control. Thousands died. Men, women and children ruthlessly slaughtered in their beds as the new reign of terror swept across the colony. And the carnage would have prevailed had it not been for a solitary visitor from the past. The history books, though, were to be rewritten. When time itself was rewound, the outcome and the future became a very different tale altogether.'

CHAPTER 44

'So what would you have done, let your loved ones and your family die? Allow another victory day parade celebrating the death of millions? Or would you have gone back in time and changed the events to stop yet another genocide?' asked the President.

They stood listening in stunned silence.

'I took action, and in doing so I made certain they would never ever threaten our people again.'

'Surely you must have killed many innocent people as well,' Gloria said.

'So how do you choose who is innocent and who is guilty? When a boy sees his father die at the hands of an oppressor, the cycle of hatred inevitability starts again. Frankly, none of you would be standing here today if it hadn't been for me.'

'And the invention my father gave you...' Godfrey said quietly as he glanced over at his friend. Charlie nodded in agreement. Before either of the two men had time to draw their next breath, staccato blasts of gunfire from outside the Planetarium turned everyone's heads simultaneously. The sound echoed around the derelict buildings outside, cracking and snapping in the night sky. The shockwave from a huge explosion rocked the Planetarium, vibrating through the viewing platform. The President steadied himself, grabbing at the handrail, as outside the ground shook from another enormous explosion.

'What in the name of Llar is happening now?' Mother screamed as Gloria pulled her close to her side.

The President gave the assembly a cynical look. 'That will almost certainly be your transport exploding, and it leads me to conclude that your deliverance from this world has finally arrived.'

Over the backdrop of several smaller explosions came the faint sound of something metal grating along the floor of the corridor outside the Planetarium. It echoed – steady, slow and deliberate. Crawling closer and closer, it reverberated off the mighty marble columns. The group glanced around at one another with anxious looks. Mable swiftly glided to the great doors that separated the Planetarium from the entrance corridor. 'Quickly,' she said. 'Shut this door. It's your only hope.'

Godfrey and Charlie ran across the viewing platform, followed by the lampposts, and slammed the door closed. They swung the gigantic wooden beam over on its pivot until it came to rest in its cradle.

'That should hold it back. These doors are very thick,' Charlie said, seeming confident. He didn't remain that way for long. The stream of bullets that pierced the door next to him showered the Planetarium in splinters of smouldering wood. Tongues of fire leapt through the mighty wooden structure, sending debris cascading in every direction as the stench of cordite filled the air. The two men stared at one another in abject fear.

'Move back, lads!' Charlie screamed over the gunfire, and the lampposts immediately withdrew to the safety of the granite wall that separated them from the corridor.

The President, meanwhile, stood laughing like a madman at the pandemonium. Suddenly there was silence. The smoke swirled and drifted, the air drenched in the bitter odour of gunfire and burning wood. From behind the podium, the Dheybar peered around a corner. He glanced across at the splintered remains of the door. His watery eyes blinked several times. 'They're here!'

Mother looked down at the shaggy creature next to her. 'Who's here?'

'The Legion,' he said, his fleshy feet flapping up and down with excitement. 'They've come to kill us all.'

As the debris began to settle, shafts of light from the cosmos flickered through the smoke, casting shadows across the remains of the door. A single wooden segment crashed to the ground sending up a cloud of dust. Through the gaping hole, the sound of rusty metal joints creaked and groaned as the thing clambered into view.

The President casually brushed the sleeves of his robe as he slowly walked towards the mechanical legionnaire. He stood calmly alongside the machine, its dull red eyes staring at his master's quarry peering out from behind the metal podium. The machine was battered and scarred. Blast marks littered its rusting frame and pieces of a ruined uniform decorated its shoulders. Perched upon its tarnished skull sat a dented helmet scorched with powder burns. The machine had without doubt seen considerable active service in its lifetime.

'Please stand up and welcome our new guest,' insisted the President.

'If I didn't know better, Charlie, I would have said that was one of my father's androids,' Godfrey said quietly to his colleague.

'And you would, of course, be correct,' the President informed him. 'He is, needless to say, an early variant of the ageing model we still use in Llar today. Although, unlike his cousins who can speak, this fellow cannot. He has only one purpose.'

'And that is to hunt people down and exterminate them,' said Mable. 'They came here after the Great War ended, thousands of them. It was after the Reformists had gained control of the colony. These machines were the ones who butchered every man, woman and child until no one was left alive.'

Charlie stared at the President with a repugnant glare.

'Couldn't you have found another way, something more peaceful?'

The President waved a finger at the commander. 'Don't be too quick to judge. You have no idea how hard I tried to change events, but it kept turning out the same. Those wretched elders on the Grand Council thwarted everything I did, and in the end I was left with no other choice. On that glorious day in our history when Spaceman Bob's capsule was hurtled into the void, no one knew it would result in the annihilation of our people.'

'But he did go up there,' Gloria said. 'He never mentioned another oasis before he died.'

'That's correct,' confirmed the President. 'It is another part of our history that I had to re-master. I eliminated poor old Bob. I had no choice. He couldn't have gone up there and seen the other colony, could he? I'm sorry, but Bob had to go. I emptied his oxygen tanks before he took off, then sat in a room at the Ministry drinking tea while doing a very convincing voice-over for all of Llar to hear.' The President walked to and fro in front of his audience. He was enjoying the power he had over them. He looked proudly at the legionnaire. 'Both your fathers were paramount in designing these wonderful machines.' He ran his hand over the shoulder of the legionnaire standing beside him.

Charlie went to move forward, quickly raising his fist. 'Now you look here…' he started.

The machine had lightning reflexes despite its rusted frame. In less than the blink of an eye, the android's corroded hand produced a pistol from its holster. It swivelled the weapon around its finger like a seasoned gunslinger, then aimed it straight at Charlie's heart. He stopped dead in his tracks. Gloria grabbed at the arm of his jacket. 'Don't move,' she said.

The President sneered. 'Mrs Davis, you are so right. If I give my rusty friend the command, he will happily drill the commander full of holes, just like that door.'

Charlie's face was pure rage and his cheeks were flushed bright crimson.

'Have you ever heard of Area 21, gentlemen? I doubt you have considering where it is and was and what it was used for. I doubt anyone has, apart from a privileged few. Let me enlighten you. Area 21 was a military base on the edge of the desert to the north of the colony far away from prying eyes. These machines were developed, tested and constructed there in absolute secrecy by your late fathers. And when they were completed, with the aid of the XXL I brought them here to the old city, and the rest, well, as they say, the rest is history.'

Mable drifted silently past the legionnaire. The android didn't move. It was unable to detect her presence. She faced the President, glaring at him, and stopped him in his tracks.

'Be gone, old woman. Surely there must be somewhere else you can go and haunt?' The President walked through the ghost as if she were merely mist in his path. He turned and smiled. 'These people were the distillate of everything our ancestors wanted to keep in check. They were infected with the MeMe chromosome. Besides, at that point in time, and thanks to your fathers and their marvellous inventions, we were better equipped than they were and we had the element of surprise. So you see, it seemed good sense to me to slaughter them while I had the chance.'

'Yes, and you did such a wonderful job,' Mable said cynically as she swirled in front of the President and his mechanical abettor.

'It was a simple situation,' continued the President. 'With the help of your fathers, it was suddenly possible not only to move from place to place, but also to and fro in time. I could even move legions of androids from one point in time to another, and so I did. Thanks to their brainchild and my intervention, our colony was safe and secure for all time. That was, of course, until the XXL went missing one day. Reg and Arthur had secretly constructed a second device without my knowledge. For some reason they came to distrust me. They tried to go back in time and prevent me delivering my army to the colony in the north. But thankfully I managed to stop them. Then lo and behold they stole my XXL and hid it. When they were finally caught they refused to give up the location of the two devices, and, well, I had no choice. I'm sure you can see that now.'

'So with both of the XXL's missing, and the blueprints beyond retrieval, Reg and Aubrey thwarted any further attempts at building another device,' Mother said, leaning on her walking stick.

'Precisely,' agreed the President. 'And I have searched long and hard to locate them ever since. The blueprints' encryption code on the mainframe is so complex that no one has ever managed to unravel it. I've had teams working on that quest for years, but alas they have not been successful.'

Godfrey nervously tugged at the sleeve of his jacket. He had no intention of letting the President know that at least one of the XXLs was close at hand. He tried to change the topic. 'There's one thing I don't quite understand and that's the MeMe chromosome you spoke of?' Godfrey said, looking up at the plaque. 'Why didn't our ancestors want the cosmos launched?'

'Ah, yes, the inscription that so many people were unable to decipher. You see, our ancient ancestors soon realised when they created us that we were, as a species, intrinsically flawed. We carry in our genes a chromosome so virulent as to be the source of our own downfall. We are, in fact, our own nemesis. You should consider the carnage that ensued in this vast metropolis before my legions arrived here. It was played out by the hands of men, not machines.'

'If, as you say, we all have this chromosome,' Godfrey started, 'why doesn't it affect our colony?'

The President threw his head back and laughed out loud. 'Godfrey, it does affect our colony, every single day of our lives, though thankfully for the masses it is kept in check.'

Mother twisted her expression as if she already knew the answer. 'And how is this mutant gene kept in check, Mr President?'

The President drew in a long breath that served to raise his shoulders. He turned and faced Mother. 'By me,' he said with a patronising smile.

'We saw the oasis and it is littered with the wrecks of transports. Were they sent here by you? Transports full of people you considered too dangerous to allow them to continue on in our society. Were these men those who knew too much or people who spoke out against the system?' Gloria questioned

'People like our fathers,' muttered Charlie, scowling at the President.

'Yes, sadly, Commander, people like your father. But you have to view their sacrifice as something greater than the deaths of two men. Without their help our colony would one day have been overrun and millions more would have died. It was for the greater good of the greater number.'

'So are you suggesting that the human race is in fact a flawed species that will eventually destroy themselves?' Godfrey asked.

'I'm not suggesting anything. I'm stating a fact,' said the President. 'Without control it is inevitable. Once the level of greed and selfishness rises within the masses and remains unchecked, the bell will toll, I assure you. All it will take is some catalyst to provoke it, as it did here so long ago. We all have that chromosome deep inside of us, and some of us know how to live alongside it and put it to better use. People like me, for example!'

'Three cheers for the despot,' hollered Mother.

'If that is the title you wish to bestow upon me, madam, then please, I accept it most graciously. But just think of this for a moment,' he said, pointing out across the cosmos slowly ascending into the night sky. 'Look at those countless tiny microcosms shining down on us. The creators of the cosmos were responsible for every human life form that exists out there and every single one of them has the same genetic flaw. There are countless billions of them all infected with the MeMe chromosome. I suspect that even as we talk they are arguing, and bickering, and fighting, and killing one another and causing all manner of mayhem imaginable. And now that the cosmos has been finally launched, something our creators never actually wanted to happen, the human race is free to roam the void forever.'

Mother bit her lip, and she glanced at her daughter. Gloria gave the old lady's arm a reassuring squeeze.

'I may have managed,' said the President, 'to have preserved our colony and given it stability, but who, I ask, will maintain order out there now that the cosmos is finally free?' The President walked slowly around his mechanical servant. He brushed his hand over the remnants of its uniform. Dust and splinters fell to the floor. 'As none of his colleagues have turned up, I can only assume that this one is the sole survivor. Still, never mind, one is all it will take to tidy up the last of these loose ends.'

The gathering stood silently watching. Godfrey and Charlie exchanged glances. Both of them knew how this impasse was about to end. Only Number Nine moved, silently edging forward in the shadows beside the granite wall. The President's oration had led him in a circle around the legionnaire. It was only when the President's back was turned that Number Nine finally made his move. He lunged forward, grabbing at the pistol. The sound of a single shot resonated around the viewing platform. Nine lay on the floor in front of his assassin, his column split almost in two from the blast.

The President glared across the platform at the motionless group. 'That saves me one job, I suppose. Are there anymore heroes here amongst you?'

Godfrey took one step forward and glared at the President as the legionnaire's pistol sounded an ominous click of another shell entering the breach. Godfrey ignored it. The inventor held his head up high as his eyes welled up with emotion.

'No, Mr President, there are no more heroes amongst us, nor are there any tyrants either.'

The President stood spellbound for a brief moment, staring at the inventor. 'My word, Godfrey, that was wonderful, so full of passion and conviction. It's a shame they will be your last words.' The President positioned himself beside his robotic henchman and smiled. 'This is the end of the line, my constituents. Please don't take it personally. It is, as I said earlier, for the greater good of the greater number. But, unfortunately, it's now time for you all to die, so goodbye.'

Godfrey looked helplessly at Gloria; she was clutching the little Dheybar in one arm and her mother in the other. Mother had her eyes screwed into their sockets as deep as they would go. Charlie tugged nervously at his jacket trying to make himself more presentable for the final moment. In an act of complete desperation, Godfrey shot a glance at the battered Phlegm-O-Matic pistol in the legionnaire's metal hand. He was thinking on his feet.

'What's the weather forecast for tomorrow?' he asked, stalling for time.

The President sighed in dismay at Godfrey's ploy.

The weapon gave a rusty croak. 'I don't normally do weather reports anymore,' the gun informed him politely.

'Why is that?'

'Ever since the demise of the old metropolis, there has been no control of the weather systems. Anyone who would have appreciated a weather forecast perished an awful long time ago. Besides, every time I started to inform my potential victims of the current cloud formations, or wind velocity, or barometric pressure, or potential precipitation, they simply ran away.'

'I wonder why?' the President muttered sarcastically as he gazed up at the cosmos.

The gun continued. 'That was the question I repeatedly asked myself. It took me ages and ages to come up with a plausible hypothesis,' the Phlegm-O-Matic informed Godfrey.

'So what was your conclusion?' Godfrey asked, trying to lead the gun into a lengthy and meaningful conversation.

'I know it may sound crazy, but to be completely honest I think I was boring them,' the gun replied.

The President, becoming impatient, clicked his fingers and pointed to the group. 'For pity's sake, just do it, will you, and we can all go home. Well, only me, actually,' he said with a smirk.

The platform was still and almost silent. In the background the steady hum of the generators deep beneath the building droned on relentlessly. The murky air flickered with light from the twinkling stars far out across the cosmos. The legionnaire twisted from side to side, squeaking on his rusty hips. He pointed his weapon this way and that, unable to decide upon a target. After a while he stopped.

'Is there a problem?' asked the President.

The Phlegm-O-Matic coughed nervously.

The President took his usual deep breath when things failed to appease him. He glared down at the pistol beside him. 'Come on then, let's hear it,' he snapped.

'I can't shoot them,' said the gun.

'What?'

'I said I can't shoot them,' repeated the Phlegm-O-Matic.

'I just don't believe this,' the President said, turning on the spot.

The Phlegm-O-Matic cleared its throat. 'I'm sorry, but it's simple enough. Reg Davis and Aubrey Albright co-wrote my software, didn't they?'

The President gave a little nod. 'So?'

'Therefore, I can't shoot Godfrey or Charlie as they are related to them. And that lady there is Mrs Davis, and beside her is her mother. I can't shoot them either. They're related to Godfrey.'

Mother stopped squinting and opened her eyes. 'You're a very, very nice gun, thank you.'

'Don't mention it, you're very welcome, madam.' The gun continued. 'You see there's a protocol written into my software excluding themselves, their families and any of their relations from ever being killed, maimed or destroyed.'

The President laughed out loud. 'I'm sorry, but I can't believe this can be happening.'

'I know,' said the gun. 'It is something of a paradox, I must admit.'

'Oh, absolutely,' said the President in a derisive tone. He thought for a moment and then turned to the unreceptive weapon. 'So you're telling me you can't shoot any of them, ever?'

'Yes, sir, that is correct.'

The President shook his head and sighed. He glanced around at the debris on the floor and grabbed a stout piece of wood. It resembled a club. 'Stand aside, your conscience is beginning to irritate me. It looks like I'll have to resort to a little "*hands on*" and finish off this job myself.'

'But, sir—'

'Don't worry. I said I'll do it,' snapped the President.

'But, sir, there's just one other thing.'

The President held the club in his hands like a seasoned baseball star. He glanced over at the Phlegm-O-Matic resting in the legionnaire's rusted hand. 'What?'

'That protocol doesn't include you.'

The President's shoulders sank and the air left his lungs in a rush. The legionnaire turned and aimed the gun at him.

'Sorry, but like you said, it's for the greater good of the greater number, and I'm only doing my job, after all,' said the pistol.

The President gave a little huff, his face twisting into a maniacal smile. 'I know, and in the end no one ever appreciates it, do they?'

'Never,' said the Phlegm-O-Matic.

Raising his club, the President took a desperate swing as the viewing platform of the Planetarium resonated to the sound of another single shot.

CHAPTER 45

The sound of exploding fuel cells shattered the silence of the decaying metropolis, stopping the group in their tracks. Several streets away, red and gold flames leapt into the night sky, dancing between the thick black pillars of spent combustion.

'That has to be Mr Davis,' Semilla said with an air of complete confidence as she stared at the inferno rising above the rooftops.

'How can you be so certain?' Burt asked, looking slightly pensive.

Semilla gave a shrug. 'Let's face it, he's been in the vicinity of one or two little disasters lately.'

'You can't just assume Mr Davis has anything to do with that fire over there,' Ethel said defensively.

'I know what Semilla is trying to say,' Baz interjected. 'You have to admit, though, Godfrey does seem to be having a run of bad luck lately, doesn't he?'

'Well we won't know for sure if it's anything to do with him until we take a look,' Burt said.

Ethel shook her head. 'Let's just stop and think for a minute. We could be walking into something dangerous. What caused those explosions?'

'Ethel's right. Perhaps we should be asking the question *who* caused them?' Baz said.

'It looks to me like we have landed in the middle of a war zone, and maybe the war isn't over yet?' Ethel said as a cold chill overtook her. She was frightened, and right now she wished she was tucked up on her sofa with her feet up, watching the TV.

'You're shaking,' Burt said, taking off his jacket and wrapping it across her shoulders. He put his arm around her to reassure her. Ethel felt the security and forced a smile. 'Right,' he continued, taking control. 'Baz and Arthur will go ahead of us and report back if anything moves; you're the ones with the sensors. I will lead the rest of the group, and Nigel and his colleagues can take up the rear.'

Shortly afterwards, they stood and watched the two scouts cautiously skirting the smouldering remains of a wrecked transport.

'My sensors indicate this was not Godfrey's vehicle,' Baz said finally. 'However, we have found this.'

The android held up the smouldering remnants of a *Llarinian Celebrities at Home* magazine. Semilla stepped forward and examined the cover in Arthur's hand.

'Look at the date; it's this week's issue. This has to be something to do with Mr Davis.'

'Arthur and I can assure you there was no one on board this vehicle when it exploded.'

'Oh, thank goodness for that,' Ethel said. 'But if they did get here, then where in the name of Llar are they?'

'Hopefully close by,' Baz said, but he didn't get a chance to continue. He was interrupted by the sound of grating metal. It came from far above them, beyond the summit of the granite steps of the Planetarium entrance. Slowly, the legionnaire's rusted frame came into view. The battered hulk stood for a moment surveying it's domain with powerful sensors. The dull red eyes focused, the head turned, and far below, an array of human life forms registered in its electronic brain. It began to descend towards them, creaking harshly with each step it took, its tattered outline silhouetted eerily by the remaining flames of the smouldering transport and the light from the cosmos ascending in the night sky.

Burt swallowed hard and withdrew his gun from his coat pocket, holding his finger on the trigger. 'Quickly, all of you take cover,' he shouted to the group as he darted behind the remains of a nearby wall.

Semilla decided it was a good idea to offer her support and she quickly joined him. Grabbing Burt's old pistol from inside her bag, she pointed it towards the menacing sound now obscured by the billowing smoke in the foreground.

Semilla's Phlegm-O-Matic promptly made an observation. 'Wow, Semilla, look at that shuttle.'

'Keep your voice down, Raymond, we're in danger,' Semilla hissed.

'Raymond?' Burt said incredulously.

'I had to give him a name, didn't I?'

The legionnaire had now descended the Planetarium steps, as Ethel, Arthur and the programmers peered around the derelict wall of their shelter. The machine rounded the remains of the wrecked transport and suddenly it creaked to a halt. The robotic hand withdrew the Phlegm-O-Matic pistol from its holster and the legionnaire swung it round his metal finger at an amazing rate. The pistol stopped in an instant and aimed directly at Burt and Semilla.

'Okay, you punks, who wants it first?' asked the gun in the legionnaire's hand.

Ethel's heart pounded as she watched the standoff, her hands drawing Burt's jacket tightly around her shoulders.

'Get real, you're out of ammo. I have sensors too, you know?' exclaimed Raymond as Semilla levelled him and took aim.

The legionnaire's gun began to laugh. 'Yeah, you're right, but it was a great line, though, don't you think?'

Burt and Semilla slowly lowered their weapons.

'It's all right, everyone,' said the legionnaire's Phlegm-O-Matic. 'I was only joking. I couldn't harm you if I wanted to. He's absolutely right. My last shell's gone.'

Baz hovered over to confront the pistol. 'Have you seen the occupants of this transport? We are looking for our friends who we believe to be somewhere in the city?'

'What transport?'

'The one that's on fire behind you,' Baz said, pointing his delicate metallic digit.

'Oh, that transport there,' said the pistol.

'Did you blow it up?' Baz asked incredulously.

'Look,' pleaded the Phlegm-O-Matic. 'It's really very difficult to resist taking out one when you get the opportunity. You know, they really light up when you hit the fuel cells.' The legionnaire spun round and the pistol did a re-enactment of his earlier deed. 'Kapow, boom, bang, whoosh.'

'I can only imagine,' Raymond said in an almost envious tone.

'So you know that group up there in the Planetarium then?' the pistol continued. 'Hey, they say it's a small world.'

'Are they all right?' asked Semilla, darting forward.

'Yeah, they're all fine, apart from the President. He's rather dead actually. Oh, and one of the lampposts. I'm afraid he copped it too.'

Baz's beacon flickered with emotion. 'Which one?' he asked.

'There was only one president as far as I know,' said the pistol indifferently.

'I meant which lamppost?' Baz hissed.

'Oh, sorry, I have no idea,' the Phlegm-O-Matic replied. 'You all look the same to me.'

'What about the President? How did he die?' Ethel asked.

The legionnaire's pistol seemed slightly surprised by her question. 'Actually, I'm no doctor, but taking a wild guess I would say he died from a rather large hole in his body. I shot him, of course, that's what I do. Okay, that's what I did do, but hey ho, now that I'm out of ammo I guess I'm retired.'

'Lucky old you,' said Raymond. 'Have you got any plans for your retirement?'

The legionnaire's motors and wires spun the Phlegm-O-Matic round and faced the gun into the new phenomenon above their heads. 'To be honest,' the pistol said in a nonchalant tone, 'I've always fancied a spot of fishing actually. After a thousand years or so of all this *"Kill, maim and destroy"* stuff, I think I need a bit of the old "R&R", don't you?'

'One hundred percent,' Raymond said, agreeing wholeheartedly.

The legionnaire's pistol returned to face the group. 'Anyway, I think it's time for me to vacate. It was a pleasure to meet you all, and I'd like to say it makes a real change to hold an intelligent conversation with nice people like yourselves instead of shooting them dead. After a while it can become a little enervating, trust me.'

'Wait up, cousin,' Raymond said. 'Before you go…we didn't get your name.'

The legionnaire's pistol gave a little chuckle. '*Me…*' said the pistol. '*I'm the gun with no name.*' The legionnaire's hand performed another amazing act of dexterous pistol action, spinning the weapon so fast around its finger that the gun became a blur. The pistol stopped dead. The rusted machine silently slid the Phlegm-O-Matic into its holster and the pair disappeared into the night to the sound of the legionnaire's creaking joints.

'You have to learn how to do that with me,' Raymond insisted to Semilla. 'That was so cool.'

'Too right,' she agreed, and they followed the others up the steps of the Planetarium.

CHAPTER 46

The realisation of all they had heard and witnessed left them silently taking stock beneath the splendour of the cosmos stretching out across the night sky. Godfrey glanced at Mother as she held on to her daughter tightly, clearly distressed by the President's corpse lying in front of them. The magnitude of the deception he had enacted upon the colony and her people would take some time to fully register, and the implications that it held were far-reaching. In the meantime, though, Godfrey was grateful that his family and friend had survived their ordeal.

Number Three approached his creator. 'Godfrey, how are we going to get back to the metropolis without a transport?' he asked as several of the other lampposts anxiously crowded around.

'I fear we are somewhat stranded, don't you?' Charlie said.

'There's no need to worry unduly,' said a man stepping smartly through the hole in the Planetarium door, following a pencil beam of light from his torch. 'The President's battle cruiser is just a few streets away. They will escort you back to the colony.'

Godfrey's heart sank. He gazed over at Jack Marsden dressed as he always was in a sharp suit and tie. The man never seemed to collect dirt on his shoes or creases in his clothes the way other people did. Following closely behind him was Miranda Short, eyeing up the gathering from the upturned collar of her leather jacket.

'Isn't she the Presidents contract killer?' whispered Number Two.

'Yes, she is, I read about her in an encrypted file. She's a ruthless, coldblooded psychopath,' Number Eleven added, pushing Number Ten in front of him.

Miranda scowled at the lampposts as she skirted slowly behind the group, her eyes transfixed on their hovering forms.

Godfrey ignored the torch in Jack's right hand as he swung it around the Planetarium. He was more concerned with something in his other hand that resembled a weapon.

Jack stared down at the President lying twisted on the floor. 'So who shot him?' he asked, squatting down beside the corpse.

'A legionnaire,' replied Godfrey, nodding over at Charlie. He motioned his head at the object in Jack Marsden's left hand. Charlie acknowledged him by raising his eyebrows.

'Are you here to arrest us?' Gloria asked.

'We didn't kill him,' added Mother. 'We didn't do anything wrong –well, not much anyway.'

Miranda walked up to the old woman. 'What do you mean "*not much*"?'

Gloria stepped in front of her mother. 'Just leave her alone. Don't you think we've suffered enough? Didn't you see the legionnaire leaving? It was him. If you go now, you may catch him.'

Jack raised his hand. 'It's all right, no one's blaming you, Mrs Davis. Frankly, I'm not surprised it's ended like this. The President was getting somewhat out of control.'

'*Really!*' Mother snapped.

'What I meant, madam, was that the President's quest to find the XXL was becoming harder and harder to contain and he was beginning to take too many chances. He was hoping Godfrey would lead him to the device here in the old oasis.' Mother pursed her lips and looked Jack and Miranda up and down with contempt.

'Several days ago I had to dispatch six of our programmers

out into the desert. Thanks to Godfrey's inventions, the mainframe has become more and more idiosyncratic and liable to distribute classified information into the public domain. The President had an awful lot of hidden treasures on the mainframe, and they were percolating closer to the surface by the minute.'

'And those hidden treasures, as you call them,' Mother said, 'would have seen the end of our President and his cohorts, such as you.'

'No doubt I too would have fallen from grace in the eyes of the colony. However, ask yourself this question: how many of us did as we were told and without question? How many of us undertook unsavoury tasks in the name of the colony and the greater good? We all lived in fear of our lives knowing that one unguarded comment could lead us to our fate at Area 21.' Jack looked at Miranda. 'Or shot dead on the courthouse steps perhaps.'

Miranda and Jack traded an engaging smile before Jack turned back to the group.

'You could have overthrown him; you had the power,' Mother continued. 'You could have put an end to his tyranny years ago.'

'Were you really that oppressed? Did you live in fear of being murdered in your beds at night? And when was the last time you witnessed insurrection on the streets of our colony? Getting rid of the President wasn't the answer, madam. What would that have achieved? As soon as he had been ousted from power, the misery would have started again just as it did here in this colony. The jostling for pole position by another horde of megalomaniacs intent on gaining control would have plunged our colony into civil war. As things turned out, however, the President's obsession with finding the XXL has culminated in this, and another civil war could now be a very real possibility,' Jack said, glancing down at his leader. 'Frankly, I could see the writing was on the wall when the President got ahead of himself and produced his own home video.'

'What home video?' Gloria asked.

'The President used the mainframe to produce the news footage of his forthcoming shuttle crash.'

'*Forthcoming?*' Charlie blurted.

'I was instructed to plant several kilos of plastic explosive in the cockpit,' Jack told him. 'The President had planned to remove the political opposition as they were becoming too ambitious.'

'You mean we were sat on that shuttle with a bomb all that time?' Ethel said from the doorway. Everyone on the platform turned in astonishment as Ethel's group walked into the Planetarium.

'So you didn't get a weather forecast then?' Jack said, smiling.

'Should we have?' asked Burt.

'In reality, no; you shouldn't have even been on the President's shuttle.'

Burt blushed at Jack's comment.

'I set the programme to detonate the bomb when the autopilot gave out the barometric pressure,' Jack informed them.

Semilla huffed. 'That's why Tucker kept asking if we wanted a weather report.'

'Who's Tucker?' asked Jack.

'He was the on-board computer,' said Ethel. 'He blew himself up after he dropped us off here.'

'Well, the Reformist Party will never know how lucky they were, eh? By the way, what's with all of these names?' he asked. 'The mainframe's now calling himself Tarquin. Has it gone—?'

'Completely potty?' Charlie said nonchalantly. 'It would appear so.'

'I think the mainframe has had a liberal dose of AI, if you ask me,' Jack said with a laugh as he glanced at Godfrey.

'Possibly,' Godfrey said, admitting to nothing.

'Anyway, as much we would like to stay and chat, I think it's time to say our goodbyes and we will be on our way,' Jack continued.

Miranda glanced at him and nodded at the gathering. 'And we are going to let them go?'

Jack gave the group a benevolent look. 'Yes, let them go back to the colony. We need someone to break the news,' he said, looking down at the President.

'And what about you two?' asked Charlie. 'You are not intending to return?'

'I don't think that's such a good idea, do you? No, we are going to start a new life out there in the cosmos. There are millions of species who would appreciate our talents. Thanks to Reg and Aubrey, this will enable us to get there.'

Godfrey and the others watched as Jack tugged on the sleeve of his jacket. Perched neatly on his wrist sat a gold bracelet identical to the one on Godfrey's arm.

'Good grief,' Charlie choked. 'He's got the other XXL. Where did you get that from?'

Jack glanced down at his wrist. The bracelet had a warm comforting glow in the light from the newly formed night sky. 'Ironically, your fathers must have hidden it under the President's desk when they were working for him. I think they knew he was about to double-cross them, and hiding it there would have been the last place in Llar the President would have thought to look. A little over a year ago, one of the office cleaners noticed it and called me in to take a look. Honestly, I couldn't believe my good fortune.'

From the edge of the group, Burt moved forward. His hand was clasped tightly around his new Phlegm-O-Matic pistol. Semilla, too, moved to join him, levelling Raymond menacingly at Jack and Miranda.

'I'm sorry, Mr Marsden, but I think you need to come with us. You have a lot to answer for back in the colony,' Burt said.

Miranda slid her hand inside her jacket and produced what resembled a pistol and aimed it at Burt's head. The red dot of a laser guidance system steadied itself between Burt's eyes.

Raymond suddenly chirped into life and greeted the President's aide. 'Hello, Mr Marsden, and how are you today? Blimey, is that some sort of weapon your friend has in her hand?'

Jack nodded. 'Yes, it certainly is.'

'I must admit I haven't seen a gun like that in our colony before. It looks really rather fearsome,' Raymond said.

'That's because it didn't come from here, and that's why you don't recognise it. And yes, it really is quiet fearsome. It projects a powerful beam of energy, and it's fantastic at melting houses, or people, or even other weapons,' Jack said.

Raymond coughed nervously several times. 'Look, that's absolutely terrific, Mr Marsden, and I'm really pleased for you, but guess what, I've just remembered I've got a couple of updates to download for my programs, so I'll let you get on with your evening. It was great meeting you both.'

Semilla stared down angrily at her gun. '*Raymond.*'

'Okay, call me a coward, but that weapon is smaller than me and it can melt a house; are you serious?'

Godfrey gazed back at the bracelet on Jack's wrist. 'Can I surmise that you have mastered the controls of the XXL and in fact you have been venturing into the cosmos already?'

'Yes, I have, Godfrey, and do you know, it really is quite a place,' Jack said. 'With the President becoming unstable in his old age, I felt it was time to look outside of our wonderful colony for something new. If he had the opportunity to discover the worlds up there above our heads the way we have, he may have had a different outlook altogether. Who knows, things may have turned out differently for all of us.'

'You never felt like sharing your little secret with him?' Charlie asked.

Jack tapped the bracelet several times, and a few feet away a huge chromium zip ascended out of the Planetarium floor accompanied by a deep humming sound. The letters XXL were clearly visible stamped on the pull tag. Jack walked towards the device, and pushing one side of the zip with his hand, the Planetarium was immediately flooded with brilliant light.

'No, I didn't, Commander, and frankly I think it's a good job the President didn't get the opportunity to preside over this,' he said, glancing up at the cosmos. 'Don't you?'

Charlie frowned at the prospect and shielded his eyes from the light emanating from the XXL.

'Just remember, Godfrey,' Jack said turning back. 'When you use the XXL and you travel in time, be careful not to alter anything before you return. Tell no one where you have come from or where you are going to. Definitely don't tell them your name, and never ever leave anything behind after your visit. If you do you will run the risk of altering the space-time continuum. You may end up altering the course of history and the future of the cosmos irrevocably.'

Godfrey held his hand up across his face. The light was intense, and he could barely make out Jack Marsden's outline. 'What makes you think I can travel in time like you?' he asked. All Godfrey heard was Jack Marsden's laughter as he and Miranda Short entered the light.

'Because I can see the other XXL on your wrist, that's why.'

Godfrey glanced down at the gold bracelet glistening as the brilliant white light receded and the giant zip descended to the ground, vanishing just as quickly as it had appeared. He looked at the place where Jack and Miranda had been standing before they had stepped into time itself. For a moment he wondered where in the vastness of the cosmos they now stood. Looking up, the night sky above his planet was a new experience; the myriad of dotted lights twinkling overhead would take some time to get used to. Godfrey twisted the bracelet on his wrist and considered the responsibility he wore. In the wrong hands the device had delivered pain and suffering to his fellow man on an unimaginable scale and countless deaths, including, ultimately, that of its inventor –his father. He considered that no matter how badly humanity behaved, no man, woman or child deserved the wrath that the XXL was capable of delivering to the past or to the future, and as the custodian of his father's invention, that would be his pledge for the rest of time. He looked at the bracelet again. It was a noble gesture, but then he had only one of them.

CHAPTER 47

Several months later, Godfrey Davis stood at the bench in his newly constructed workshop at the bottom of his garden. He had laboured long and hard to complete the structure, and this evening saw the final item installed and ready to be tested. Godfrey pressed the button on the intercom three times and waited.

It had rained earlier, as forecast, from four o'clock to five o'clock precisely, and left the garden with a freshness only a shower can bring. Tarquin once again diligently controlled the weather systems across the colony, much to the relief of the populous, and most were glad that at least the climate had at last returned to normal. There had been many changes in the colony after they had returned, and life had taken on a different direction for all of them

'The new intercom is working, Godfrey. Can you hear me?' Gloria asked.

'Yes, perfectly.'

'Good, now you have finished that, you can come indoors and get ready for dinner. I will be serving up in twenty minutes.'

'I'm on my way,' he said.

The intercom went silent and Godfrey gave a contented smile as he looked proudly around his new workshop. He now had the perfect place to sit in peace and quiet and study the reams of drawings and sketches that Tarquin had so kindly produced for him. Since the demise of the President and the influence of the artificial intelligence from Godfrey's creations, the colossal machine had opened itself up to the people of the colony. The information hidden deep within its data banks was now in the public domain.

Godfrey cleared away the drawings from his bench, rolling them neatly and securing them with an elastic band. He took one last contented look at his handiwork. There were questions, though he knew he would never be able to answer, even with all of the drawing and data at his disposal. And one of those questions was the location of Jack Marsden and Miranda Short; he had often wondered where they were. The thought concerned him, but nowhere near as much as another question that gnawed at his mind. It was the prospect of that terrible chromosome the President had spoken of. Godfrey reasoned that if it were true, then there was a possibility that one day the genetic flaw their leader had described would come back to haunt them as it had with the colony in the north. Were they and the cosmos truly infected? It was a question he would have to continue to ponder another day. Right now, it was time for dinner.

The XXL glowed invitingly in the workshop lights as it sat on his wrist. He had worn it constantly and never let it out of his sight for fear it may get into the wrong hands. In recent weeks he had experimented with the device, undertaking short leaps from his workshop to the front garden and back again. The prospect of travelling in time, though, had proven a somewhat bolder option and something he had not yet tried. It was then that the idea struck him as he tidied up his bench. With his father's device he had the ability to leave his workshop and return again the moment after he had left. The thought germinated in his brain and very quickly he was unrolling a chart and studying it intently. The star chart had been produced with Tarquin's help to show the positions of the heavenly bodies that now surrounded them at night, and it was expanding everyday as new galaxies were being discovered and catalogued. Godfrey

288 · A R MERRYDEW

pondered the multitude of dots upon the chart until one in particular caught his eye. There was a note beside it in very small writing. Seeking the aid of his magnifying glass, he took a closer look. 'Small, blue and shaped like an orange,' he muttered.

It would surely make little difference which planet he visited, although this particular one intrigued him from the description. Godfrey peered through the workshop window; he saw the shape of their home in the early evening shadows. He bit his lip as his fingers feverishly tapped the chart. His mind was made up. Picking up his old green briefcase, he quickly grabbed a torch and several items he thought may be useful and threw them in. Punching in the coordinates from the chart, he was confident he would be back in time for dinner and Gloria would never even know. The intense light from the window of Godfrey's workshop spread itself across his lawn, flashing over the back of the house, and was gone in an instant.

Gloria sat with her glasses perched on her nose as she read the evening paper in the lounge. The heavy, lined curtains had shielded her from the light of the XXL and her husband's departure. Five more minutes, she thought, and then she would call him again for dinner. Godfrey had always been thoroughly useless at managing time.

CHAPTER 48

On a small blue planet far across the void, the sun stretched out that morning on a land mass now known as the Iberian Peninsula. It brought with it the promise of another fine day for the local population stirring in their huts blissfully unaware of the chain of events that were about to take place. Smoke rose from the previous night's campfires and drifted aimlessly across the settlement as chickens strutted in every direction searching for their first meal of the day. A scruffy hunched figure clad in smelly animal skins stood outside the hut of his neighbour, casually scratching his genitals through his lice-infested loincloth. This individual knew that today was a special day, not so much for the lice, but for himself, his friend and his tribe. The lowly Neanderthal had brought something to show him. It was an invention he had crafted with his own hands, and he was convinced that this device would benefit them in surviving to see another day in this beautiful but treacherous country. Emerging from his hut, an equally unkempt and smelly figure stretched his skeletal frame. With one hand disturbing a colony of parasitic life forms in his uncombed hair, he yawned loudly.

'Morning, Steve,' Thomas said, scratching his grubby face. His breath drifted across the space between them, making Steve's nose twitch involuntarily.

'Morning, Thomas. You have to see what I've got,' Steve said with a broad smile that exposed his stained and rotten teeth.

Thomas rubbed his bleary eyes. 'What is it?'

'I'll show you,' said Steve. 'Come on.'

Leaving their primitive sanctuary, they took off, heading up into the tree line at the foot of the mountains, the sounds from the camp drifting away behind them. Thomas asked Steve several times what he was carrying in his hand as they trekked through the forest. Steve explained that it was a secret and that he would understand soon enough. Thomas was not the brightest of individuals and he struggled to understand his friend's statement. He reasoned that a secret was something no one knew about, and if Steve knew, it wouldn't be a secret.

Late in the afternoon as the sun began to settle on the distant horizon, Steve suddenly stopped and raised his hand. 'Shoosh,' he whispered as he lowered himself and crouched at the edge of a clump of bushes. 'Over there, can you see the pair of rabbits on that mound?'

Steve slipped behind the foliage, appearing again with the sticks he had been carrying. The larger stick was now bent in a crescent shape and held in place by a long strand of thin animal gut. The second stick had four feathers at one end and a nasty looking point at the other.

'Those feathers are really pretty,' remarked Thomas.

Steve ignored him, concentrating instead as he pulled the animal gut back as far as his arm would stretch. Choosing his timing carefully, he let go. A loud twanging sound resonated through the forest.

Thomas stood gaping at the rabbit that the pointed stick had dispatched. 'Wow!'

'That's what I've called it,' Steve said, smiling modestly. 'It's a wow and arrow.'

The men wasted no time in lighting a fire, and after some butchery with a sharp flint, the afternoon's spoils were spit-roasting nicely over the hot coals. They feasted as night fell, and apart from the howl of a distant wolf summoning his pack, nothing disturbed their meal.

The Neolithic hunters accepted what happened next remarkably well. A humming sound became more audible and the flames of their campfire turned lime green and then stood completely still. Appearing out of thin air a few feet away, the jaws of an enormous chromium-plated zip materialised on the red Andalucian soil. Clearly stamped on the pull tag were the letters XXL. Ascending silently to the height of a tall man, the zip opened, flooding the campsite with a shaft of light.

'This is new,' Steve said approvingly as he shielded his eyes. The Neanderthals looked down at the pair of dusty brown shoes as the owner straightened himself up, brushing one hand through his slightly ruffled greying hair, the other firmly clutching his green leather-bound briefcase.

'I do hope I haven't startled you with my entrance,' Godfrey said.

Thomas stared at their visitor and his unusual attire. He leant forward and tugged at Godfrey's trouser turn-ups.

'What's this called?' asked Steve, standing up and pulling at his green corduroy jacket as he began to circumnavigate their guest.

'I'm sorry, but I can't tell you,' Godfrey said, feeling slightly perturbed at the level of interest his hosts where taking in his attire. Thomas and Steve continued inspecting his clothing like a pair of Savile Row tailors.

'Look,' Godfrey said, becoming slightly impatient, 'I have just travelled an unimaginable distance through time and space to visit you. I think the least you could do is ask me why I'm here.'

'So, why are you here then?' Steve said, lifting Godfrey's arm and stroking the corduroy material back and forth with his grubby fingers.

Thomas casually explored the jacket pockets. 'Yeah, so why are you here?'

'I am here because of a sequence of events that occurred on my own planet a long time ago. I need to know whether or not your species has succumbed to the effects of an insidious chromosome,' Godfrey explained.

'What's a chromosome?' asked Steve.

'Yeah, and what does it taste like?' added Thomas.

Godfrey lowered his lofty frame, sitting himself down beside the warming fire. The aroma of spit-roasted rabbit filled the night air and reminded him of his own dinner when he returned. 'Basically, a chromosome is a microscopic gene-carrying body in the tissue of a cell.'

'Where does this gene thingy live exactly?' asked Thomas with a studious expression.

Godfrey was now staring intently at the remains of the rabbit. 'It lives all over the inside of your body,' he said in a matter of fact way.

Thomas jumped up and began frantically beating his thighs and chest, 'I've got it,' he shouted, 'I can feel them biting me inside.'

'Just listen to me, will you? I'm sure everything's fine. There's probably nothing wrong with you at all,' Godfrey told him.

Thomas stopped jigging about and sat back down. 'How can you be sure?' he enquired nervously. 'I mean, really sure we haven't got it?'

'This is a mutant chromosome,' explained Godfrey. 'We even had it on our planet. In fact, to be completely honest with you, that is where it came from in the first place.'

'What happened on your planet?' Steve asked.

'Good question,' Godfrey said, getting himself comfy. 'I shouldn't really be telling you any of this, but I can't see what harm it will do. On our planet a long, long time ago, an ancient civilisation created the cosmos, which is all of those beautiful twinkling lights you can see up there. They also created this blue orange-shaped planet that we are now sitting on.'

The Neanderthals looked up at the star-studded night sky and back at their visitor.

'Through a bizarre sequence of events, my colleague Charlie

and I discovered the cosmos suspended in the Planetarium on the oasis in the north. It was when my mother-in-law became involved that it all went terribly wrong.'

'Your mother-in-law, you say?' asked Steve.

'That's right,' Godfrey said.

Steve leant round the campfire and offered him his grubby hand.

'Here's to mother-in-laws,' he agreed, shaking Godfrey's hand vigorously. 'They're nothing but trouble if you ask me. The other day I came back from hunting and my mother-in-law had eaten my brother. Can you believe it?'

Godfrey failed to hide his shock.

'So where does this chromosome thing fit into the story?' Thomas asked.

'Well, when the ancients were constructing the cosmos, they allegedly infected it with the MeMe chromosome, which is why they left it inanimate. You see, it was never supposed to be launched at all, not even by my mother-in-law. So all of the planets you see up there in this incredibly clear night sky could all be infected, including yours.'

Godfrey watched his new acquaintances jump up and scream loudly as they ran aimlessly around in circles. Finally, he shot to his feet. 'That's enough,' he declared, angrily pointing a solitary finger at the ground. 'Now, both of you listen to me,' he said as he paced in front of them, his patience dwindling. 'This MeMe chromosome is more likely to affect your behavioural patterns than anything else. It can make you become egotistical and greedy, turning you into self-centred spiteful angry individuals who only consider themselves and have no time for their fellow man. That's why they called it the MeMe chromosome. Me, me, me, me – get it?'

Godfrey surveyed the rabbit as his stomach reminded him that his own dinner was now overdue. Suddenly an idea formed in his mind.

'It can also make you unwilling to share with other people, for example,' he added with a devious grin.

The Neanderthals sat quietly and listened.

'There you have it, nothing too much to worry about really. It can't kill you, technically speaking,' he said frowning deeply. 'Although, to be completely honest with you, it did result in 50 million people on my planet dying rather violent deaths.'

The sound of screaming filled the night air again as his audience jumped and jigged around again, beating themselves raw. Godfrey casually sat himself down and enjoyed the aroma emanating from the Neanderthal's meal. Finally, the pair completely ran out of breath.

'There is a simple test I can perform,' Godfrey continued as they both collapsed on the ground. 'It will prove one way or the other whether you have the MeMe chromosome.'

'What is it?' Steve asked, panting heavily.

'I will ask you a simple question, and depending on your response, I can determine whether or not you are infected,' Godfrey informed him. 'It's that simple.'

The two bewildered hunters looked at one another and nodded in agreement.

'Okay, let's do it,' they said impatiently.

'Right, here's my question. Now listen carefully,' Godfrey said, pausing for a breath. 'I have travelled a long way through time and space and I'm very hungry. Can I eat the last of your rabbit?'

After some hesitation, the Neanderthals closed ranks and leant across to whisper to one another. Finally, after some muted conversation, Neanderthal Steve informed him of their unanimous decision. 'Yes, you can, but what's it worth?'

Godfrey was hungry and his sugar levels did nothing to maintain his composure. Instead, his blood pressure soared to new heights as he leapt to his feet.

'I knew it, I knew it, I damn well knew it,' he shouted. 'The President was right. You're all infected with this wretched MeMe chromosome, even at the dawn of your pathetic little planet's evolution. You do realise, of course, that there's no hope for you. It's all going to be a complete and utter waste of time. You and your little planet are all doomed.'

Thomas and Steve gazed at their guest, totally spellbound.

'Besides, blue is such a dismal colour for a planet anyway,' Godfrey continued, turning to sarcasm. 'Give it another half a million years and there will be nothing left here but a giant hole in space.' Godfrey's stress levels had finally reached critical mass. Stabbing his finger angrily on the gold bracelet strapped to his wrist, the wormhole immediately rose skyward behind him. 'If this is an example of how greedy and selfish your species are here, what's the rest of the cosmos like, eh?'

Thomas and Steve said nothing.

'Anyway, I'm off,' he blurted. 'I hope you gluttonous selfish examples of prehistoric stupidity enjoy your meal. Oh, and by the way, there's no cure for the MeMe chromosome, none whatsoever. It's completely terminal. It's in your genes.' Godfrey's cheeks rode high on a contented smile, until the thought occurred to him that he was, in fact, returning to the planet where the MeMe chromosome had originated. His cheeks suddenly collapsed, and with a very perplexed look, Godfrey walked into another dimension. The light from the XXL briefly flooded the Neanderthals campsite, and then vanished completely as the zip closed and the chromium pull descended silently to the ground. The letters XXL reflected briefly, as Godfrey, the wormhole, and the knowledge that earth was doomed, faded together into the night.

The hunters remained rigid; their visitor's display of temper had left them flabbergasted. They stared vacantly at the spot where Godfrey had disappeared.

'He was a real party animal,' Steve said. 'What got into him?'

'He obviously didn't know the answer, Steve.'

'You're right there.'

'It's always worth a please and thank you,' they said laughing.

After the humour subsided, Thomas noticed the dark green briefcase their visitor had forgotten in his haste to leave them. 'Look, he's forgotten this.'

The two pals eyed up the briefcase.

'What did he say his name was?' Steve asked.

'I don't think he told us.'

They stared at the initials beside the handle of the briefcase, the gold leaf reflecting back the inscription embossed in the leather.

'GOD!' they said together, in agreement at the initials on Godfrey Owen Davis's briefcase.

Later that night, the pair settled down and examined the contents of GOD's forgotten briefcase. It had been easy for them to open as GOD never locked his briefcase because he couldn't remember the code for the little tumblers beside the catches. There was a wad of undecipherable blueprints describing the design, construction and operating techniques for a device called the XXL wormhole transportation system. Fortunately, neither of the men possessed the technical prowess to build, perfect and operate such a device that could slingshot them across the cosmos and back in the blink of an eye. So they agreed the papers were more suited as fuel for their failing campfire, and so they burnt them. Oblivious to the path they were about to tread, the Neanderthals continued to rummage further. Thomas had found an interesting object that had all manner of shiny devices folded inside it.

'Look how this thing cuts up meat, Steve,' he said,

experimenting with the multipurpose camping knife on the remnants of the rabbit carcass.

'If you think that's good, take a look at this lot,' Steve remarked, excitedly handing his companion a selection of brochures and catalogues. One particular magazine had caught his eye. It displayed a range of men's clothing. 'He said something about having jeans, do you remember?'

As they tucked in for the night, they both agreed on one thing. Whoever this GOD person was, he had certainly done them a massive favour forgetting his briefcase. With the discoveries they had made, it now meant that tomorrow was going to be the start of a whole new life for them.

Several weeks later, on a beach not far from where modern-day Torremolinos now stands, Steve walked into the kitchen of a new straw-thatched Chiringuito close to the water's edge. He thumped down a selection of red mullet, squid, two seagulls and the head of a sardine onto Thomas's kitchen table.

'Look what I've caught,' he said, his face beaming. 'I'm getting better by the day with my wow and arrow.'

Thomas glanced across at the produce of a morning's hunting. 'Where's the rest of that sardine?'

A boyish grin swept across Steve's face. 'I got peckish, sorry.'

Thomas nodded at the kitchen table. 'You'll need to do better than that, Steve. Maybe you didn't see the queue out the front.'

The entrepreneurs glanced out of the servery window at a line of hungry customers stretching out across the silvery beach.

'And another thing, while you were out, I booked three more families in the last of our beach huts. That means we're now full for the summer.'

Steve shook his head in amazement. 'If that GOD person hadn't left that case, we wouldn't have any of this.'

Thomas agreed. 'Personally, I can't praise him enough.'

After some reflection, Steve's thoughts returned to the queue outside their Chiringuito. 'Listen, tonight I want to discuss my idea about these rabbit-fur jeans. They will catch on for sure this winter. Besides, like the man said, it's all in our jeans.'

Thomas laughed. 'Maybe we can also sort out a name for this little enterprise and get ourselves an image, something people will remember?'

'We'll think of something,' Steve said, glancing at the long queue of hungry customers. 'But in the meantime,' he continued, 'we have to feed this lot. So its cook, Thomas, cook.'

ABOUT THE AUTHOR

As an electrical engineer Anthony Merrydew has spent a lifetime surrounded by machinery in factories, industrial plant rooms and data centers. Nursing ailing generators back to life and chasing the gremlins out of switchgear has become a normal day.

Over a decade ago he and his wife moved to Andalucía and bought a property at the foot of the Sierra Mijas mountain range. In the junk left behind by the previous owner they found a discarded garden lamppost.

Somehow the lamppost became Nine and the story began from there.

Today Anthony and his family still live at the foot of the mountains, and Nine now illuminates their garden every night.

15772908R00180

Printed in Great Britain
by Amazon